TO PASS IT ON

Scott Duka

DEDICATED TO

J.P. Nelson & John C. Hampsey
for your guidance, your words, your courage.

And to everyone else that has been
a part of this, one way or another...

CONTENTS

I know what I __can__ know;
therefore,
I know everything.

PREFACE

I was always a curious young man.

Of course, most every young man is curious.

Perhaps it begins at the age when he's still young enough to get his tongue peppered for using profanity—which was all along a simple attempt to be like his father, for that's what most young men try to do at that age anyway.

He grows up bit by bit, as his curiosity wheels a sharp turn and lunges forward all because he overhears the older kids talking about this idea much bigger and taller than him called *sex*. It's then that his eyes get big over things. He starts to really see people as people: boys as boys, and girls as, well, girls. It's maybe in some adolescent Springtime, when the blonde girl sitting in front of him in class has decided to put her hair up that day. Small, white hairs play invisibly across the back of her neck. Her pink blouse is sleeveless. Freckles from the sun stretch over her shoulders, and he wonders if she and him could ever fall in love.

And sure enough, growing up one year at a time, little instances like this go on to feed his curiosity about the smallest of things that he'll later discover to be the biggest of things.

〇

I assume that, by now, most of us have heard the reports that curiosity killed the cat. What a calamity—this damned curiosity—killing innocent kittens for sniffing around foreign corners. But it's a good thing, a blessing even, that the story of the cat doesn't end there. If you've heard this much, if you've heard that the cat was killed by curiosity, then surely you've also heard about that same cat having nine lives. Perhaps this means something. Perhaps some slant of light, some bit of wisdom, hides itself in this intertwining of childhood mythology. And it seems there's only one way to make sense of it. Sure, the cat is—one way or another—killed by curiosity; yet, it's reborn so soon afterward, with another eight lives to go. So it must be that the cat is *reincarnated* by the discoveries of curiosity, not dispatched by them. Perhaps what's going on is the death of the cat's naiveté; not the *cat* at all. So the headlines *should* read: *Curiosity Kills Cat's Ignorance: Cat Lives to Tell.*

To fasten this around the human race and our own endeavors, and to relate it to existentialism or transcendence or whatever it is they're teaching in schools nowadays, I'll leave it at this: Without curiosity, the mind would never see fit to walk barefoot through things. You'll know what I mean if you've ever walked barefoot across the things that were here before us—sand and dirt and grass—and felt the millions of sensations grip you from the sole of your foot up to the soul inside yourself. Being curious—walking barefoot—is quite essential to who we are: to where we've been and where we're headed. If man was never curious to turn over a stone, he'd have never seen the wisdom coiled up and nestled beneath it. So curiosity is a good thing, a blessing, not a doom, not killing *us*, rather our illusions of things. And all we can do is applaud that cat—that furry, little, nimble-pawed, nine-lived empiricist—for reminding us of this.

And so, what were once two said truths floating around our childhood minds now come together as nothing more than: *Curiosity killed the cat who had nine lives.* It makes you think; perhaps mythology of the likes isn't as set in stone as we once believed it to be. It's a real wonder how differently we believe in things as children and as whoever we are now. It's because of all the movement surrounding us, all the change. Maybe nothing's really *set in stone*, as they say. And even if some things are, perhaps the stones are quite small and moveable, pebble-like; perhaps they're the same stones we fetch to skip on the surface of a lake, only to watch them jump off into the orange horizon, splashing once or twice and then disappearing forever.

I'll say it again; I was always a curious young man.

Growing up, I'd wonder about things like the idea behind a two-piece bathing suit and why women didn't just wear their bra and underwear in the lake or the pool; or, if gardeners are secretly at war with each other, with one blowing leaves to the right on a Tuesday, only to have them blown back to the left by another on Thursday; or, if people remembered things more than they forgot them; or, why rainbows look like frowns instead of smiles; or, why your piss smells like popcorn sometimes; or, if music heals itself, filling its own holes—like for every sad song there's a song about something lovely; or, why male science teachers had the pretty girls sit up front; or, why we wait until the first of January to decide we're going to be better people; or, why funerals aren't just called *sunsets*.

My age moved toward double digits, and I got into the habit

of ruminating about everything stupid or little or sad. I mean, really giving attention to things in a kind of second-guessing or paranoiac way—things that didn't need to be ruminated about, things I'd heard or overheard people say, or hiccups of nothings from my past. I wished I could just look at something and accept it for the song it sang, right then and there. That's what everybody else was doing. But I always had to cut into things. I'd have trouble hearing the song, trouble listening for it. I'd be too busy squinting, looking for the singer, digging deeper, maybe deeper than I was supposed to. Looking back now, it's kind of like this: I think that while you can learn a tree by studying its roots, you can miss what's real and in front of you if that's all you study. It's a hard thing to find yourself stuck in the underground of things. It's even harder to pull yourself out. And what put *me* underground in the first place and kept me there for so damn long was really only one thing, and it actually wasn't a *thing* at all. It was an idea.

And this idea would rush through the channels of my body like a hot, red river, and it would come in both the quiet hours and even the louder ones. Once my curiosity let it bleed into my mind, it wasn't long before it went for my heart. That's what began all the heaviness in my life. I was barely a teenager and was already uncomfortably conscious of this idea I mentioned. There was no peace to be found with it either. I just thought about it and thought about it and let it bruise my heart while all the other kids in the neighborhood were growing up just fine, sunshine warming their backs. Perhaps the only way to avoid getting ripped up by a thought is to write it down on paper and then rip it up yourself and be done with it. But I didn't know that then. Humans are tempted to think about the things they know they're better off not thinking about. It's built into our curiosity. We know we don't belong looking in some directions, but we do it anyway. Just look at how we bend our necks to see a bad car wreck on the highway. Or look at those who came and went

4

before us. Look at Nietzsche. Look at Eve, at Adam. Just watch, even the last human on Earth is going to be curious as hell.

Sure, amongst other things, this story is about curiosity. But at its core, that which gives this story its pulse and its purpose comes from nothing more than a passing idea from my teenage years that I finally feel okay in the head enough to talk about.

PART ONE

1

It all started in the place I grew up—Mayhaw.

It was a little place, just barely a suburb, just outside of town. A unique plot on the map, smaller than a thumbprint. Wind always blew through Mayhaw, and you'd see all four seasons drop down and dance to their own music and then swiftly exit the stage for the next act. You'd see things like original brickwork around houses and good-sized yards and children on squeaky bicycles. There was a bigger-than-small-but-smaller-than-big family of streets that paralleled and crossed each other and a whole load of trees peppered throughout the neighborhood. The southern end of Mayhaw was what we called *town*, and up at the northern end, past my high school, sat wide a small lake—Lake Wisley.

Mayhaw carried similar colors you'd find in Monet's 'Bridge at Giverny'. I really mean that. And if you're not familiar with the painting, find it in print somewhere and look at it for longer than you think it would take to look at.

The seasons would chase each other around in circles, leaving drags of themselves behind like paint across the sky. Each one of them looked at me differently. Some looks were nostalgic, others motivating, some daunting. And though I could never trace the *why*, I always knew that the changes that came with the seasons—those in the wind and the sky and on the ground and in the bird's song—were somehow deeply, deeply significant, like they told a story, perhaps the same one, over and over again. And each chapter of that story would always be able to mimic how we were feeling inside. Weather will do that; perhaps it knows us better than we know it.

◊

Summer always had a real buzz to it. A sort of hot and dry buzz. People would complain about the sun being too hot right after they'd gotten through complaining about the snow being too cold. But they'd get over it by way of air conditioning and ice cubes floating indifferently at the rims of mugs. People are happier in the Summer anyway. That's how it's always been. Perhaps the heat from the sun fills in the chip on everyone's shoulder with its invisible warmth. This chip develops during the other seasons. It comes as a result of feeling that the world owes us something for having to put up with things like idle Tuesdays during the Fall, or streptococcus in the Winter, or pollen-sneezing and bee stings in the Spring.

Poor Mother Earth is so damn accused.

But Summer, if anything, was a loud and bright invitation back outside, and perhaps all the Earth wishes is for us to come back outside.

◊

Spring was a whole other whirl of happenings, in its wetness and its colors, its letdowns and its magic. Bouts of rain would fall with weight from the sky, never halting on time, keeping the ground wetter than we wanted. The people would say to each other from underneath their umbrellas, "It'll pass, it'll pass." And it always would. Spring rain is on its own schedule like that. There was something elusive, something beautiful in a forbidden kind of way; hell, there was something theatrical about Spring. You could never trust the weather to be one way or another, and I'd even find myself feeling sympathetic for the sky—it was just as confused as we were.

The many faces of Springtime carried smiles that even the most astute painters and poets could never entirely acknowledge or smile back at in the right way. One poet would try, and he'd go on to call the month of April *cruel*, but even *he* was only halfway there. Sure, April had its sadness, its shadows. But any time there's a shadow, there must be a source of light as well.

Growing up, I personally couldn't ignore God's despondence in April.

He'd cry enough tears for everybody to see and feel—plants, animals and humans alike. I used to think that those tears would fall right along with the natural drops from the gray-beard clouds, and if you stood out in the rain in the right place, and stuck out your tongue, you could maybe catch a salty drop. All those tears, I'd reason, could only mean one thing: we all must've been doing something terribly wrong. Maybe it's because everyone hurried inside when it was wet outside. No one was living *with* the rain, no one dancing in it like they used to. They'd miss out on the smells it would bring to the low air, the life, the vitality it secretly brought out in things. I'd hear people say they liked the rain if they didn't have to be out galoshing through it. They liked the rain if they were nestled inside, in the corner, a favorite chair, a favorite book in hand. But that was the sound of rain they liked, not the rain at all.

One of these people was, well, my mother—"The only ones

crazy enough to parade around in the rain are tireless, jacketless children, or hippies, or the homeless who can't fare any better." Rain was just one of the many things that taught me how different my mother and I were, how apart we were from each other on things. I never minded the rain; in fact, there might have even been something I loved about it. It carried down something very honest with it, something tangible yet elusive in a flirtatious way, something I'll never be able to fit into words.

I'd watch Spring and its eccentricities hit Mayhaw every year and wonder what Mother Earth thought of it all—people rushing around, right and left, into car doors and buildings, avoiding the sky as their ceiling. She had to feel the way a lot of mothers feel when their children start giving rushed hugs before shooting out the front door to somewhere else. Children start acting that way once they realize they might finally be teenagers. This is all, of course, quite contrary to the mommy-don't-leave-me days—the days that seem to be miles into our past, but were really only yesterday.

Spring was strange as hell, really. It would make you think in weird ways. It was easy to get stuck out in the rain of my own curiosity, stuck between the question and the answer. Kids can get stuck like that. Their bodies slow down and their minds gallop on and on and on. Some parents will sense that in their children and snap them out of it. And then of course, there's the other kind of parents: parents who believe that the mind is designed to gallop far and wide, parents who see everything their child does—good things and bad, rises and falls—as nothing less than paint added to the canvas.

If Spring itself were a canvas, perhaps it would have every color on it, and twice. Or if you could look at the paint in layers, you'd see the colors stacked on top of each other, graduating from cold and muddy to bright and warm. You'd see April slowly giving birth to May.

A woman would later tell me that those drops of saltwater I thought I could catch on my tongue were never really God's tears. She said I was imagining God's sadness, that I was being a fool and trying to justify Nature. She told me that the salty drops were, instead, beads of God's sweat. After all, *someone* had to garden the Earth for Spring.

And so, the sweat would fall from the sky in its warmth and soak into the dirt along with the rain, and flowers would shoot up from the dirt like children coming up from pool water. And just like that, Spring was transformed, and you could see that April wasn't, in fact, a cruel month. Perhaps we're cruel to think it is. Because without April, we wouldn't have as many flowers to pick from and hold in a tight fist behind our backs while we knock the other fist on the door of someone we love, or almost love.

So maybe it's about being both patient and still in April, and then walking around in May. That's the only way we're going to be able see it: Mother Earth singing like a freed slave and shoes becoming strangers again as barren feet saunter across new grasses.

It's all going to be there—right there, where it's always been.

2

Just like Spring and Summer, Fall would come around every year as well. Fall told a different tale. Fall was when school always wanted to start.

Fall was when I'd return to Texana Hills High School—to those laughter-filled, freshly waxed, bustling-yet-lonely, locker-lined hallways—where my shyness was more certain than my refrigerator-worthy grades. I wasn't a bad student; I just got distracted easily. Maybe it's that I could never see into the importance of grades; I just couldn't chase after them like the others. I'd run out of breath wrestling with the difference between having knowledge and having wisdom, and grades didn't seem to measure much more than what you did or what you didn't do when you were in a classroom. How could a grade—one twenty-sixth of the alphabet—capture what you really knew or understood deep, deep down in the pit of yourself? I wouldn't waste my time trying to make sense of something that didn't make sense in the first place. And even if I didn't get the grades the others got, life would go on just the same—the sun would come out every morning and set every night, flowers would still grow, dogs would bark, seasons would change, and people would drive their cars to and from work.

School is a hell of an environment.

There's so much going on, and so much not going on that should be going on. Physically, I blended in just fine—blue eyes, expected five-foot-nine, brown locks with a random streak of blonde down the side. But so often what one looks like is so contrary to what they feel like. I had a removed feeling about myself, you see, a feeling that I wasn't only on a different page, but in a whole different book—maybe even a book without words, hell, a picture book. Unlike the students in the squeaky desks around me, I could never commit to those timeless wonders you'll hear in school, like how geometry is secretly related to sports, or how without mitosis and meiosis we'd all die, or why a certain man bellowed some Latin phrase after shooting Abraham Lincoln in the back of the head.

I'd wonder *why* I didn't care about the things that everyone else was busy memorizing for life. This was, of course, before I started to understand that it's okay, perhaps better, to feel alone sometimes, different, outcast from the normal batch. You can learn a lot when you're alone. Some things you can only learn *if* you're alone.

And that's the thing.

I *wanted* to learn; I *wanted* wisdom in my pockets and books in my hands. I just didn't know which direction to wander or even *wonder* into, or who I could trust enough to ask. It was like I was dangling an empty wicker basket down by my side. With each step, it would bounce on the side of my leg, and I'd walk on, head up in the trees, looking for the right fruits to fill the basket with. But for some reason, I didn't want the kind of fruit everyone else was picking and eating. I walked past all those trees with my gaze down at the ground, my eyes nearly closed. I wanted something else; I just didn't know what it was. Hell, I hadn't the slightest idea where to even find it; I just knew I wanted it—whatever *it* was. And perhaps wanting that *unknown it* is how any adventure begins.

◊

School is perhaps the most commonly footed terrain that people trudge across in attempt to discover something about themselves. It teaches people what they're good at and what kind of mental or physical environment they were born to be in. It moves most people along, through the years, offering incentives and plateaus of sorts, promising that the future is only brighter than the present moment.

But then, of course, there's a small population—maybe not that small after all—who can't help but wobble under its weight, barely able to stand still on both feet in between the morning bell and the three o'clock bell. And I, Aydenn George Price, happened to be one of them—especially once high school and I came nose to nose.

The worst for me was maybe English class. It was my first language and my only language. Sure, I could speak it well, but I couldn't write essays and I'd rather have stapled my nostrils shut than put up with assigned reading. The books were never really what you wanted to read. Assigned reading was like eating sugar-free candy. There was no freedom in it. And all I'd get out of it were some tiring encounters with ghosts of fiction, meddling around in their lives and trying to make sense of their nonsense—as if I didn't have non-fiction problems of my own to sort through. Writing was a hell in itself for me. Maybe it was because it wasn't really *writing* after all, but something else posing as writing. My essays would turn out like crooked collages of cut out dictionary pages—words across the page, nudged shoulder to shoulder, like a group photograph where no one really likes each other enough to be standing that close together.

Sure, we've all heard from some graying adult that being able to write good will pay off some day, but more often than not, it takes a long time to understand the things graying adults say. There's no fiction in saying that my relationship with literature wasn't a romantic one. I hated it. And maybe it hated me back. I just couldn't see into it like my teachers could. If I tried to look deep into a story or a group of words written across a poem, I couldn't see the movement at the depth, just the reflection of my confused face bouncing back at me from the surface. But I swear on both my mother and my father that it wasn't because of laziness. Like I said, I wanted to fill that basket of mine; I wanted to fill it to the goddamn brim. Even if I had to amble up a tall and limber tree that I didn't even trust with my own weight, just to pick the right-looking fruit, I'd do it.

But at the time, as nothing more than a high schooler in 1989, my basket was as empty as wind. And it's a hard irony that emptiness can somehow give you a feeling of heaviness; having no anchor can somehow make your ship feel even heavier.

I look back now and wonder: if I were to have squinted even harder into that empty, metaphoric basket of mine, would I have maybe noticed something? Perhaps something small: a leaf or a blade of grass or *something* would've been in there as some sort of hint. Maybe even a caterpillar, nestled in between the basket weaves, cocooning itself.

I wonder if I missed something, anything.

But then I remember that all we can really do is wonder.

3

Ever since I saw an animated monkey sneaking around on television, being followed and corrected by a voice from underneath a big, yellow hat, I found it funny that *George* was my middle name. When I asked my mother why she gave me the name, she said nothing more than that it just seemed to fit. I looked more into it when I got old enough, and I found out it came from Greek origins. Apparently it meant *farmer*, and, still young, I had a hell of a time trying to make the hiddenness of my middle name relatable to the life I'd been born into, or fallen into. It was a sturdy name though—George. It took full use of the lips to say. I never used it on school papers though. And not a lot of people knew it was my middle name. It's not that it wasn't important to me. It's just that things tend to stay more yours with the less people you tell.

There's one last season worth a few more words. Perhaps it was the most cryptic of them all, casting shadows in places where there was supposed to be light. There's supposed to be a lot of light when you're still a teenager. And if there's not, well, it's going to be a hell of a walk through the night.

And so, like hard cheese with wine, the season of Winter was always paired with the two-word question, *Why me?* It was a question that carved itself deeper and deeper into the wall of my consciousness as I got older, and the moist and blue-black air of that season always led me down the same hill into the same cave, where I'd sit down and stare up at those two words in the form of a question, carved crookedly into the wall.

The weather would get colder; snow would sneak into the clouds to fall whitely with intention while we slept. My house would start to feel larger than it actually was and colder than the season alone could account for. The Winter of 1989 found me to be sixteen.

I couldn't drive. Couldn't smoke. Too quiet for dating. Too skinny for team sports. I had a best friend, a television set, a mother I wasn't close with and a slow-growing pile of paperback books in my room from an aunt and uncle who still had the delusion that I was a bookworm. I was a junior in high school then, slowly walking the halls of Texana Hills High School, wondering when life would lift its weight from the top of my back.

◊

Being out in the snow too much would make my bones ache, so I was always indoors when I could be. It always started snowing around November first. Sure, it wouldn't technically be Winter for another fifty-one days, but if you grew up in Mayhaw, Winter began whenever the ground started turning white. That

Winter in particular, when I was home, you'd maybe find me on the couch, legs dangling over its arm, *The Brady Bunch* playing in between commercials while my mother had her evening glass in the kitchen. Or maybe I was nosing through homework I didn't understand or maybe understood really well but didn't understand why I needed to understand it. Or, if the hum in the air was right, you could maybe even find me sitting low in my closet, under a few jacket sleeves and shirt tails, opposite the growing stack of books. The sliding door would be cracked three inches to let just enough light through to spread across a spiral sketchbook that held a few hundred sketches of a man's face. All of the faces looked different. Some were of an older man, a sadder man. Some were of a young and strong-faced man. They were all done in pencil. Most of them were done pretty quickly, just to get something on the page. They weren't very good, but they were mine, and I drew them with the soft side of the pencil. And maybe they helped me have some sort of anchor in this *passing idea* I mentioned.

You see, with the white tufts of snow came a cold-blood current that passed through my body at the most random times. I got to know the feeling pretty well. It was the passing idea. I'd get heavy in the chest some nights, and wake up with a knot in my forehead from it. You can't always control what you think about or even when you think about it. And it would leave me there—the ruminating—with no real answers to move on with. Perhaps it's a coming of age thing: the questions multiply as the answers hide behind trees.

◊

It was just after Halloween—after big bags of candy shot off of store shelves and plastic pumpkins or old, off-white pillowcases full of treats had left the tight grips of children; it was after people had gone back to wearing their other masks

It was the time in my life when this passing idea was no longer just something that mattered, rather, it was the only thing that mattered. And maybe it was just because I was getting older, and when you get older you're more concerned about the things that you could once treat as butterflies—you'd notice them and stare at them, with or without judgment, then they'd fly away and you wouldn't really think about them until you saw them again.

But this passing idea became less of a butterfly and more of a mosquito that Winter—hell, a mosquito *bite* even. I'd scratch at it until it bled, and then it would itch even more. The thoughts and images and textures of feeling that went along with the idea would pass through me like cold, thin wind through tall and naked pine trees. And that wind always flirted with the idea of knocking me down completely.

It made the sweetness of being sixteen go to shit, really.

And it didn't make sleeping at night any easier.

I'd wait for sleep to come, studying the deep purple backs of my eyelids without any real emotion. It would get cold in bed, up there on the top bunk. My mother would run the heater late in Wintertime, and even if I had my bed dressed in flannel, the cold would still be there. Perhaps it was a cold coming from inside of me. Whatever it was, it gave me the kind of chill you'll get from sitting on a stone bench in the shade for too long. And so I'd lie up there, in between awake and something else, rolling over intermittently to look out my bedroom window down at 8th Street where my mother and I lived.

The bunk beds I had were my mother and her sister's from a long time ago. My grandfather built them from solid wood with his own hands. And they were moved down to our house in Mayhaw when I was old enough. There were times I wished I had a brother like how my mother had a sister, but I adjusted well enough, taking out the bottom bunk to slide my desk in its place. I wasn't embarrassed about having bunk beds in high school. It wasn't like anyone important would be coming over. And sleeping up there wasn't something I could complain about—a big view out the window, warmer Winters, warmer Summers.

Out my window and across the street, sitting plump and permanent, was an oak tree. It filled a sort of empty lot between houses. It had an arch cut out of its trunk, straight through and down to the ground, and you could walk right through it without touching your shoulders or head. Everyone in Mayhaw knew about it, and everyone had photographs of it and with it. It always made me feel protected. Perhaps trees do that without people even knowing it—they protect us somehow.

I don't blame you for wondering what the hell this passing idea was. It sounds pretty simple, yet, it carries a whole lot of complex weight with it. Perhaps that's how it is with everything—simple things are always complex and complex things are actually quite simple.

In essence, the idea that would pass through my mind, marching with heavy feet, sounded something like: *What did he look like beyond what my mother had said? What did his voice sound like when he was serious, or sad? Would he hold my tiny body when I cried and even when I didn't? Was he strong and intelligent like the other fathers? Did he know he was going to die right before he did? Did he think of me, his newborn and only son, right before he closed his eyes one last time? Was he still around in some way, and would I ever see him again, even in traces, even in heaven?* The hatred and confusion and the dizziness of anxiety would pump at my chest as it finished me off with something like: *Why him? Why did he have to die?* And of course, *Why me?*

My father was someone I'd come to know solely through the retellings of my mother.

But you can't create a sustainable, pulsing image of a person from someone else's words alone. I wanted to know him for myself. I wanted to know the fleshiness of the man who I was supposed to grow up underneath, the man I was supposed to look up at and get the same feeling of protection I'd get from that oak tree across the street.

It was hard for my mother to talk about him. And you couldn't really blame her. It was a sad story. It made it tough for me though, growing up. As I saw the pain eat at her more and more over the years, I learned to keep my mind about him to myself. That's why I'd make sketches of his face while nearly hidden away in my closet.

And no one would ever know if the sketches even came close to the truth, but it was the only way I could feel that he was real, the only way I could look at him looking back at me. I kept at those sketches because I wanted more, I needed more, more of the man who'd become a hiccup in my thoughts that even a hundred teaspoons of sugar wouldn't cure.

The passing idea was nothing more, nothing less, than my deceased father.

4

Earl Price was his name.

When I was of age, my mother tried her best to illustrate it all. She recounted what'd happened to my father, and how young I was when it did. I was just a year old the night he died.

She gave me snippets over the years, and each thing said was said with difficult emotion. The older I got, the less she'd talk about him. I grew to feel guilty just asking questions. Perhaps she needed me to stop asking altogether; perhaps she felt it was the only way she could move on—we could move on. And that was the biggest plight between my mother and I; that's really how our relationship slipped into such quiet, with so much unspoken distance between us. She wanted to move on from words about my father and cope silently; I, on the other hand, wanted to hear the stories again and again and again until I could maybe fall asleep under a nice slant of peace or hope or memory.

Another ugly and tough thing was this: we didn't have any

photographs of my father. Not one. My mother told me how they were all lost on the night of the fire. *What a night that must've been*, I'd think. You see, infants can't grasp much, which is why I sure as hell didn't remember anything about a fire. My mother assured me that I was much too young to remember, and I kept my distance with it because I could see it swell up in her cheeks that she didn't like to talk about it. In truth, she always avoided opening little doors of her past, especially doors that my ephemeral father stood behind. It killed me, but I couldn't hate her for it. It was a real, red-blooded wonder to see what the death of a lover could really do to a person. It made me a bit terrified to fall in love myself because you just never know when you'll lose the thing that you've spent your whole life looking for.

This fire she told me about happened a few months after my father passed. We were living in the same apartment he'd lived in with us. It was a one-bedroom, one-story, square apartment. I couldn't even imagine the weight of my mother's loneliness then. She recounted that our apartment was no bigger than a classroom and that it was situated in some urban corner, hours south of Mayhaw, deeply inland.

I'd get chills just imagining what that night was like. She recounted how she was just a step outside the front door, perched on the stoop—most likely with her glass—when she smelled the smoke. I imagined her letting her glass fall and shatter as she shot up and pushed back through the door, flapping through the haze like a seagull in flight amidst a hurricane.

My crib stood on its feeble legs right next to the kitchen, where the fire started. "It came alive so quickly," she said. "A hot orange lined half the apartment, right by you. I snatched you right up in all your blankets and ran outside and watched it from the cold curb, watched it all burn on the inside." She'd been cooking with some sort of grease, and the oven was pumped up to five hundred degrees. And that's a hell of a recipe for flames.

Sometime later in my childhood, I'd overhear her on the

telephone, saying something to someone. Perhaps it was a friend or her sister or someone who cared enough to hear that her life was *like hell* the first couple years after I was born. Perhaps that was the first, big thing that unsettled me about who my mother was and our relationship as mother and son.

I'd grow up to think about that fire from time to time, ruminating, *If only my father had been there. If only he'd been there, he could've extinguished that night from my mother and mine's past.*

But he wasn't. He was long gone by then.

◊

Growing up, the only sliver of peace I could extract out of my father's death was knowing that he'd died for a purpose: he died a warrior, a gentleman, a martyr; he died in the battle of his craft. He died a firefighter.

And that's all I really had to hold on to—that, along with his red helmet that the squad lieutenant gave my mother the night he died. I'd done a handful of sketches of him wearing it.

I never learned every precise detail of the night my father passed. And I couldn't just go back down to the fire station for answers or stories or photographs. It had been shut down and boarded up and stripped of all its rusty insides, and a new one had already been built elsewhere by the time I was three or four years old.

The saddest thing was how my mother noted it was my father's first night at the station. He died in his *first* fire! Even *if* any of those other firefighters there that night were still around, how many stories could they really have to share with me?

But maybe there wasn't much to know about that night after all. Maybe I knew enough already. He'd run back into a house full of smoke and flame to try and rescue something. And somehow, I got along okay with only that much. Not knowing the exact details wasn't a bad thing; it enabled me to think of his heroism with no limits—like how all boys should be able to think of their fathers.

That red helmet of his was something real, something I could hold onto. I put it up on shelf above my dresser. There it sat, trophy-like, beaten up good and textured with scratches. Stitched on the inside, in capital letters, it read EARL PRICE.

When I was a young boy, I'd put it on my head and stand tall in front of the bathroom mirror. It would tilt down over most of my forehead, but I stuck out my chest anyway and pretended to be him, talking in a low voice, talking with my hands. Without photographs, I'd never know how much I looked like him, or how much he looked like me, but I think wearing that helmet from time to time helped me get along with that. But eventually—like too many other things you used to do as a child—I stopped one day. I couldn't wear it any longer. It was my father's very own crown of thorns, not a toy. I put it back up on the shelf for good, where it would watch me grow up as it quietly collected the dust of days passing.

◊

It should've brought my mother and I closer together—my father dying. That is what's supposed to happen. But it didn't. Most words between us were only the necessary or considerate types of words; there wasn't anything extra with us, nothing noticeably special.

Dinners were routinely quiet, but she was a hell of a cook. I'd watch her from the couch in the living room, standing there in the kitchen, aproned. So carefully would she go about preparing the little things and stirring wooden spoons as if she were playing the violin. And she'd always ask twice if everything tasted okay when it came time to eat. She was always a better cook than a conversationalist, but, I respected her privacy and she respected mine, although at times I wished she wouldn't have.

There *was* this one thing we had together.

It was stupid and silly and a hundred years from now, no one will even know or care that it existed. But at the time, it was ours. It was important in a little but big way. I never knew if it was as special to her as it was to me, and I never asked. All I knew is that it was something we had together.

Right around the time I tripped and fell into my early teenage years, we started the tradition. Every Christmas Eve, I'd light the fireplace and we'd watch our tape of *A Christmas Story*. We'd laugh in breaths together at all the same parts that wouldn't get old. The warmth coming from the belly of the fireplace, us in our pajamas, my hot mug of tea, and her glass of red wine: again, it wasn't much, but it was ours. That's really the closest we ever got, the closest I ever got to really feeling the love between us. Sure, I'd see love paint itself across her face at random times, and I could almost always taste it in her cooking, but we never said *I love you* to each other or anything. Whatever kind of love I was getting from my mother never felt the way it should've felt.

But maybe love never really feels how it's *supposed* to feel; maybe that's what makes it love in the first place.

5

Tea always helped in the Wintertime.

The Winter months can drive everything around you inward and make you feel lonely. But there's never been anything lonely about a mug full of tea, even if you drink it all by yourself. Hell, when we look back at our lives one day, we might even say that tea was some of the best and most honest company we ever had.

Emma's Café was a small and familiar place. It sat on the corner of town, cozily situated in one of the few little shopping centers down there. There was a memorable liquor-cigar-baseball card shop across the street from the café; there was a toy shop that hung around too, also a men's suit shop, and even a narrow, high-shelved place where you could buy just about anything for a dollar.

I hated shopping—even more than I hated shoppers. Shopping can be a real pain. It's the reason people end up with hills of junk they never really needed in the first place and then grow neurotic as hell under the weight of it all. I was a teenager then. I didn't have a lot of money, so I didn't have a lot of things. It made sense. Things will just get you into trouble anyway. But the one thing I did have, from time to time, was my tea. And fifty-five cents for a big and round mug of Earl Grey was always fifty-five cents well-spent.

A good café is a hell of a place. People get together in them. Some are seeing each other for the first time; others, for maybe the last time. Regulars come in every day with new emotions, yet they order the same thing.

A good café is like a bar for those who thrive on comfortable, wide-backed chairs and decent lighting and, of course, words—to listen to or read or even write down. A lot of authors start their careers in cafés. It's a funny thing how authors begin anyway. You wonder if writing something is a decision of theirs, or if it just falls into their lap with the weight of responsibility. Or perhaps authors write things simply because no one else but a few hundred blank, ninety-degree-angled pages would really listen to them, really understand them. I guess blank pages give people a lot of room to think.

Emma's Café was a good café. You'd walk in the door and the wall to the left was mostly all windows. Ceiling to floor windows. It made it cozy in the cold months—being able to see the cold temperature outside while feeling the warm temperature inside. Black and whites hung at random across the other three walls—big prints of places and people you'd never seen, but the more you went in there, the more they felt like places you'd lived and people you'd loved. Some of them were framed, others just tacked up easily—faces of people with wrinkles, or trees, or boats on water, or old couples in kitchens, or boyhood friends squinting up at the sky from front porch steps. Old photographs will always show how simple it still is underneath all the color.

Waiting in line, my eyes would spend time with their

favorites, and getting closer to the register, you could see up on the wall, behind the girl taking orders, the portrait of a young woman with fair skin and a sharp jaw line and big, round eyes that rested under thin eyebrows. It was Emma herself. Who knew what year the photograph had been taken. She couldn't have been much older than twenty-six. But age, of course, doesn't matter; it's the presence of the person or the experiences they've had in the years they've had. And I'll say that the way Emma smiled up there—with an easy dent in the corner of her mouth that maybe hinted at her belief that everyone's always welcome—made the tea taste better.

I never wanted to ask when she'd passed away. Perhaps it didn't matter.

◊

The girl behind the register always looked like she wanted to greet me by my first name, but she never remembered it. I couldn't blame her. No one remembers anyone's name anymore; now it's all by the shape of their nose or their height or their squeaky shoes. But she did always remember my order. Perhaps she should've just called me Earl, like my tea, like my father.

I'd sit at the round table in the back corner, along the windowed wall. It was the perfect-sized table for two elbows with a mug in between. It was the only round table in there. The arm of the cushioned, teal chair I'd sit in would rub itself right up against the low part of the window to a good, crisp view outside. I came in one day and found a man and his wife playing chess at that table. That was the day I got my tea and drank it outside, leaned up against the window with my back to them.

There was so much to see from that table. You could see everyone in the café, but no one could see you. Older men who maybe had wives would read through their sun-brittled newspapers or their Hemingway, writing in the skinny margins with dull pencils. Couples would flirt or break up. Fathers in a rush would burn their tongues on coffee, and women with purses would ask for extra cream. And maybe, to blend in, I'd flip through a stale travel magazine that'd been lying dead in the rack down at the foot of my chair. But I couldn't get interested. No one really likes reading travel magazines.

Cars would pass by the window, parking, leaving, circling. Often, and I don't know why, I'd feel sad for them, like they were lonely. But it wasn't them that were lonely. It was the sixteen-year-old on the other side of the glass that was.

〇

Eventually, the achy-boned month of December retired along with my routine dawdles down to Emma's Café. Walking in the snow is fine, but when it's really snowing, the snow will start to walk on *you*.

It had really started to fall on car hoods and rooftops; Christmas and New Year's had passed; it was 1990: the year of impossible things. The first half of January, just before I'd find myself back at Texana Hills High School, was spent mostly with my childhood friend, Dillon Rubenson. He was my best friend. A real solid guy. He had this air about him that most people don't really get until they're well into life and know where they are and where they've been and where they're going. I'd known Dillon for as long as I could remember. His was one of the only black families that lived in Mayhaw then.

〇

My mother and I first met the Rubensons shortly after we moved to Mayhaw for me to start kindergarten.

We moved down to Mayhaw from Maygood, where we'd been living temporarily with my Aunt Jodie. We sort of had to, being technically homeless and all after the fire.

My mother and aunt grew up there together, in Maygood. It was a place that leaned up against the sea. My Aunt Jodie still lived up there, with my Uncle Lou, in the same house she and my mother had grown up in. It was my grandparents' old house. They were the only grandparents I really knew about—my father's parents had died long before I was even born.

We'd visited Aunt Jodie and Uncle Lou a fingercount of times over the years, in that broad, two-story house that was light blue with a faded white trim. It was an easy house and it had a flat and open deck off the second story that looked out at the ocean, at the horizon, where everything was different every day—everything except the straight line that made the sky 'the sky' and the ocean 'the ocean'.

I was too young to remember, but when my mother and I returned to Mayhaw—however many months later—we moved into the small apartment where that kitchen fire would soon happen. It was yet another knife to her heart, but she walked on, against the slanting, wind-blown rain. Soon after, she'd land a job that she'd have for a long, long time. And she'd become good at it too. It was in realty, and there's a hell of a lot of irony buried in that—she'd sell people *homes* during the day only to return to our *house* at night.

Her name is Emily, my mother's. Don't forget that. *Emily*.

6

As I said, Dillon was my best friend.

His family, the rest of the Rubensons, took to the road a lot of weekends throughout the year. Hell, maybe even twice a month. Growing up, I'd go with them almost every time I was invited. My mother wouldn't mind.

We'd go on short trips and even a few longer, distant, fall-asleep-with-your-face-against-the-window-and-your-headphones-blasting-crookedly-off-your-ears trips. They parked their camper outside their house under a tree that leaned diagonally into the street. It was the kind of tree that dropped down a load of spiky cherry-balls in the Spring that could pop your bike tire.

Perhaps Mr. and Mrs. Rubenson knew how important movement was. Perhaps they'd bought the camper on a whim because it was a good deal and the kids were still young. Either way, they seemed to use it whenever they could. And though tiffs weren't uncommon to their family, I always knew they liked being together in it. It kind of showed me how home travels with you; it doesn't stay behind when you leave.

◊

I lived on 8th Street, and Dillon lived on 13th.

The walk over was always a good walk. Just enough. Good in any weather. Walking is one of the biggest things we learn to do when we're new to life, and it amazes me how such an accomplishment—such a rewarding ability—somehow loses its magic, and people stop going for walks. It amazes me how people stop walking for the sake of walking. Perhaps the only way to learn to value something is to witness other people taking it for granted. Like breathing, too. That's a big one.

I had this mountain bike back then. It was red with good, bumpy black tires and it would scrape through snow on roads and sidewalks with a sort of vengeance. It was a spontaneous gift from my mother one Spring, when the city and school bus drivers went on strike. I even rode it a little in the following Summer with Dillon when he wasn't away.

But the bus drivers found their way back behind the big steering wheel in the Fall, and my long bike rides to school stopped; so did my riding altogether. That bike ended up like a lot of other things, crouched in some corner of the narrow, dust-gray garage behind our house. It was a sad image seeing it in there, leaned up against the cold wall, cobwebs thrown across its frame. But perhaps it wasn't a bad thing, surrendering it like that. I learned to walk places instead. And because of that, I learned how to watch the world slow down.

◊

I was having my walk over to Dillon's after dinner one evening as the sun was disappearing far behind everything and the colors typical of early January flirted with the sky. It had snowed a little the night before, but ceased once the sun came up behind the clouds. We still had a few days before school would start up again. It was in the middle of the week. No one else was out walking; the snow had stopped falling for a little while. It just lied flat and soft all around me as the air hummed with a buzz of buried melancholy. Overhead, the faces of old, tough clouds blanketed the sky.

I always walked down Main Street to Dillon's. Sure, there were other ways, zigzagging through neighborhoods and cutting corners over front lawns. But Main Street could get you anywhere in Mayhaw. Across Main Street stood a line of trees that had this promising permanence about it. All the branches, stubbly with black twigs, were powdered white with weather. They stood like troops, but their posture sagged nakedly.

In other seasons, when they had leaves on them, they'd catch breezes and keep the streets warm. But on that day, the streets had a stiff, cold stillness about them. The round-trunked trees were achingly unacquainted with life, like they'd been left behind, forgotten about, abandoned. It was like seeing children standing lost, crying helplessly—as much as you're moved to pick them up and embrace them and stroke their hair, all you can do is stand there with a pumping heart and wonder where their mother is. I couldn't stand there forever looking at them though. People have places to go. I myself wasn't a tree. I was born to move.

"Spring'll come; Spring'll come," I reassured myself, looking away.

On to Dillon's again, my snow boots crunching along, I left footprints that wouldn't be there tomorrow. But I loved walking. It puts you in good touch with the ground. It gets at your senses.

I pulled my red scarf down, off my mouth and nose, beginning to make my way to Dillon's in inches rather than feet. A cool smell peppered the breeze and it burned my nostrils

34

clean. I opened up real wide as dry air stuck to the insides of my mouth like plaster.

Walking slower, slower, almost stopping, I heard silence. Beautiful. A symphony of nothingness. Free and natural and thinly invisible. Odd how no sound is still a sound, like how even darkness is still measured by the amount of light.

I was on the same street I'd always walked on. But somehow, this time, it was different. Perhaps *all* familiar things are different when you slow dance with them. Because if you do, then it's like stumbling upon a page in your favorite book that you'd somehow never seen before.

Dillon's house fell into eyeshot as I loosened the scarf completely from my neck. A thin chill whispered its way down the hollowing between my collar bones, down into my shirt. I hooked a left onto 13th Street from Main and peeked at the houses to my left, their fog-framed windows half-concealing families doing nothing together. There were a lot of big, square lawns on Dillon's block, all speckled with tufts of white. I strayed from the sidewalk every few steps and walked across them, feeling grass and snow mush under my rubber soles. People hate when you walk on their lawns, and *I* hate that people think they can honestly *own* a lawn when it's all coming out of the same shared Earth underneath us.

I mushed along with that chill in both my nostrils and down the front of my neck as grass blades would fight to spring back up inside the footprints behind me. It's such an earthy feeling to walk across a surface outside and hear it and feel it respond. It reminds you of something—something distant and real and homey. I thought about that bike of mine, and how it would've eradicated that. It would've thrown out this whole sense of touch. And what's life without touch? Not much at all. You learn that as you get older. Touch is everything.

I felt like the only person outside that early evening. And what a wonder that feeling is. You might get it late at night too, when everyone else including the moon is asleep. So much room to stretch out. So much room to *be*. So much of time and space is yours. And it's a time that epiphanies tend to show up. They show up in quiet times, sleepy times. They show up on trains you didn't even know ran through your neighborhood. But that's one thing about epiphanies and transformations: no matter how or when or why they show up, they always do show up.

It was the first time in a long time it actually felt okay, even good, to be alone. But then again, there's always the chance I wasn't entirely alone out there that day. Those neighborhoods had a good amount of kids. Bored kids and funny kids. There could've been a handful of freckle-faced kids standing slim behind trees with lopsided snowballs clutched in their hands, watching me walk, vulnerable as hell. That's something to love about youth though—we've all been freckle-faced at some point, one way or another. And that simple truth, as we get older and older, will always make us smile.

I cut across the street for Dillon's, hoofing along in zigzags to the sidewalk on the other side. I looked up again at the swollen and puffy-eyed, gray sky. I got the same feeling you'd get lying on your back on a bottom bunk, the mattress above you slumping heavy and close to your face. I hopped up the curb and halted on the sidewalk right in front of Dillon's. I closed my eyes and cocked my head back and stretched out my arms the way kids do. The air was sticky and dry, free of falling snow. I took a long and easy inhale through my nose. It went in cool and straight, up and around my troubled mind, then down the back of my spine like a thin waterfall.

7

The narrow walkway up to Dillon's squeezed itself snug between two square lawns. Both of them were unevenly powdered white; the one to the left had the imprint of a snow angel about the size of Arietta, Dillon's younger sister. Up three steps, through two pillars, I came onto one small porch. The pillars were nothing fancy; it was just how the houses were built on 13th Street.

I hadn't been to Dillon's since Thanksgiving. I was usually there every year for it. They'd put out a seat for me between Dillon and Mr. Rubenson, and we'd sit and talk easily about nothing and everything, like families do. And my mother didn't mind that I was there. She'd always be out with people from work on Thanksgiving, volunteering in kitchens to serve the homeless. I was never invited, and I never asked to go. It's like I said: she respected my space, and I respected hers. Well, it was more like I had to *learn* to respect hers.

Before knocking, I noticed that the Rubenson's front door had little splinters beginning to run across it in certain areas, worn out patches and the paint drying out and chipping off in one of the corners. The sudden Winter weeks had lifted the life right out of the usually warm and painted-red surface. I ran my fingers across it. It killed me because the Rubensons were the only home I'd seen in Mayhaw with a red front door; it made it *their* home. Mrs. Rubenson even said herself that it was her way of showing passersby *some sorta love*. They'd get to repainting it soon enough, I was sure.

I went ahead and knocked.

"I'll get it!" A small voice echoed from the other side of the door. It was followed by the music of small feet on hardwood floor. The youngest member of the Rubenson family took a minute to work the lock and pull the front door wide open. Warmth from the inside of the house flooded my face. The door was about two and a half times her size when it opened.

There was something unique about Arietta, but I couldn't figure out what it was. Dillon made her out to be the typical brat—loving vegetables one day and hating them the next; wanting to be treated like a lady and then behaving like a baby. But she had a sweetness about her; it was that sort of honest innocence—the kind that usually fades with age. Dillon said she had a crush on me, and it was pretty obvious in her sudden, silent shyness when her parents and I were both in the same room with her. Arietta was bright like most younger kids are. Not just bright by intellect; bright by presence—a smile too big for her face paired with those roundly curious eyes. From inside of the doorway, she leaned to one side and squintingly studied me to maybe see if I'd grown any taller. She smiled for no reason, accidentally showing off a big black gap in a row of white teeth.

"Aydenn," she said benevolently. She had feather-light eyelashes whenever she spoke.

"Hi, Arietta."

With the warmth from the house at my front, I really started to feel the cold spread its fingers across my back. I stuffed my hands deep into my jean pockets and leaned forward, into the doorway, staring right at the gap in her teeth.

"What happened here?" I said as I put my finger up to my own tooth.

"Ice cream," she said.

Kids never need to elaborate.

"Did you lose a tooth?"

"Yes," she said flirtingly.

Adults are always asking kids questions just to hear the answers. And the answers are always obvious, but we just love to hear kids talk. And perhaps adults are so quick to reprimand their kids nowadays because they are simply jealous of them. Perhaps adults are jealous that, after a life of education and growing up, children are still somehow smarter—living in moments, knowing to sleep when they're tired and to eat when they're hungry, always remembering to play nice, and responding to questions with few-word, simple answers like *Ice cream*.

"What'd you get for Christmas this year, Ay-denn?" she begged with excitement.

You'll wait an eternity for a kid that young to formally invite you in. Her teeth disappeared into a different smile as she leaned against the big door, looking up at me.

"Well Arietta..." I started.

"For Heaven's sake, child, let the boy in!"

Mrs. Rubenson's voice sailed into our conversation from somewhere inside the house. She came into sight from down the hallway, her slippers shuffling over the hardwood. She walked closer, with an upside-down hand on her right hip. She fell tall behind her daughter, her presence just as soft as the pig-tailed girl that came up to her waist in front of her.

"How do you do, Mrs. Rubenson?"

"Aydenn, you gentleman," she smiled, "you know what my name is."

It was hard for me to call her by her first name—Jane. All mothers need that *Mrs.* In their name. And there was just something wholesome about saying 'Mrs. Rubenson'—perhaps I'd give her a toast next Thanksgiving: *Here's to you Mrs. Rubenson, Jesus loves you more than you will know.*

"Well come on in Aydenn, he's in the family room." She always called it the family room. I'd heard *living* room or *sitting* room, but theirs was without a doubt the *family* room. She opened the front door as wide as it would bend. She herself saw the red paint too and rubbed her hand over a small patch with a frown.

I stepped into the foyer and bent down to take off my snow boots. By the time I looked back up, Arietta had disappeared up the carpeted staircase to my right. A pattering of small, soft feet tumbled and faded above me. I followed Mrs. Rubenson down the hallway as we talked about how cold it was out there. She walked in front of me, still holding her hip like that. Halfway down the hallway, I did what I always did and stole a glance at their family portrait. Dillon couldn't have been more than eleven then; Arietta was maybe two or three. The hallway shot out into the kitchen, with the family room just off to the right. Walking over to the sink, Mrs. Rubenson asked, "Tea for ya, Aydenn? Cocoa? Somethin'?"

"Maybe in a little."

Dillon was sitting quiet and unbothered in his chair off to the right, in front of the fireplace. It actually wasn't his chair at all. It was his father's. It was a darker crimson color of leather and it squeaked whenever you moved. He just kept it warm while Mr. Rubenson was at work or in the den on the other side of the house. It's funny how we're drawn to things of our fathers. Dillon sat in that chair the same way I used to wear my father's fire helmet. Most of the time it's true: boys that are growing up can't help but want to be like Dad.

The chair faced its flat, sleek backside to me. The top half of Dillon's head appeared like a black and fuzzy sun, setting over the top of the chair. In front of him, in the opposing corner of the family room, was the television. Much newer than ours. It was on with low volume. Their home stayed pretty quiet in the nights, after Arietta had run out of energy and fallen asleep somewhere, sometimes even in her own bed. But it was a different quiet than what you'd find in my house. It was a good and warm kind of quiet.

I guessed that Dillon spent a lot of his free time in that chair.

Come to think of it, *free time* is a phrase I've never been able to get at. All time is free. Utterly free. So why is some time considered *free* while other time is just *time*? Perhaps free time is nothing more than the time when people do the things they're dreaming of doing all the time—the colorful and textural things that become so damn difficult to do. Who knows? Time's always been a fish, and it always will be. And there *we* are, standing on the shore, without bait, without a fishing line, barely even fishermen.

8

The leather let out a quick squeal as Dillon readjusted in his father's chair.

I got closer and saw that he was sitting on one of his feet, face concentrated downward. In his lap he was fiddling with something. I had a feeling Dillon spent a good amount of time alone like that. Hell, maybe that's why our friendship worked out as well as it did. I was okay with being alone; Dillon was okay with being alone. In a way, perhaps we both spent our alone time waiting for our fathers to come home. We understood each other, even if it was through our unconscious, I guess. And as you know, empathy is a hell of a glue between people.

Whatever it was he was fiddling with was cube-shaped, each side charted with smaller, colored squares. A Rubik's Cube. It was a very *Dillon* thing to have—something that appeared simple but wasn't, something to squint at and figure out, something that'd lesson you on patience, determination, failure.

Everyone had these at school. They were the new most-hated things by teachers. But that's how it goes—there will always be *something* that's new that every kid wants and that every teacher will have to go to war with.

I remember one kid in particular having one. His name was Ernest—*Learny Ernie*, I called him. He brought his cube to school every day, fiddling with it in the halls and in between bells and putting it on the table next to his tray at lunch. I swear I'd even see him talk to it. He'd go at it in Biology class, too, turning it and switching the sides and twisting and bending the colored squares around, and if the teacher would catch him and call on him, Ernie could sit up straight and bellow an answer just like that. And it was usually the right answer. He about killed me.

I wasn't usually bothered much by kids and their ways, but Ernie was just so damn smart. But at the same time, he wasn't. He was so smart at school and in the classrooms. But outside of all that, he looked and stood as dumb as they come. He taught me what it meant for someone to be *pretentious*, and he talked through his nose. A big, nasal, know-it-all. He really annoyed me. I'd see him sitting under a tree before and after school sometimes, reading his textbooks. It's funny how books come from trees. Funny, too, how reading the leaves in books somehow becomes more important than watching the leaves of trees.

One time, I told him to go jump headfirst in the lake.

Of course our teacher heard me, and I got after-school detention for rest of the week. It was a Monday, and I guess that on the previous Saturday something big had happened out at Lake Wisley. Some senior at Texana Hills had drowned in the lake over the weekend. But I hadn't heard anything about it. They hadn't made any grand announcement. It's not like I made the comment on purpose. But you know how sensitive people are, especially in schools.

I later heard that the girl drowned just off the Northern

Park of Lake Wisley.

It was strange because you'd never hear of anyone actually going all the way out there, let alone at night. I never got the whole story of what exactly happened. Sure, people talked, but you never know who or what to believe in high school. I just couldn't understand what she would've been doing all the way out there, up the road and over the hill from our high school, in the thick of the pine trees, alone.

Even more, I couldn't believe it when I found *myself* in the same place just a handful of months later.

"Hey, Cubes!" I said, walking around the side of Mr. Rubenson's chair.

"Aydenn, Aydenn, Aydenn," Dillon smiled. He didn't break eye contact with the Rubik's cube. "My man. How goes it?"

"Eh," I offered. "What do you got there? Is that your new girlfriend?"

"Ha!" he nodded with a grin.

I continued, "How far along are you two now?"

His smile faded into a seriousness as he found his focus again, twisting his hands to the right and left.

"We met a couple days ago, on Christmas," he said, "Dad introduced us."

"Well I'm happy for you guys...I see you've gotten pretty 'hands-on' with her?"

He laughed with a quick burst. He kept his eyes down as he sat further up on his leg, the leather moaning again. He went on, "I've almost got one side all the same color...that's the objective, you see. Tough thing is...I can't get *that* son of a bitch," he pointed to a bright red square in the middle of an otherwise-yellow side, "to be the same as the rest." He fiddled some more, twisting and turning, angles and sides and clicks of plastic, his mouth moving to the left side of his face while his eyebrows shifted downward. "It's like fitting a square into a goddamn circle."

Dillon swore a healthy amount. Never in poor taste. He was good at swearing.

I formed a smile that he couldn't see, "A square into a circle, eh? Sounds like someone missed 'Shape Day' in kindergarten."

"It's a saying, jackass."

I snickered, "I know, I know. Just a little humor. Don't be such a *square* about it."

He shook his head with a loose smile, stopped his fiddling, and just kind of looked down at the cube. "Dad said it'll make me a better architect." Dillon always listened to his father; he revered the guy. He bent forward, let out an exhale, and set the cube down on the ottoman next to his cup of tea. He didn't like tea, but Mrs. Rubenson always made a whole damn potful whenever she herself wanted only a single cup. Things like that are what make a mother a mother. Sure, I liked tea, but whenever we'd drink it together—Dillon and I—he'd get that look on his face with every gulp. Maybe he liked the idea of it but not so much the taste. It's funny how you can like something as an idea, but in actuality, it's nothing you'd really miss if it went away.

I plopped onto a nearby stool that kids use to stand on to help with dishes or brush their teeth. Dillon finally looked up at me after picking up and taking an awkward sip from his mug.

"So how was your Hanukkah this year?" he with that smirk.

"Oh, shut it."

My mother was raised Jewish—which Dillon somehow knew—but religion never made it on her to-do list. We didn't go to church or do anything like that, and I thought it made me an Atheist or something. Religion could really worry me. I felt guilty about it all the time. I wondered how many other people felt guilty—guilty about the same thing that was supposed to be liberating them. Nonetheless, my mother and I always had a Christmas. It wasn't real colorful or anything, but it could be okay. It had some warmth to it—a fire, a tree, a tea, a wine, some presents and, of course, our movie together on Christmas Eve, after she'd gotten back from serving dinner to the homeless with her coworkers.

"My *Christmas* was just fine. Nothing unexpected…lotta sweets," I added. "Oh, and—surprise, surprise—guess who I got *two* more books from?"

Dillon exhaled a chuckle as he leaned forward to put his mug back down on the ottoman. That mug was so damn stupid. Painted on the side in balloon letters was: *It's always Summertime in here!* It made me laugh every time I saw it. I hated it, but I wouldn't want to change it.

The books had come from my Aunt Jodie and Uncle Lou. They always gave me books for presents. They were my only aunt and uncle, so it always seemed wise to appreciate them no matter what. But they didn't know me very well. I didn't read, and if they would've looked in my closet at the pile of dusty, un-creased books they'd given me in the past, maybe they would've learned that. But I'd never let them see. They were too nice to be let down.

But both birthday and Christmas, it was always books. Perhaps they were encouraging me. Perhaps they knew something I didn't. Perhaps it was simply because Uncle Lou was a literature teacher at some small college out in Maygood, and Aunt Jodie was a part-time librarian. What *could* I expect but books, really?

My mother and I had a curious relationship with the two of them. Every now and again, they'd stumble through Mayhaw—usually unannounced—and pay us visits that were never more than a day or two. They were those people who loved movement in their lives. And when the Springtime would hit, they'd load up that camper of theirs—sky blue with a beige stripe running down the sides—and get on the road for maybe two weeks, all the while proving that love and travel is a marriage that cannot fail. They didn't have any kids. They were light; they were terribly simple. And they brought some bit of *home* into our house whenever they'd come visit.

My Aunt Jodie was born a few years after my mother, and though they were definite opposites, they were still sisters. Sisters can always find some way to get along, even if it's only whilst along the sidewalks of memory lane.

Aunt Jodie had an easy way about her. What you saw is what you got. She was always interested in me—what I'd been doing and what I'd be doing down the road. She'd throw out the word *college* and sneak in, with a hinting smile, "Perhaps you'll be seeing your Uncle Lou a little more often after high school, Aydenn."

It was a sweet and innocent thing to say. I'd nod back at her and my uncle with the kindness they deserved. They didn't know about my plans after high school; they didn't know about my plans to join the fire academy, my plans to follow in my father's footsteps.

Dillon lifted the mug to his mouth one last time.

Apprehensively, he looked over the rim—inside, at the tea—only to put the mug right back down on the ottoman where it would slowly get cold. In the dimming background, you heard Mrs. Rubenson quietly beginning with the dishes. She didn't look at us or make too much noise. She knew how teenage boys liked their space to banter and talk about the nothing-importants.

Dillon started again, "You rake in any Christmas greens?"

He had a funny language about him sometimes. All the Rubensons did.

"Not quite, but I have hope for my birthday in May."

"*I* know when your birthday is, man," Dillon said with a smirk. "And now I know just what to get you."

I laughed it off. "Oh, and I got this from my mom." I unzipped my jacket and pushed my scarf away, and the insides of my hands glided down the front of a new, wool sweater. It was soft as hell. But it was too nice to just wear around. I'd save it for special occasions like a lot of people save a lot of things for. It's a tragedy, however, when those special occasions never show up; that's how closets get so full.

"Well cool, man. Sounds like a damn good Christmas to me," he smiled. "Guess you gotta be warm when you're reading." Dillon always understood things, and he had this way with words that would comfort you for no reason.

Before I could ask him about what he'd gotten for Christmas—other than that damn Rubik's Cube—he started, "Hey whaddya say we go up to the roof? The sky ain't as bad tonight. We'll throw on some heavy jackets of Dad's." He jumped out of the leather chair, almost knocking over that mug, which, in itself, would've been a late Christmas gift to me. "Maybe we can see some constellations," he added as he stood up, finding his balance. Dillon always liked looking at things. Just looking at things. Not looking *for* anything, but just looking *at* something. It was child-like and perfect.

I got up off of Arietta's step stool and followed her big brother back down the hallway to the stairs by the foyer. Mrs. Rubenson kept to the dishes, not missing even a beat of her deep, deep humming as we clunked by.

Up the stairs, I started to skip and Dillon turned around to hush me when we got to the top landing. Arietta had gone to bed, and the hallway up there was as quiet as the color black. Her bedroom door was always left open at night, and you could hear faint and sleepy breaths escaping her little mouth. It was Dillon's favorite time of day—well, second favorite to when his father got home from work. Waiting for your father to get home from work was a warm wonder I'd never experienced.

We footed softly down to the end of the hallway, and Dillon flicked on the light to his room. He doubled back in front of me, out of his room, back to the other end of the hallway, to his parents' room. I waited there for him, studying the mathematic wallpaper that striped his walls vertically. I heard muffled closet doors sliding and cabinets shutting with a click in the thin distance behind me.

He came back with arms full, his face barely showing. Two jackets, both lined with wool, one brown and one dark blue, sat atop another pile of something in his arms. Two sleeping bags, rolled up tight.

He threw me one of the jackets. It hit me with its weight, and I began to put it on over my own three layers. He let the sleeping bags tumble to the ground and leaned over to slide his bedroom window up. He climbed out onto the roof and signaled for the sleeping bags. I threw them out to him one at a time and mimicked his footing on the windowsill to climb up myself.

Just before lifting out into the night air, I saw there on his desk the framed picture of him with his father standing behind him, his hands on his son's shoulders. They were next to Mr. Rubenson's drafting table in his office. It was take-your-kid-to-work day from maybe ten years before.

I stood up into the quiet breath of Winter.

Dillon's rooftop was patchy and white with little, round fists of snow. You could see other rooftops from up there, and I couldn't help but wonder what everyone else under them was doing or thinking about or not doing or not thinking about. Dillon unrolled the sleeping bags and tossed them to me in a big nylon and flannel heap. He fetched the wooden push-broom leaning up against the brick chimney and cleared a dark, square shape for us to lie down on.

Once zipped into the sleeping bags, the sky was ours. The snow had ceased since my walk over, and the wind was taking a long inhale. We laid side by side on our backs watching the thin fog run away overhead. The stars stepped out from behind it, one by one. I'd still never seen a shooting star at that point in my life, but I didn't think about it then. I just looked upward, without expectation, without reason.

It's funny: that view—the one upward—it's always been there. And it's always been enough, just enough, to suspend yourself entirely for a few moments. Everyone's been looking up and wondering about God and who He is and if He was, and of course the philosophers had a whole train of words about it, and even today you get these people over their tea for hours debating what can't be debated: heaven and hell, ethics, and who is right or wrong about something. And all along, I've been wondering when people are going to quit all that and just look up at the sky, into the clouds, and take a good clean inhale for the sake of *now*.

Into the air just above us, without turning his head, Dillon whispered my name.

"*Aydenn.*"

Transfixed on the stars that were all supposedly dead, I answered him back in the same volume, not looking over at him either.

"Yeah, man?"

I heard movement in his sleeping bag, and after a good minute of his ruffling around, I looked over and saw his hand come up and out of it. He was firmly holding two short, brown sticks. "I found these little sons of bitches hiding in my dad's sock drawer," he said with pride. The wash of moonlight revealed the two Castella Classics.

Cigars.

My smile started to unfold as he added, "It's been a long

time, my friend."

You'd never guess Mr. Rubenson smoked. You'd never smell a hint of it when he was around. He hid it pretty well and didn't tell his kids. Maybe his wife knew. In the end, all adults have at least one secret they keep from their children. Maybe they do it because having secrets somehow keeps you young and childish and far away from aging.

Dillon and I had only smoked a handful of times like that before, but we acted like old pros anyway. He pulled out a lighter with his other hand, and the sound of its spark seemed like the only sound in Mayhaw that night. The nighttime aged right along with us, up there on that roof, zipped up in those sleeping bags, gazing up and sucking in hollow drags from our cigars.

It was January of 1990, and school—like it always is—was just around the corner.

I can still see us up there—together, but in our own heads, worried about nothing and worried about everything at the same time. And all we could really do was watch the warm smoke roll out of our mouths. It would dance nonchalantly just above our faces, a curtain between the stars and us, and before we could render any image in it—like kids do with clouds—it all dissipated into the dark blue canvas of night.

We'd gone up there to maybe *chew the fat*—to talk about academic strife, females, certain teachers, our plans for Summer, for life. But the words never arrived. Perhaps we didn't have much to talk about after all.

Our flame-dipped cigars crackled with each bitter drag that somehow resounded brotherhood and understanding. We just lied up there like that, taking turns breathing, forgetting what season it was altogether. We were nothing more than prisoners of the moment, surveyors of stars, captains of the night.

We were just kids, but perhaps much, much more.

9

The following morning, the Rubensons would all pack bags and board their camper and make the trip up north a ways to the cottage where Dillon's grandparents lived. They'd jump on the highway a few miles past Lake Wisley and drive on father north for however long it was. His grandparents lived in a town even smaller than ours, but I can never remember the name of it. But they went there a lot. They'd even taken me once or twice. But I didn't go with them that year, and they wouldn't be back until the night before school would start up again.

◊

Lake Wisley sat pretty quietly at the northern edge of Mayhaw. It was a curious place, split into two different parks—Northern and Southern. The Southern Park was good size for a lot of things, and people did things out there in the Summertime.

Ducks would eat rips of bread crust from children, and cynical geese would try and knock those same children down; family reunions would maybe find their ground there; birthday parties and barbeques happened; Dillon and I had ridden our bikes out there a handful of times, along the widening and thinning dirt trail that ran through the park like a dried up river.

I'd go with the Rubensons and would borrow Dillon's old, squat and squeaky bike because I didn't have one yet. We were much younger then. Mr. Rubenson would strap them both on the back of their station wagon while Mrs. Rubenson strapped Arietta in her car seat. She was so little then, and she'd sit there looking out the window with a serious focus, waiting to see the pine trees that meant we were there, a paper bag of old bread crusts clutched firmly in her hand. Dillon and I sat in the way back, in the reversed seats, and we'd be boys and make faces or pretend to get stabbed and fall forward or pick our nose at the innocent people driving behind us.

I can still taste those Summer days and afternoons out there. We'd pedal along the winding path, under pine trees of all ages, and your whole nose would be cleared up by the freshness of it all. I remember a thermal wind at my face and a loose grip on those sticky handlebars, riding around the Southern Park's contours long enough until our stomachs growled for the whitebread sandwiches Mrs. Rubenson had packed with patience. It seemed like nothing then, but it's everything now.

Nostalgia burrows itself in little things like that. Scenes and memories. And it's always been odd how happiness of the past can bring on a heavy woe in the present. It's a sad trap to be in, itching to get back to something you once had, itching to get back into the lightness of youth, the good freedom of it all. Perhaps if we would've known *then* that we might look back with nostalgia at what we were doing, we would've jumped right off our bikes and just sat still in the shade of a few trees, eyes closed, barely breathing. But then again, perhaps you can't avoid nostalgia the same way you can't avoid change. Plus, any memory *must* be a good memory, because, whatever the hell it is, it's going to remind you to *remember* and teach you to *feel*.

Mr. and Mrs. Rubenson would always keep an eye on Dillon and I as we rode. They made sure we didn't go too far in the direction of the bridge that sat where the trail turned thin and undefined. It linked the two parks together. There wasn't much for kids to do in the Northern Park.

There wasn't much for anyone to do there. There wasn't much else but a few tents, scattered about, and a few quiet, shadow-like people breathing in oxygen from the pine trees and dealing with the dizziness of life and its circumstances.

It was the place where homeless people passed through or ended up. And you just kind of left it alone. Sure, you heard old stories about seniors at Texana Hills going out there to drink bottles in the deep and distant dark, but that all stopped when that girl drowned.

◊

I had a little over a week until school would start up its engine again for the second and final half of my junior year at Texana Hills.

It was January. The snow had kicked back up, and I could see it fall in shy tufts out my bedroom window. I was tired of television reruns and I wasn't much for going into town, so the only logical thing left to do was to empty my hamper into the washer, vacuum, and claw down the cobwebs that hung high and gray in forgotten corners of my room. Funny how it's just as easy to hate the idea of cleaning your room as it is to love the sight of your room after it's cleaned.

With intervals of Winter sniffles, I cleaned and organized, all the while convincing myself I'd be more organized from then on, like we always do. In the far corner of my room, between dresser and closet, I fetched up a jacket that I wore in heavy snow as an outer shell. I'd lay it over the seat of the stool so it could dry. It was lying dead there with its cold, nylon skin, and when I lifted it up and off the stool to go hang it up on a hanger in my closet, something showed its face from underneath.

Sitting squarely there on the seat of the stool were my aunt and uncle's Christmas gifts, stacked on top of each other. *Damn books,* I thought. It was like they'd been waiting there for me, the two of them. Books will do that; they'll linger all their lives in dust, just waiting there. I hung up the jacket as planned, and in doing so, I saw down there on the closet floor the even taller stack of books. On top was a brown-covered sketchbook that held my drawings or tear-stained sketches—or whatever you want to call them—of my father; under that was old schoolbooks I might've been interested in later on in life and long after school; under *that* were the past books I'd received from my aunt and uncle, unskimmed and unread. The stack teetered as the closet door slid open into a slam against the frame. If I would've added even one more book to it—let alone two more—the whole thing would've timbered over pathetically.

Aunt Jodie and Uncle Lou were good people, nice people, the kind of people you'd want to be friends with until you're older, the kind of people you could have tea with and not talk about a whole lot but have it still feel like you're talking about so much. Maybe I'd been wronging them by not reading their books. Maybe I was wrong for not believing them, not trusting them. After all, they *were* my aunt and uncle. Maybe they somehow knew what I'd like, perhaps even what I'd needed.

Surrendering to the guilt, I picked up one of the books from the stool and flipped its pages. I watched the paragraphs chase each other like brothers and sisters do outside before being called in for dinner.

I mentioned that they lived by the sea, Aunt Jodie and Uncle Lou.

By the simple color of their clothing, you could sort of tell that—soft blue or salmon colored cotton and khakis and baseball caps. Aunt Jodie was one for photography. She took pictures for no reason, or maybe even the accidental reason of showing things—in their stillness—to people who'd long forgotten about them. She took pictures of little things and big things. People's hands and smiles and wrinkled eyes and the ocean and the sky when it was changing. You'd spot her pictures in humble frames around their house, on the mantle and tucked a ways back on weighty bookshelves. She and my mother were both born in that house—not in some hospital up the road, but literally *in* that house.

Oh, to be born by the sea!

Their parents—my grandmother in particular—thought that the best place to start a family was somewhere where you could sense the nearby washing of water and befriend the salty echo in the breeze. And that's exactly what they did. They started their family right there, seaside, in Maygood.

My aunt had shoeboxes of old shots—them all there on the sand, my grandfather, my grandmother, my mother and aunt. Old fashioned swimsuits and a blanket spread out with things like French bread and jam and fruit. It was beautiful and sad at the same time, looking at those yellowed and square little coaster-sized photographs. My mother's hair was so curly back then.

My Aunt Jodie would tell me stories about my grandmother. I never got to meet her. She'd passed before I was born, and my grandfather passed a few years before her. But she sounded lovely, my grandmother. She was a painter. Not a big-time one, not a famous one. Just a painter.

"She's probably *still* painting up there in heaven," my aunt would joke with glassy eyes and a smile that was her own. "She was by her easel more than anything." It was an easel built by my grandfather, so he was always right there with her, even after he'd passed. "She painted because she had to," Aunt Jodie would say. "She'd sit out there on her sundeck measuring time only by the sun's rising and its setting, and she loved every minute of it."

Her name was Ira.

She'd perch behind her easel with rounded posture, and with little wrinkled eyes, she'd squint out and put her study on the horizon. It was the loyal line that always gave repose to her mind of colors and shapes. She'd only paint outdoors. Maybe the indoors is just too small for some people. She'd sit there and take slow, little breaths and "She never let anything get in the way of her painting," my mother chimed in once. "She'd even paint out in the rain if she had to."

"Yeah," Aunt Jodie agreed, "that was her stubbornness, her *need* to be outside. She'd make your grandfather stand out there in his rain boots and hold an umbrella up over her and her easel. And you'd better believe he'd do it too!"

I guess, before he died, my grandfather would tie a thin and light paintbrush around her wrist with a ribbon so she could still paint. See, she'd lost most of her grip once the arthritis got her good in her hands. But like my aunt had said, she had to paint. And that's exactly what she did.

◊

My mother had a few of Grandma Ira's canvases up in our house. There was an especially large one in our living room. It was up to your left when you walked in the front door, above the couch. A blend of oil and water, it was a painting of the early evening ocean—the water placid blue, no waves or whitecaps, just a barely-there current rolling shyly atop the shallow water, trying its best to blanket a few rocks that poked their noses up to the sky.

The real personality of the painting was *in* that sky, where paint was laid down generously in puffy textures, thick and shapeless clouds changing their robes at sunset. It romanced the horizon beautifully. The sky tinted the water with a deep red, and it was all so still across. No swooping birds, no sea foam; just the invisible movement of light.

You could never just walk by that painting. It would catch you and make you linger for a minute. That was how I could really see my grandmother. Much like I'd only gotten to see my father by way of his firefighting helmet, I only got to see my grandmother in her paintings. But maybe that was okay. Maybe it reinforced that art does, in fact, immortalize the artist—not the other way around.

My aunt met my uncle at some art festival in the local streets up there and married him pretty soon afterward, and, with my mother's consent, they moved into that same seaside house with the sundeck where my grandmother used to paint. Down in the basement still remained the big collection of her paintings. They hung along slanting walls—some in frames, some not—and the air down there was damp and dusty but quiet and cool. You had to shuffle down narrow wooden steps to see it all, and the roof followed your head nice and low as you walked. She had a few unfinished ones leaned against the concrete basement walls. There were two or three unwashed paintbrushes, neatly lain out and dried stiff with orange and light blue paint.

Aunt Jodie and Uncle Lou left the basement just like that.

They never went out on the sundeck either. They even locked up the door leading out to it. All that was kept out there was the easel my grandfather had built. Set in it was a big, blank, square canvas. And they let all the seasons pass right over it, rain and sun and clouds, without taking it inside.

That's how Grandma Ira would've wanted it.

I remember visiting them this one time when I was younger, with my mother, for Aunt Jodie's big photography display at one of the nearby galleries. It was the *Sea Me Now* gallery that my grandmother used to show her paintings at.

Aunt Jodie really took after her.

Every time she'd come rolling through Mayhaw, she'd have that 35-millimeter around her neck like some sort of oversized necklace. She'd always take a photograph of me, then my mother, then my Uncle Lou would take one of the two sisters, side by side with widened girl smiles. She could talk about photography forever and about how she, long ago, ran into Ansel Adams in some big national park—she loved to tell that one and we'd always let her. A nameless, warm color would fill her face when she'd talk. It wasn't vanity. More of a gentle pride. My Uncle Lou would just sit and listen to her. I'm sure he'd heard the stories three-hundred times, but the way he twisted his short, graying beard and smiled as he looked at her mouth move when she talked showed how warmly he felt about her.

And for however long it was, the four of us—my mother and I and my aunt and uncle—would sit there in our living room underneath that quiet painting of Grandma Ira's and talk like families do. Maybe those were the times our living room became our family room.

I'd do my best to keep good eye contact with my aunt or uncle, but often I'd flick over, out the window, to the sight of their camper parked out on the street. Sometimes I just wanted to go with them, wherever they were going. It's a strange and round, swallowing feeling to want to *go* for the sake of going. I guess I just wanted to be anywhere but *here*. But I'd soon learn that *here* is the only place you *should* ever be. More than that, it's the only place you've ever really been.

Aunt Jodie was one of the few I'd met who remembered to do just what she loved. She remembered to be passionate about something. Active in it. She embraced her craft, and it gave her a hell of a glow. Perhaps we all need that. Perhaps that's the great secret—having some sort of artistic outlet, something that allows us to feel the fire changing its hot shape inside of us.

She spent half of her time behind a camera, the other half behind the circulation desk at Maygood's public library.

Librarians are a wonder. They're like priests in a church of hardbacks and reference numbers who become excited when new people poke their heads in, half-frightened, half-curious. She wore glasses, librarian-like glasses—the ones with small square lenses, a floral-printed plastic frame and a small chain attached to the arms in case they were to fall off in an intense bout of reading.

I could imagine her sitting there—behind that desk, behind a little plastic sign that read *Please interrupt,* thinking about what book to get next for her only nephew, Aydenn.

I shut my closet door, ducked under my top bunk and plopped those two books from the stool down on my desk, bringing the stool over to sit down on. I flicked on my orange desk lamp and, in the light, I held the first of the two: *The Adventures of Tom Sawyer.*

Perhaps it had been my Uncle's when he was my age. It was old as hell and the pages had turned brittle-orange and it had that smell about it. He was always telling me when-I-was-your-age stories, and it seemed like the kind of book he'd want to pass on to me. It's all pretty ironic that *Mark Twain* was a pseudonym and everything. Pseudonyms can be a real buzz when you actually meet someone who has one. And later that year, I would.

The second of the two books was from my aunt: *Jonathan Livingston Seagull*. I lifted the cover open to find her dedication in bold blue handwriting up in the corner.

Aydenn,
Merry Christmas! This one is a favorite of mine.
Read it slowly. Don't be afraid to fly alone!
Love, Aunt Jodie

With a patient cursive, I wrote my name on the insides of both of the books.

Aydenn Price.

Doing that makes a book your own.

10

Tom Sawyer saw the world as some sort of playground, throwing his squintingly curious eyes all around shabby, little St. Petersburg. Some people, especially mothers, will go on thinking he was too damn young to be pioneering through why-not adventures like that. But everyone's too caught up with age as it is. If you sit on it long enough, age is much more irrelevant than we've made it. Because it's never really about age; it's about experience. And I'll believe *that* much until the day my age runs out.

Reading that old book of Uncle Lou's at the tail end of Winter break, I finally got to use that bookmark I'd made in the sixth grade or so. I still had it lying around somewhere—you know how teenagers hold onto little sentiments. It had been an art project in the sixth grade; we made them with real leather at Mayleaf Elementary School. It was a little ways away from Mayhaw, close to where my mother worked. Dillon and I were classmates there, and it was where we became best friends.

Our teacher handed out twenty-eight scraps of full grain leather. None of us really knew what the hell they were for, but, at that age, you just liked getting things. He also handed out twenty-eight needles and twenty-eight tiny spools of polyester thread. We all fought each other for the good scissors in the old cabinet that faintly read *ART SUPPLIES*.

We cut out any shape we wanted to, as long as it had the same contour line on both sides; that way, we could fold over our cutout and sew the two opposite sides together with the polyester thread, and there we'd have our bookmark. Teaching us how to sew took two days of art time.

Being left-handed introduced me to a few accounts of classroom prejudice growing up. It was something I half-hated, half-laughed at. One of them was right-handed desks, the other was how all the scissors were right-handed, and they'd hug the inside of your thumb like hell when you'd use your left with them. It made me turn my scrap of leather into God-knows-what. I tried cutting out a spade, like what you'd see in cards. Not even close. Jealousy kneed me in the ass when I looked around at the others cutting out their perfectly organic shapes, especially the girls. They were so patient and lovely and horrible about the way they did things.

I got the thread through the needle and folded the leather shape in half and sewed its sides together. It was hell. It ended up looking like a crooked flame, like what you'd see atop a candlewick. But it was okay. Art is never perfect. And it ended up getting its use, being thrown in and out of *Tom Sawyer* that last week or so of Winter break.

It kept me company in a weird way, that book. Perhaps that's what authors try to do. Perhaps authors are a lonely people, and they feel that their work is nothing more than company to their lonely readers. Reading is a real buzz. I've found this to be the case over the years. And you won't understand why reading is a buzz until you've sat down across the table from it and clinked your glasses and thrown back a few.

Reading is like walking into someone else's house, seeing what his or her life is like on the inside, ambling into the kitchen of smells and sounds while someone like Mark Twain is hunched over the stovetop, cooking dinner. Sometimes books will become real, four-walled places for people. It's like you can walk into them and stand on the chapter title and lean over, glancing down at the first sentence, or even sit right *on* a sentence for a good and generous while and dangle your feet down into the margin. Books are all just a jungle of words for us animals of thought.

And the next jungle for me was the book from my aunt. It was told from the eyes of a seagull, and the last person I'd heard about who'd really listened to what a bird had to say was Edgar Allan Poe. Sure, he was a nut, but I didn't care. We're all nutty, nutty as hell. And if you think even for a second that you're not, then you're even a bigger nut.

◊

Break was over and Dillon came back and school started up again for the last time until Summer, and there I found myself, sitting with a shoulder-slouch in a school desk built for people who wrote with their right hands.

It was a brand new year, 1990.

I'd turn seventeen in a few months, then it would be Summer, then Summer would pass and I'd be a high school senior in the Fall. It was a time of new beginnings, a year of new weather, new babies, new friends and boyfriends and girlfriends, new music and fashions, new cars, new news. We resumed our classes at Texana Hills about two weeks after adults everywhere had gotten drunk enough to convince themselves they'd be better people *this* year. New Year's was funny—people waiting until the first of January to really look at themselves in the mirror.

I quickly made four new friends that semester: *Biology II, Geometry, History of the United States,* and *Introduction to Analyzing Literature.* It was going to be a lot of weight in thoughts and books and studying, but sometimes that's what the bare bones of school is. Never much for grades myself, I was naturally put off by people who were—except for Dillon. He had a way about him where he could just pick something up and learn it, like that Rubik's Cube. He got things that other people would *almost* get. He listened to and understood things like biology and geometry; he took school seriously, just like his father had. Dillon sort of smiled at academic challenges like an 8th grader might smile at a 5th grader before a tetherball match. He was real bright all across the board and a lot of teachers knew him and acknowledged him around school, but I was never jealous.

You see, jealousy is a choice, and so is admiration.

◊

History of the United States could be a hell of a time in class.

It was a lot of looking into the past, and you really need to have a balance with that kind of thing. Not just with history written in books, but your own history as well. Some people can get stuck in the past like it's mud; others won't even look back because they can't deal with it; some know exactly what to take and what to leave behind. Perhaps learning the relevance and importance of the past without living in the past is a fence that we're all placed on to sit for a while. Some sit on it their whole lives. Some decide which yard to hop down into. Some stand right up on the fence and slowly begin footing themselves forward, toe to heel, along the top, with their arms stretched out bird-like for balance.

History is the place where all things once existed. It's the book where most of our stories reside. And it seems like, more and more, stories are all we really have. Reminiscence, conversation, coffee shop talk, war diaries and perfumed letters, books and newspapers and so much more lost and unwritten words. There's something real and hard and stone-like about the past, like how the story of yesterday has happened only one time, forever.

Things stood under a different light in my *Introduction to Analyzing Literature* class.

It was a mouthful of a class, but you'd hear good things about it around school. It was with a teacher that everyone, faculty and students, loved. She was young and real spirited about the stuff. Pretty too; she wore skirts. She threw a slew of new words and sentences into our lives. Not much poetry, but short stories. Oates and Joyce and Faulkner and Hemingway— *Poor Hemingway*, I always thought.

She'd teach us to feel the textures in words, to hear the voices of themes and to find the things the author may have hid between the lines by accident or even on purpose. The more we dissected and discussed, the more we were adding to the history of the texts; perhaps that's how all literature works—sure, it was written on a certain date in the past, but it's always being added to, amended each time we look at it or think about it or talk about it out loud.

One day, in late March of that year, just around the time the rain began to rinse Mayhaw with notes of Spring, our teacher introduced the word *novella* to the class. It was a new and curious and romantic kind of word. With a long piece of white chalk, she wrote up the title of a novella that we'd read next. A grandmother-like cursive ran across the middle of the blackboard, reading:

Jonathan Livingston Seagull

The *same* book from Aunt Jodie!

Sure, it was curious, but all things are. You see, coincidences don't really exist. Magic does. The sooner you learn that, the sooner life becomes its true self.

Later that day, right as the sun lowered and the late afternoon yawned, I reclined back on my top bunk with the book on my chest, and through the big, still clouds and thin sheets of rain, a ray of sunlight jetted into my window right onto my face. I closed my eyes as a blanket of heat worked at my eyelids like paint was drying on them. I lied there like that, propped up on elbows, facing the window. Fiery-orange shapes blossomed on the insides of my eyelids, only to dance and die and then reappear bigger and more circular.

I fell back on my pillow and held up the novella in the overhead stream of light. Every word I read was read with my index finger underneath it. I read from cover to cover right there, and anytime I was outside after that and looked up at the sky on a clear day and saw a bird cut across, it was all different.

It was like Aunt Jodie knew.

11

By the middle of that semester, I started to see less and less of my best friend.

That's just how it gets toward the end of high school, when everyone wants to grow up. A whole lot of them start pairing up and falling in love and having sex, and best friends slowly become only friends. The month of March matured, and so had Dillon's relationship with *her*.

Her name would slip from his lips from time to time, but I never made anything of it; I never knew he'd really go for it with her. But things are always unpredictable as hell, and since the third week we'd returned to school, it seemed like they'd been binge drinking love potion together in between bells. And by early April, it was no surprise catching them in the halls with their magnetic hands. Sure, they'd wave to me, and we'd talk a few words; they were so light and easy, floating off the ground. And it was fine. Dillon was growing up, and I figured boys become men when they're supposed to, when they need to. And it was just his time. I just thought he might get distracted by it all. He was supposed to keep his A's and be an architect like his father; he was supposed to keep a focus on things.

But perhaps only fools waste their time wrapped up in the romances of others. Instead, I figured Cupid knows best. And hell, maybe *that's* why God or Zeus or whoever it is has kept Cupid on the payroll for all these years. All the guy does is shoot arrows. He must have pretty good aim by now.

Perhaps Dillon's new girlfriend was just another thing to study, just like that Rubik's Cube of his. And if she was, I couldn't help but wonder which one he'd figure out first.

()

All the snow was melting into water on the streets and front lawns and rooftops, and April started off wet as hell. The school year was creaking slowly to an end, and pretty soon the season would change again. Summer. And then it would change one more time. Fall, and I'd finally be a senior at Texana Hills. Being a senior was always the thing you'd dream about, and it seemed like only real-life part of high school. It was a dream you couldn't wait for to materialize.

But the twisted truth is, when you get to any dream's hatching—when it comes true and you become what you'd been longing to become for so long—it all somehow shifts backwards, and you start dreaming about the time when you were first dreaming. And just like that, you begin to dream backwards, further and further, and suddenly, childhood becomes the greatest thing you'll dream about. But it's hard because we can't ever get back there. Or perhaps we can, even if only for a minute, and I guess that's what you do when you're an adult— you dream about childhood.

You'd think Dillon's absence would've made the rain fall harder, but it didn't.

We were still best friends. Sure, he had a girlfriend, but a woman can't come between certain things. Of course, *girls* can. But Dillon's girlfriend wasn't a *girl*. She'd had a boyfriend before. And she carried herself well. You could just tell she cared—about him; about herself; about the Earth she walked on.

It's a coming of age when you get your first, real girlfriend. It's another coming of age when your best friend gets his first before you do. But you can't feel bad for yourself. In fact, every time you want to go ahead and feel bad for yourself is just another opportunity to, instead, feel good for someone else. That's what separates the strong from the weak, the selfless from the selfish, the hearts from the minds.

I was happy for him. Sure, there was a new distance between us, but that's just what happens. Much like the trail of Dillon and mine's footprints in the snow when we used walk home from somewhere together, at some point, separation always had to happen. And I think it's these separations that are important in friendships. We were still the same rooftop philosophers at heart; we were just taking to our private studies––he, to the hand of her; me, to the pages of a few books. And such a circumstance was nothing more than a new branch on the tree of friendship that we'd planted hard in the ground over ten years prior. And trees don't just disappear. Sure, they go through the seasons and change color and blow in the wind and lose their leaves and grow new ones, but they never just go away. They never disappear unless someone actually cuts them down.

My mother, like Dillon, became more and more absent as

the year continued to unfold.

That's because, really, up until the night everything happened, she was just kind of in the background of things—there, but barely there, a soft hue in the far sky of an oil painting. Mothers and sons should be close. Mothers and sons without *Dad* should be even closer. It wasn't fair, but nothing is. Fairness is just something people made up to help them try and justify what's already been written out and what is to be.

The last rains of April washed away everything. Well, almost everything. I still stole to my sketchbook from time to time, maybe not even to draw, but just to look or cry or whatever it was I did. That was the thing about this passing idea, about my father. Thoughts of him would leave, only to return again at random with their intensity. It's like how even though you can watch a train leave the station, and it feels like it's its final departure and it's never coming back, it always does come back. My mind was the station of course, my father the train. Whoever was conducting that train could've been time or fate or God. The ruminations would always return, and they'd be on their own schedule, but then they'd pass. Some things you can't escape, like thought. Thought can be a hell of a time. It really makes you wonder who has control of your thoughts—you, or the world you're thinking in.

〇

May came after April, and though you always knew it would, it still managed to surprise you.

Flowers showed up and trees were trees again and the roses were all extroverted with their full, red lips. There was this house I'd walk by on the way to Emma's Café that had a whole slew of roses right under its front windows. It was a big, yellow house and it was older than anything else you'd see in Mayhaw. There were only a few like it in the neighborhood. It had pillars on the porch—much larger than the ones out front of the Rubenson's house. A wide and deep shape of green grass separated the house from the fence at the sidewalk, where I'd stand and gaze at it. The grass was mowed short and stood vacant, with only a small black iron table and two matching chairs directly in the middle of it. But they were always empty. It's funny how empty chairs can sometimes look like people themselves, sitting there with straight backs. The house seemed wise with its angled architecture and little extra peak up in the roof—a small window was tucked under it; there weren't any drapes and I doubted anyone could actually fit up there, except maybe for Arietta.

But at the base of the house—all right there in front, under the windows and on both sides of the porch steps—sat the roses. I loved to look at them. Such care was put into them. You could just tell. I'd never seen who lived there or who watered and pruned the roses. But whoever they were, they understood what it meant to have intention. I never really told anyone that I'd stop to look at those roses, or that sometimes I'd purposely take a different way home, a longer way home, just to catch them before the day ended. No one knew I loved roses. Maybe the roses knew. Maybe they loved me back.

They were only there in the Spring, right around the time the air changed.

Change is a wonder. We'll always be one way or another with it. And all you'll ever learn about it is that, often, it's the only thing left to rely on. It's the hero of monotony, the hiccup in the mundane, the coin that always remains deep down in our pocket, under the lint. It brings us right to left, to and fro, up to down, from lightness to darkness to heaviness back to lightness. The existence of change makes our lives into simple flickering flames upon the wicks of candles. The flame flickers and dances and dims and brightens, but it never disappears until someone blows it out.

May was always the best month. By then, the sky had figured itself out and everyone was calmed down. Plus, it was the month that I'd turn a year older.

For some reason, Aunt Jodie and Uncle Lou gave me money that year—just straight cash—for my birthday. No books. They mailed it down from Maygood. I couldn't believe it—straight cash. It made me feel like an adult; there was this inexplicable freedom in it. The money had hid itself in a store-bought birthday card. My aunt always made sure to underline whatever words were printed inside. It was to say that, though she didn't write the words herself, she still really meant them.

My mother did her German Chocolate for my birthday cake, like she always did. And it wasn't one of those family traditions that you wish would just stop. It was always the best cake, and it was how she said *I love you*. While there wasn't much of her love manifested throughout the year, I always found it then, on my birthday, in that first moistened bite of coconut and chocolate.

Funny how love hides itself in things.

12

A handful of weeks before school was out for Summer, I was walking down the hall after dropping a few brick-weight books off at my locker. Something was posted up on the wall, begging for attention. Some sort of flier that someone felt was important enough to post eight times. Kids never read those things, so they needed to post it eight times. Next year it would be nine

They were all written in big, bold letters. I got closer and squinted up at what they had to say. My eyes weren't bad or anything; I just squinted at things because you can see things better that way. The bell rang when I was only a few words in. From behind me, lockers slammed and feet shuffled. It meant you had five minutes to get to class. But the bell was just a bell. It was just a silly noise that occurred when two pieces of metal rattled against each other. Funny how only the noises of Nature used to mean something—the wind or the rain or the howl of something in the depth of the trees. But now it's all different.

Now we move like cattle to man-made noises, forgetting the difference between sound and noise altogether.

Bodies hurried out the door to my right as I stood still and read the flier two times through—enough to be interested. Seven fliers wouldn't be all that different from eight. I leaned forward to snag one of them from the wall. Balancing on my toes and reaching up, some man bumped right into the side of me as he hurried out the door. He squeezed in between students of all shapes and heights. I didn't see his face; all I saw was the back of him. He was clearly a teacher, carrying some sort of briefcase—it turned out to be an attaché. I didn't recognize him then because he must've been clutching the red beret in his hand instead of wearing it on his head like he usually did. More students piled out as I ripped the flier from the wall and folded it in half, starting to walk to class myself.

I look back now at the irony of that teacher bumping into me right then and there.

Funny how irony flirts with you when you're asleep like that.

And the flier? It was simple:

TEXANA HILLS POETRY COMPETITION

All subject matter welcome.
Turn in your typed submissions to Room G22 by May 31st.
English faculty will elect judges and post results toward semester's end.
Prizes awarded to winners.
Remember, a poet lives within all pens!

Does a poet really live within all pens?

I'd never been in any kind of love. I'd never been given another's heart. Never had I broken one or had mine broken. I hadn't studied literature on death, or religion, or the death *of* religion for that matter. And that all seemed to constitute more than half of poetry. But if a poet lives within all pens, it must've meant there was *something* I could make words about. Perhaps with poetry, it's never really *what* you're writing about; rather, it's *how* you write what you're writing about.

Introduction to Analyzing Literature turned out to be a class made up of a fleshy body of ideas rather than dry-bone, skeletal facts. Our teacher talked about a lot of things—some new, some old, some old that became new again. One day, she mentioned how the *long for yesterday* could be a pretty powerful theme in literature. But what the hell could someone like me be longing for? I hadn't found a girl with the right eyes yet *to* long for, and it couldn't have been my childhood I wanted back. Hell, the only thing I longed for was something that was foolish to long for in the first place. It made no sense to long to see someone who wasn't even alive. It was nonsense to long for my father. But it was real. Perhaps it's the case that poetry often evolves from nonsense.

And so I took the bus from school that day, down, down, past my usual stop, and got off at the edge of town. I walked the blocks over to Emma's Café. The sun was out and on my back as I made it closer. I ordered my Earl Gray from the same girl behind the register who, again, almost remembered my name. In the spirit of the changing season, she was showing more skin than usual, up by her collarbones. She had shorter hair that would just barely entertain the idea of resting on her shoulders. I paid for my tea and she smiled at me and I smiled back and went to sit down and wait.

From the chair by my round table in the back, I looked out through the glass. I never knew what you would call a wall of glass. Is it a window or is it nothing? Or is it nameless and perfect and not in need of a name?

I slung my backpack off, onto the ground, down heavy by my feet. A thud and then a loud and quick zip open. I felt the eyes of a few regulars on me. They were calm and quiet and monk-like, but they could have these scowls about them. Maybe they were unhappy. Maybe they were happy to be unhappy. Either way, we were all in there for the same reason. You see, people are lonely, and they go to cafés to be lonely together.

The girl brought my tea over along with another smile. She put it down on a napkin and turned and walked away, swaying the arm that had a small tattoo tucked on the inside of it. It was the outline of a bird, maybe a sparrow. I thought I might tell her she was beautiful. Instead, I went right for the tea and burnt my top lip.

I let it mellow, and I pulled out the folded-up flier from my backpack and flattened it on the unpopulated round table and read it again. Eyes still on the flier, I leaned down and slid a piece of lined paper out from a binder in my backpack. I finished reading those words for the last time and laid the lined paper over the flier for padding. With a dull pencil, I began to write. I wrote real slow. I didn't know what exactly I was writing. Words will come at the strangest times, but you always feel good when they do.

I wrote for the passing idea.

I wrote for my father.

And I still have that first draft.

In My Fabric but a Thread

by Aydenn Price

Buried under the Earth.

The same earth which I tread.

Present in ideas, not memories;

In my fabric but a thread.

Left behind this poet.

Left behind his wife.

Entered the fire on Earth,

but not in afterlife.

Perhaps a saint, from the little I've heard.

Just proud should I be of his act?

Or do I dare ~~inquire~~ *inquire* more,

showing poor mother no tact?

13

Just like that, the competition results arrived.

They were posted on a white sheet, only one time, at the end of that same hall. They came quick, but that's how it is with everything. It was the first week of June. It was almost Summer, but then again, it's always *almost* Summer for kids in school.

To make the competition judging fair, participants had to use a pseudonym for their entries. It made me think about Sam Clemens or Mark Twain or whatever you want to call him. The name I used was okay. I liked it. I thought it was clever of me. It was *A. B. Seedy*.

But neither *A. B. Seedy* nor *Aydenn Price* found its way up there on that white sheet with the other winners. It was real shitty, but you can't let little things like that break you. If you do, then you've only made yourself breakable, and that's no life to live.

It's just that it was such a personal poem.

For people to let themselves go like that and be more open than they'd ever intended on being and let their hearts bleed by way of their pen, and then for it to not be *good* enough? How can you even measure things like that? There was so much in there that the judges probably missed. But I couldn't blame them for it. You can't show people a tree and expect them to see the roots. But perhaps the biggest accomplishment, bigger than winning, was just writing it. You'd be real surprised at how heart-squeezing and difficult and real writing can be. Words are like hell sometimes. And they come from nothing more than the same letters of the alphabet you learned back when you were five. Words are really something. Words are like tools, dictionaries like sheds, books like father-son projects built in the Summertime.

I'd turned 17 a month prior to all that, in the middle of May.

I wouldn't have to rely on Dillon—well, Mr. Rubenson's secret pastime—to enjoy a good smoke anymore. Sure, the smoking age was 18, but it was different down at a little liquor store on the way into town. It was a hidden and quaint store, tucked off the street, neighboring a video rental store that had pornography magazines on the back wall behind a black, velvet curtain.

You'd usually be one of only two or three others in that liquor store. But maybe that's just how liquor stores work. The walls and ceilings were dusty and quiet and wood-brown, and it made you feel like maybe you shouldn't have been in there at all. But they had trading cards and bubble gum for sale too, and sports posters along the walls, so it always felt okay. It was called *Mayhaw Cabinet*, but you'd hear the neighborhood kids on bicycles call it *Sil's*. That was the wrinkled man's name who owned it—Sil. He was always dressed in his crisp, rodeo-looking button-ups, hunched over the counter, tapping his ring against the glass surface. His vision would trade between you and whatever the hell it was he was reading. He was somewhere between 70 and 100 years old.

There was a good amount of cigar boxes inside that glass counter—some beveled with illustrated women and men, others with painted-on trees or landscapes. Castella Classics were in there too, the kind Mr. Rubenson would buy. But I had to go for the cheapest ones, and I can't even remember the name of them. They were alright. And I could buy one, just like that. Sil could never see the difference between kids who were 17 and kids who were 18. He couldn't see much at all for that matter. I even saw him try to put on glasses over his glasses once. It was so easy to just walk in and look around at nothing for a minute and then point into the glass at the cigar you wanted. Sil wouldn't even ask for a picture ID. He'd unlock the glass and slide it open and strategically finger a cigar out of its box with his bony, purple-veined, white hands. He'd ring me up while I'd avoid eye contact and look behind him at the different-necked liquor bottles back against the wall. I'd do it like I was old enough to be interested. I'd see the dark and mature wine bottles there too, toward the bottom, and I'd think of my mother.

I'd pay him and thank him and he'd give me a head nod. He was never much for words, always squinting down at the register or whatever it was he was reading. I'd return the nod and fetch a blank-white matchbook from the neat, four-squared stack next to the *Take a Penny, Leave a Penny* tray. Sometimes I'd light up just outside the store, and have the whole cigar on my walk back home. But I wouldn't walk by the roses if I did that. I didn't want them to see me smoking.

I had a cigar-walk-home the day I found out those poetry competition results. I walked home from Sil's, thirty-nine cents poorer, through neighborhood streets I almost wished I lived on instead of 8th, under trees of new colors. People were outside doing outside things, but I smoked anyway, walking over the cracks in the sidewalk. I thought more about my poem and everything, and then I let it go with the breeze. It would now be just another memory.

And it would've stayed that way—just a memory—if a certain yellow note hadn't arrived for me in class a week later.

◊

It happened the second week of June, 1990.

It was during pre-Summer exams. We were right in the middle of our history test. It was silent as hell aside from the pencil work. And then there was a knock at the door. There's always a knock like that when it's been quiet for too long in a classroom. Mr. Aldridge hated the interruptions even if he wasn't lecturing but just sitting and watching us do good or terrible on his tests.

We called them *runners*. They were students. They'd knock and deliver notes from the front office around school during their free period. And you'd always be caught off-guard when *you* were brought a note. Some notes sang the blues of discipline. Others reminded you to leave school early for the dentist or doctor—the people you hated visiting otherwise. I imagined that, over the years, runners had learned by word of mouth to knock softer and softer when they knew it was Mr. Aldridge's door. He'd been there forever. He was as old as the history he taught.

The knock quieted. The room quieted. A girl pressed open the door like it weighed a thousand pounds. She looked around like she was entering a dark cave. Mr. Aldridge, sitting down, tucked in his chin and peered at her over the top of his glasses. You just knew she wanted to get the hell out of there, and she wasted no time whispering, *Aydenn Price.*

I waved a hand at her, and she trotted over and dropped a

little, yellow note on my desk. It landed right next to the spot where someone had carved into the wood: *Where's the PASSION?*, and by the time I picked up the note and read my name on it and looked back up, she was gone. The scratching of pencil work resumed as the door eased into a silent close. I'd never seen that girl before, and I never saw her again after that day. She was real pretty, angelic and innocent in that little girl way, but I never saw her again.

I began to read the note, squinting at the writing, forgetting I was in the middle of a test. There wasn't much to read. Only a few lines. Again, it wasn't that my eyes were bad. It's just that, with squinting, you tend to see more. It's the kind of squint that painters will do when they step back from their easel and tilt their heads from side to side, as if to get the water out of their ears.

I'm always challenging myself to not be a sentimentalist.

If you become a sentimentalist while you're young, then by the time you're 40, your whole house becomes a thrift store or an antique shop with nothing for sale. It's the truth. But we can't help holding onto some things, which is why I've held onto that note all this time, just like I've held onto that café-written poem for my father.

TEXANA HILLS HIGH SCHOOL
STUDENT NOTIFICATION SLIP

FOR ___Aydenn Price___

DATE ___6/26/90___ TIME ___11:45am___

MESSAGE

Aydenn -

Really enjoyed your poem. Something real there. Perhaps there's more to be gardened. I think you'd find comfort in my "Literature as Philosophy" class in the Fall. I invite you to enroll.

Til September,

J. Kristiansen

14

J. Kristiansen.

I knew the name; we all did. He was one of the more talked about English teachers at Texana Hills, and obviously one of the judges in the poetry competition. You'd see him around campus just like you'd see everybody else, but he was always on the move, to or from a significant somewhere. He stood out in the throngs of kids with that faster pace of his. Perhaps he could hear his existential clock ticking, giving him the momentum to walk as fast as he did. He took bigger strides than everybody around him. He'd always been a curious sight. A distant, curious sight. And I never expected he and I to make acquaintance by way of a little, yellow note. But with anything, what we expect is never what is.

He taught seniors in both English and Spanish classes, and I was never sure how a conversation might go with him. My guess was that bilingual people got their tongues tied more often. And then I'd think about what language they thought in, bilingual people. Since I'd started high school, Mr. Kristiansen had simply been the English teacher in the cherry red beret. Word of mouth around campus would let you know that he was Norwegian, but didn't have the accent. You also heard that he'd storytell like hell. Good stories—the crazy and crooked and wise ones you don't really forget. Stories with a lot of untouched culture. Stories you'd cackle about and admire with friends, but then go home after school and really think about.

He'd recount events of his past, illustrating the essential stupidity of young ambitions: selling your car for a one-way plane ticket, traveling somewhere strange with a few friends and a few dollars, men growing their hair long, women chopping all of theirs off. Upperclassmen would say he made you want to have a hell of a past too; he made you want miles on your feet; he made you want to go and just live big and see things.

I'd meet him face-to-face the following semester, but until then, I'd only see him from far away, squinting his brown eyes from behind his thick-framed glasses, his attaché case bumping into his hip with every step he took. If you were close enough, you heard the sound of its buckles, which were never fully buckled shut. And maybe, if you were lucky, one day you'd be reading a flier posted on the wall about a poetry competition, and he'd bump right into you.

◊

I finished Mr. Aldridge's test and slipped the note into my pocket where it would stay quiet. Funny how Mr. Kristiansen had sounded almost certain I'd enroll in his class. It wasn't much of a request at all. It was more of a notice—*Til September.*

Pre-Summer exams concluded my junior year at Texana Hills High School, and Summer began to spill over onto things. Things got real light in Mayhaw, and you could see into the life of things again. Everybody was ready for it, and you could tell by the way they took an extra second to stretch in the sunlight like window-sill cats in the morning. The sun was especially hotter that Summer. Everyone mentioned it at least once a day. Usually whenever the easy topic of weather floods into a conversation, you know the conversation's gone to shit. But it was different with that Summer. The sun numbed faces into a good and round and warm happiness. Colors flourished outside, in the sky and on the ground, and birds you'd forgotten about reappeared in the air, dancing on the wind.

Expectedly, Dillon and her remained under that spell, spending very little time apart. As the month of July came along and matured, the Rubensons took their annual camping trip. It was to somewhere miles away from what was familiar, underneath redwood trees. They'd meet up with other families out there, wherever it was. I'd gone with them a few times. Mrs. Rubenson would pack everything two weeks early, and Dillon's father would have to leave his smokes at home. Arietta would fall asleep for most of the ride. She'd retreat up to what she called her *castle*, which was just the loft in the back of the camper just above the narrow bathroom.

But I didn't join them that year. I knew Dillon's parents liked his girlfriend a hell of a lot. She had that kind of face, an easy voice and thin arms. She'd make Arietta giggle and she'd help Mrs. Rubenson with after-dinner dishes and things. And Mr. and Mrs. Rubenson were high school sweethearts themselves, so it all fit. Dillon invited her with them that Summer. He invited me too, out of that *Dillon* consideration he'd picked up somewhere, but everyone knows that three wheels don't roll too well together. Of course, a third wheel works just fine on a tricycle, but we were all much older than that.

I *thanks-but-no-thanks*ed him, and I knew he understood. I didn't want to witness the two of them giggling and sneaking up into Arietta's *castle* during the day, while everyone else was out hiking or picnicking or throwing lines into freshwater streams.

Sometimes when I'd think about them together—Dillon and her—I'd think about Dillon fiddling with that Rubik's cube. I'd wonder if he'd thrown it into some drawer and forgot about it once he and her started dating. I thought about it because I really wanted him to finish it—the Rubik's cube. I really wanted to see the cube all completed with all the colors perfectly together on each side. And that's when I'd think about young love, and I'd wonder if it takes us *to* things or brings us away from them.

◊

That Summer acted as nothing more than a quiet prelude to the Fall that would change everything I'd come to know about my life. I mowed lawns for money, read books, did Summer things and got lonely from time to time under the sun that rolled around up in the sky, burning its warmth into chests and onto eyelids. I looked at Mr. Kristiansen's note a handful of times, too. Of all the things to talk about in the world, what would he choose for the Fall? *Literature as Philosophy* was a hell of a family of words. It made the whole idea of Fall less daunting than it had been in the past. Maybe the class would have answers to questions I hadn't even thought to ask yet. Maybe it would give me the things I didn't even know I needed. I was excited and terrified, light-footed and heavy-hearted about it. Whatever I was feeling, it felt good. And it felt good to be really feeling something other than the dizziness brought on by the passing idea of my father.

And just like that, Summer whistled by like a pretty face on a passing train.

15

Fall's first wind exhaled on Mayhaw, and the school year began one more time—the last time—for me. Incidents became phenomena as things happened to me that don't usually just happen to people. Or, at least, if they *do* happen to people, those people aren't writing them down.

Texana Hills High School felt smaller, looked smaller. The buildings were shorter, even a little pathetic in their square brickness. But that's just how it gets with places you're around for a while. It's like how every shoe you get growing up eventually becomes too small. The wise will know when it's time to fetch the next shoe size. The even *wiser* will take off their shoes altogether and walk barefoot, because you can never grow out of barefoot.

All of us seniors wore similar grins around campus that first day. In my new-enough-for-the-first-day-of-school clothes, I felt good and light. Sure, I knew where most of the other kids would be after graduation, and I knew where *I'd* be, and that was just the way it was. But I was content. There's not a feeling in the world greater than graduating high school. It's the ultimate Summertime, really.

I'd graduate and move along. I'd be given back this freedom that we—better, our parents—sort of hand off to a few different principals as we go through the education system. Perhaps the high school diploma was sort of a write-off for the headaches and backaches and awkward right-handed school desks I'd put up with. It was supposed to be our one-way ticket into the real world, whatever that was. The term *real world* was just like *free time*; I could never really get at the meaning of either of them. I knew that, in conversations with adults, you'd find out that the *real world* is the world where you're always missing out on something because you're always doing something else. And naturally, *that* world starts to feel like reality, and you forget about the other world altogether—the world that your inner child tries and tries to remind you about. It's terrible how many people put their inner child in time out. And it gets me too how people keep talking to each other about *stopping and smelling the roses*. Hell, you don't need to *stop* just to smell something. Everything's in the air all the time. They're there all the time— the roses. It's *people* that aren't there to smell them.

$$\langle$$

It's in your last year of high school when you realize that, all along, you've been involved in some kind of relay, like you've become some sort of baton and one teacher passes you off to the next and you're carried on a bit more.

Now, I hadn't taken P.E. since my freshman year at Texana Hills, and I never would've thought that a senior year P.E. class would've had such value to it. Our teacher, Coach Fischer, wasn't a jackass like the other P.E teacher who'd shout at you to run while he stood still in the shade with his whistle and his sunglasses. Coach Fischer was softer than that. He had a softer voice about him that would just sort of make you listen.

Now, in truth, we *did* run a hell of a lot to start off the semester. But it was different. It was somehow more than just running. If he wouldn't have given that speech to us on the first day of class, we surely would've hated him for it. Kids can be so quick to hate people, you know. But the speech made it all understood. Coach Fischer would pace back and forth with an easiness when he spoke. He was a teacher—a man—and we were just kids, so we listened.

We all sat there on those wooden bleachers by the track, under the huge oak tree, on that first day of class. P.E. was first period, and the wood we sat on was still soft from the morning dew. With matching gym clothes, we all sat waiting for him to appear, trying to rub off the morning chill and goosebumps that raped our biceps and the backs of our legs. Some kids were quiet as hell, or too tired to care, or pissed off about something. Others couldn't shut up, making jokes about one another's sisters or mothers, or haircuts or privates.

The sky carried a transparent gray, kissed by whispers of blue and white. In the distance, we saw Coach Fischer appear as a mere blur, walking up the track. He had a stoutness to him. He walked toward us with an unmistakable waddle, holding a clipboard by his side, his whistle tip gleaming around his neck. Some kids laughed at the way he walked. It's kids like those who will never understand anything.

He wore a navy blue track suit, form-fitting his portliness, and the nylon made that noise as he got closer to us. Halting in front of the wooden bleachers, he paused to look the oak tree up and down and smile as if it were an old friend. He looked back at us quietly, and then onto the ground as his face became more stern. He drew a small and deep circle in the red dirt with his foot, thinking of how to say what he wanted to say. It made a little cloud of dust in the low morning air.

"Men, boys, whatever you will."

Everybody seemed to sit up straighter just then, including myself.

"Perhaps some of you see this as a break from books and a break from learning. And yes, you can see you're all outside, free from the rooms they keep you in. But do yourselves a favor and stay focused on something: so much of your life happens—and will happen—outside the walls of school. So much! Those Number 2 pencils are just one tool of the *thousands* you're going to need if you want to survive, I mean really survive in the trenches of life. It's important to look at all your environments in life as you would a classroom. Each moment, even the small and insignificant ones, contains its own lesson, its own pulse. Sometimes the lesson's little and sometimes it hurts like hell, but it's a lesson nonetheless. And it's your choice—it's always been your choice and it always will be—to take notes."

A warmth travelled nimbly up my spine as he went on.

"School and academics aren't the only ways to become an intellectual."

Some kids looked around at each other.

"School's important, of course. School gives you the canvas, the paints, the brushes. But, *you* still have to paint the picture. School will make you a painter maybe, but it won't paint for you. Go and be the artist of your own life. That's the biggest thing school will teach you.

"There's um...there's a difference between living and existing, you see. It's about chasing something, participating in your life, finding your niches and learning all you can. Not all from books, but from experiences too—real life, raw, heavy experiences. Take time to learn the things that you can't quite explain but can only understand. Lend an ear or even a heartbeat to the silent little truths around the corner."

We sat there in obedient silence, all wondering the same thing—*Where did this guy come from?*

"The world's a library. Each minute an author. It's a matter of looking at life with new eyes every day. That's what you want. Crafting questions and journeying here and there to find the answers, or, maybe not finding the answers at all, but simply doing it just to *go* somewhere and *be* on some kind of journey. That's what gives it all purpose. That's what will bring the color into your days."

He rubbed his forehead with the back of his hand, still looking down at the lopsided circle in the red dirt.

"So what I'm trying to say is, well, school isn't the end. It's the beginning. A lot of brilliance you'll find is born not just from academia, but from experiences of people who walked around and through places both alert and awake. Perhaps we're all painters by nature, but only a few of us ever paint. So, maybe what I'm trying to say is that school alone isn't always going to save you. Back it with experience. Back it with exploration. Heck, you'll even meet *homeless* people with no more than a *drop* of academic education, and they can somehow draw focus on the things you always saw but never looked at."

It was a brain-full for what we were used to in P.E. classes.

"And how does P.E.—physical education—find its way into all this? Well, the discipline out here, in the outside air—just you and yourself—has a lot buried in it. It's a sure way to get to know yourself so that you can go on chasing experiences you know you and your soul need. And this discipline isn't something I'm telling you to obey out of respect for me; it's something I'm asking you to obey out of responsibility for yourself."

He looked down at his whistle. He got hold of it and, with his thumb, began to polish it.

"Now I'm sure you all have your opinions about running— love it, hate it. Most of you are probably put off hearing me say the mere word this early in the morning. We've all experienced the tired and flat, burning lungs, the crooked breathing, the heavy-footedness you get from stomping around the track. But this semester, we're going to straighten those breaths and give ourselves some ease, finding some lightness in running. Sure, it'll be hell at first, but it'll pay off. Nothing that's ever worth learning is going to be giftwrapped for you.

"I'll tell you up front that, yeah, we're going to be doing a lot of running in this class. If you hate running, perhaps you don't know much about it. Or maybe you don't understand it like you should. You see, the track over there is like our consciousness." He twisted around to point at it. "A lot moves through our consciousness—good things, bad things, worries and ideas." He looked up at us, his eyes scanning over our own. "We all *run* at some point in our lives. And most of the time, it's not on purpose. Maybe something tragic happens—someone close dies, we lose touch with that supposed-to-be-lifelong friend, our heart is shattered by another, we question our god—and we run. We try and evade the heavy thoughts that follow tragedy. We feel the hot waves of fear and anxiety pass through our heads. We're troubled, so we run.

"But we must learn to run *alongside* our problems. To run *with* them, not *from* them. Because if you choose to run away from tribulations, you're not escaping them at all. You're just giving them reason to chase you."

He threw a foot up on the first row of bleachers and leaned an elbow on his knee, looking up at us. With morning-cold hands, we all stayed quiet. None of us had ever heard anyone talk like that. We were just kids. Or perhaps we weren't anymore.

He went on. "So when I say we're going to run a lot, what I mean is that we're going to be spending a good deal of time learning the art of reflection. This is a pass/no pass deal, and I'll probably pass all of you because I see your focus on me now. It starts with focus. This is your opportunity, as seniors, your last run, your last deep breath before entering the next world."

Next world. Not *real* world. But *next*. I loved that.

"This is your opportunity to survey yourselves, mentally and physically. I've been running all my life. We all have. But I've practiced enough to run *adjacent* to my troubles—the darker equations in my head. Some prefer taking a pen to a journal, and that's fine. But I've always taken my feet to the Earth, running out my perplexities, anxieties, my inquiries—the ground: my notepad, and my footprints: my words. Thinking about things can only get you so far, then you've got to move." He straightened up a bit. "Take this advice for what you will, but remember one thing: sometimes, a self-generated, moving body finds the answers that a still and contemplative mind simply cannot."

He shifted to face the track. "Now on your feet, let's get to it. Let's try arriving into ourselves." He blew his whistle perfectly clear. The sound it made has echoed throughout my whole life. Coach Fischer was the real thing, the first to really wake me up to the hidden art in everything. I started my feet on the track that day just like everyone else, and one simple thought filled my mind like warm water: We can all *do* in life, but it's *how* we do that renders us artists.

The art of running started to illuminate things inside myself and in my surroundings. It was a sort of zen, but people didn't really use that kind of word back then. My feet even fell beyond the school track as I cut spontaneous paths along sidewalks framing my familiar neighborhood. I wasn't much for long distance because I didn't have the lungs yet. It wasn't that I'd been smoking cigars much; I just didn't have the lungs yet. I could jog almost into town without cramping up, and if Dillon wouldn't have been so busy with her, I bet I could've ran straight to the Rubenson's in six minutes flat, especially with the snow gone and everything.

With just a few good and honest words, Coach Fischer had made the weight of Fall much lighter than it had been in the past. And that was a good thing. Lightness is good.

◊

Being a senior was a lot to think about.

I wasn't quite ready to leave the only place I'd really grown up in. Every corner evoked something. But you have to be careful around nostalgia. I hated how the past could always find some sort of way to be sad. I hated how there was always a bit of misery to memory. But perhaps that's only the case if you don't spend your time *doing*, and are lulling around in the past all the time, fantasizing about yesterday. Of course, we all think about our yesterdays, but you have to be careful. You have to be careful around nostalgia. If you're not, it just gets really heavy and cold and stupid and depressing. Like how I used to spend so many quiet moments imagining what my father might've been like, missing someone I never knew, feeling shorted by the world. I had to grow out of that. I could still *think* about him of course, but I couldn't just lie there in bed and dwell heavily in a hole like that. He'd be with me, I knew, somehow, somewhere. But I had to get him out of my head and grow out of it all. It was time for change. Time for movement.

You shouldn't spend the present in the past. It's the second hardest advice to live by. If we spend our present in the past, we can't blossom. Like Coach Fischer said, it's about making your future the way you want it to be, really confronting the bad parts of your days and chasing down something good. Unlike what a lot of the other seniors were chattering about, I wouldn't be chasing down a college education. Dillon would. He'd chase down becoming an architect. He'd be like his father. And all along, all I ever wanted to be was like *my* father. It's all I had.

A big book about firefighting—from the academy—found

its home up on the shelf above my dresser. I'd have to read through it sooner than later if I wanted to be a good firefighter. The book leaned heavy against my father's firefighting helmet, which was powdered with dust. I'd look up at it a lot and wonder when I'd become a man, or if I already had. Then I'd think about how all boys should have a shelf above their dresser.

16

It was the next day of school. The second day of my senior year. It was the day I'd have English class, the day I'd meet Mr. Kristiansen face-to-face.

Without expectations, I sat in a new classroom along with everyone else, waiting for him to come through the door. I sat comfortably, repeatedly placing my pencil at the front of my desk and letting it roll back down toward me. It was the first left-handed desk I'd seen at Texana Hills. It was the first one I'd seen ever. Other than a skinny brown-haired girl who had her face in a book, I was the first one in the classroom that day, and naturally, I made that left-handed desk my own right away. It was off to the far right of the classroom when you'd walk in—the side with the windows. The room was on the second floor, and the view got better as the semester went on. Funny how the same old view of things can start to look different, better even. And it's not the view that's changing; it's you.

More kids piled into the room. The bell rang and bounced its echo off the tops of our desks. Everyone talked through it, sharing loud or quiet nothings amongst each other. That's what seniors do. It went on for a few minutes, like it always does in a classroom with kids and no teacher. And then, with a quick wind, the classroom door was pulled open from the outside. It was sort of alarming.

Immediate quiet preluded his first words.

"Afternoon," he said at the floor, looking down as he crossed the front of the classroom with two big steps. He was three or so minutes after the bell, which turned out to be routine for him. He dropped his attaché down against the podium up front, letting out a noticeable exhale as he leaned back up to look out and study us. He had these deep and dark brown eyes. You never knew what they meant, peering there from behind thick-framed glasses. He lifted off his red beret only put it right back on, and you could see that his hair was thin. He wasn't old or balding or anything. He just had thin, blonde hair.

Attendance came first. He began and then stopped about halfway through. "Strange how I'm saying your full names before I even know your faces…names are a real wonder." We didn't know if he was talking to himself or to us. He had an uncondemnable weirdness about him—a weirdness that you couldn't digest at first, but you could tell there was something to it; it was a weirdness you could almost admire.

He finished off with the names and went on to introduce himself. It was the moment we got to see for ourselves the Mr. Kristiansen that we'd heard about for three years: the enigma, the English teacher that made you think. It was a big moment for all of us.

He went on talking and using story-words—the kind of words that are only really spoken by those who've, at some point, been in the real and hidden mix of thought and action. He illustrated a life of paths he went down and fields he ended up on, mentioning a difficult growing-up with some sort of mental disability, his days as a student, and how he was a terribly slow reader. He talked of brief and scattered days in Norway with no more than a borrowed pair of skis and a backpack with a broken strap. He also mentioned that he spoke *Spain* Spanish and said that knowing more than one language is the best way to live— "You sort of learn everything all over again, and pretty soon every*thing* starts having a dual personality, all because you know how to identify it in more than one tongue. That's when life gets bigger—when one thing starts to mean more than that one thing."

He wasn't married or anything. No kids, but he made it a point to say that kids should all be spoken to in one language by their mother and another by their father. He was big on culture, big on being cultured. He'd talk a hell of a lot about a hell of a lot. He'd talk with elbows propped up on the podium, gesticulations aplenty. He'd talk with his hands like that, as if words were never enough. There was something about him that you knew was important. It was something no one in that class could understand then, and maybe it's even something I'm still understanding today. Sometimes you witness a sort of magic in people that you can't really pass on in words. And maybe that's fine. Maybe magic isn't meant to be translated into words.

As the semester went on, I'd get wrapped up in the individual threads of his teaching. I'd hear *how* he was saying just as much as *what* he was saying. Perhaps I was just distracted, but he had this passion about the way he talked that you couldn't help but tap into. It was his real desire to not just teach us, but make us want to teach ourselves. A passion very real and honest, and something no one could take away from him. It was something I wanted to figure out, to chase down and understand. Turns out he became a Rubik's Cube of my own.

Rubik's Cubes.

Dillon.

It had been a while since I'd spent time with my best friend. He was busy as hell preparing for college—and, most likely, preparing for third base with *her* as well. School announcements reminded everyone that college applications were due in a handful of weeks, at the beginning of November. Dillon wanted to attend one place and his father wanted him attending another. Fathers and sons are like that. Either way, Dillon had a handful of those essays to write—a handful more than I would anyway. But I kept busy after school and on weekends regardless, as senior year homework is no fairy tale.

I kept up with my running too, the way Coach Fischer had taught us. I ran into town and back out of town and down sidewalks and streets that'd stayed the same over the years. Little by little, my lungs widened, my shins forgave me, and I could run without having to pinch and wince at side-cramps. It was nice to get out of the house and out into things.

At home, however, life unfolded pretty regularly.

It was the time of year when my mother would start using the word *swamped* a lot. It got like that in real estate in the Fall. But we'd eat together almost every single night regardless. She always made sure we at least ate together. I mentioned it before: she could cook like hell. She had one of those kitchens too. Nothing fancy. It was unique; it was hers. Everything was hung up on hooks: pots and pans and measuring cups, spatulas and spoons for stirring. Everything was organized in containers and jars and the counters were never left with even a bread crumb.

She'd ask about school, and I'd tell her some of it, maybe some about P.E., but never really about English class or my new teacher, and I never showed her the poem I'd written. She wouldn't have thought much of the poem. She wouldn't have wanted to hear it or even talk about it. My father and everything about him was a closed book between us.

In so many words, dinner was a quiet delicious. The food was warm, and our relationship, well, wasn't. The way she'd look down at her fork in between distant and hollowed-out conversation and twirl her spaghetti always tied my chest in a square knot. I started to feel like it was up to *me* to create a bridge between us. Up to *me* to fuse back together mother and son. It could be really heavy some nights. All we really had in common was my father's death, and that was something we never talked about—something that was, on her part, avoided almost on purpose.

◊

Coach Fischer had echoed in my head since that first day of P.E. class, and I'd often times wonder why he only taught that one subject. Why had he stopped there? It seemed like a shoe too small, a bookshelf too narrow for all that he *could* lesson kids on. But I guess it's often that brilliant minds wear simple disguises, and that's perhaps what makes them brilliant in the first place. Perhaps it wasn't that he'd stopped at high school P.E.; perhaps it was where he was starting.

His words hadn't left me one bit—*I've always liked to take my feet to the page of the Earth: running out my perplexities, anxieties, my inquiries.*

I was perplexed, anxious. Hell, *I* had inquiries.

I knew but a fraction of the truth that there was something I was in need of. Something sacred to me and only me, and it wasn't something I could find in one of the churches in town or anything. It was something inside myself I needed to pull out from underneath a rock. Something to give me the feeling of momentum, of lightness. And I knew I just had to reach a little further to get it.

There was an underlying heaviness in my life that still hung around, loitering in deep silence, and whether it was caused by the presence of my mother or the absence of my father, I'd never know. All I knew was that it was time to start living a life strengthened by the possibility of the future and not one weakened by the reality of the past.

I told you that Aunt Jodie and Uncle Lou had sent me money for my birthday that year instead of books. Well I took it, all of it, and bought my first real pair of running sneakers. I would need them to start running longer distances. The old ones with a new toe hole I'd been using would retire to my closet for use with Summer yardwork.

I can still remember lacing up those new ones for the first time. It was a real crisp day with soft light boxed in by thin sheets of clouds. There was a good tightness around my feet, an easy spring about the toes. Little did I know those sneakers would take me such places. They'd get me stoned off a runner's high; they'd teach me about the breeze that licks your face when your pace is right with the wind, but most, they'd show me the complexity that hides itself in simplicity.

17

Time moved into November.

Halloween bookended the month of October, and you only went door to door that night if you were young like Arietta or a nostalgic parent looking for a memory, a feeling, a single piece of candy.

It was nearing 1991—the year I'd graduate high school. School went on fine, and I was less confused about *it* than I was the weather. November and no snow yet, and if it rained, it was light and ephemeral, passing by as quick and natural as time or emotion. Right around then, a near-perfect day happened. It would've unfolded as another ordinary and brisk Saturday had I not had a certain twitch in my legs. It was a twitch curable only by movement in directions far and unplanned. A twitch that called for one of those open-ended, one-way-ticket jaunts that'll remind you of your freedom.

I slept long and good and woke up a snooze past noon. A

short, stand-up breakfast, and I was moved to begin my analytical essay for Kristiansen's class.

He wasn't the type to assign homework consistently throughout the week. He even said once, *I'm not sure I believe in assigning much more than what's already bestowed upon you by the obligation to think and the responsibility to live.* But when he *did* assign things, they were always a little bigger than you'd want them to be—reading a spontaneous 65 pages out of something old or something new, or an essay where you'd count your last few words as you wrote them just to make sure you hit the minimum word requirement.

Later that afternoon, once I'd pantedly painted on about a thousand and a half words, I scooted off the stool under my bunk, bending up and out from underneath, and stood up fully in a slant of light that poured in from the window above my bed. Warm light in November.

It couldn't have been later than four o'clock.

I stood on my tiptoes, stretching my arms up and back. Looking through the window up there, I saw the big oak tree across the street standing as still as the dull and warm pencil I'd just laid to rest atop the few sheets of paper—scribbled with my handwriting—back down on my desk.

There are days when the outside hints to you that you should probably stay inside. But that day, to my very good and hidden fortune, wasn't one of those days.

◊

My mother was taking some kind of nap on the couch with a half-empty glass and the television on low.

I toed into the kitchen, making sure my new sneakers wouldn't squeal across the linoleum. I slid a granola bar into the left pocket of my brown Texana Hills gym shorts and crossed back through the living room, half-hearing the weather man on television try and figure out the sky—the same sky that couldn't even figure itself out. I peeled the sticky front door open into the briskness that was November. Some wind snuck in past me. My mother twitched, but I closed the door behind me before she could wake up and ask me anything.

I was quick to make my way down 8th Street toward Main.

The air was still as hell, and no one was really outside except for a few cars chasing each other down the street in slow motion. A few fingers of sunlight pointed down through gaps of clouds, creating little hallways of light between the trees lining the other side of Main Street. The sun wasn't supposed to be out like that. It was supposed to have gone away, way behind the clouds, until the Spring. But I guess it was the same as when a mother tucks her child into bed and he doesn't want to go to sleep yet.

◊

It would be fiction for me to say I had a destination that afternoon.

I simply started a walk that turned into a jog and then a running glide, my heart pounding its drum solo from behind my ribcage. It was just me out there, cutting the breeze in half, my home inside an easy and straight breathing pattern. I noticed how thoughts would peek into my mind and then drift off into nothing. Worries would even rain down, but then they'd evaporate. Wonders and curiosities parachuted in as well; I'd watch them glow and disappear. With each hard foot I planted on the concrete, Coach Fischer became more and more right about running.

When I made it to the corner at 13th Street, I slowed a bit, looking down at the big, square camper parked under that tree, off the curb, like it always was. I could even see a sliver of their front porch—the Rubenson's. It stuck out because of the front door, but it still hadn't been painted over with a new coat of red, and that somehow made Dillon even more distant. I thought, too, about Mrs. Rubenson preparing the house—almost four weeks early—for their Thanksgiving dinner. I'd always been invited to it, and I *was* invited later that month, but I wouldn't go. Dillon had a girlfriend; it was a hard and tangible fact. And I wanted her to feel like I'd felt all those years. It was her turn. I'd played some sort of role in the Rubenson's Thanksgiving up until then, and perhaps it was simply time to pass it on, time for *her* to feel like part of the second greatest family I'd ever know.

Main Street was like a river, stretching itself long throughout Mayhaw.

You could get on or off the highway from either end of it. Way south down Main, past town, was where my mother would hop on to go out to Mayleaf, where she'd work and sell houses and find her purpose or whatever. And at the north end of Main was where the Rubensons would get on the highway to go visit Dillon's grandparents. They'd drive all the way down Main Street, past everything—even past Lake Wisley.

I saw it all differently that day, running down the long and familiar street I'd been down so many times before. Funny how familiar things can look different. Fighting cramps and hairline sweat, I kept an easy pace. I wasn't racing anyone, I was just moving along for the ease of it, for the hell of it. The more things you do for the hell of it, the happier you'll be.

Who knows how many minutes or meters had passed by the time I reached my weekend-empty high school. How the hell did I get that far? I ran on, eyeing the sports fields that flirted with the sidewalk I was moving across. A few cars were in the lot and a few brown-jerseyed kids were running around on the grass with short white pants. Football practice. And the coach was there too, in the distance, blowing short blows out of his whistle. He was sporting a navy blue track suit.

Coach Fischer! What timing! I wanted him to see me, to see me running, to see me doing it. Just for his approval or something. But I was too far away. And it's probably the worst feeling to feel too far away.

◊

A hill in the road rose up a ways past my high school.

I looked back at the team moving around together, little brown dots, as I began the incline. I was running hard, but it didn't hurt anymore. The balls of my feet tapped up the sidewalk as the previous thuds went quiet.

From the top, you could see out for what felt like miles.

My head got closer to the sky with each footplant. In the deep distance, planted right along the horizon, were the blurry tips of tall pine trees. They were the same ones that stood quietly all around Lake Wisley. I was beginning down the hill as soon as I'd gotten to the top. It had been a hell of a view, but some things are only beautiful because they're brief like that, because they die before you can give them life.

Descending down in a slowed jog, the cool and thin breath of November passed around me in curves, and the sun was still right there, subtly coming in and out from behind its cloudy curtain. Stomping, halting speed but still pushing on to nowhere, I stuck out my arms wide, bird-like, and got that feeling you'll get when you're alone in some sort of Nature and you remember how light life really is—how time doesn't *really* exist and that everything is just so fresh and light, and you can be right there with it, part of it all.

18

Lake Wisley was a curious place.

It always had been. The lake sat still in between its Northern Park and Southern Park, both of which had their good share of pine trees peppered throughout. The Southern Park is where you'd find children feeding the ducks and the angry goose who would always find his way in. You'd spot home-sewn checkered blankets finding their purpose there as well, atop the grasses that grew in between years of fallen pine needles. It was the bigger park, the one you'd hear about whenever someone mentioned Lake Wisley. The Summer months would find canoes drifting out insouciantly there; kites would maybe stretch their necks out, watching over careless laughter, and on occasion you'd be flooded by large groups of people wearing the same colored t-shirt with the same last name printed big across the back. Just the thought of family reunions could really depress the hell out of me. The Southern Park was a family place, and maybe that's why I'd only been there with Dillon, and never with my own mother or anyone else.

The Northern Park is perhaps what had always kept the lake curious. You wouldn't hear much of anything about the Northern Park. By word of mouth, you already knew everything you needed to know about it. It was never a place you'd need to go or want to go. It was much smaller than the Southern Park, and it was hardly kept up. It was mostly shaded from the sun. Obscured like that in the thickness of the pines, there was only one clear opening to the lake. The only direct light it got was at sunset. The other hours of day stayed gloomy and unshaven-looking, dusted with cold breezes. The Northern Park was where that girl drowned. You never found out if she was drunk or alone or whatever, and that really added to the place. Like I said, there wasn't much reason to be out there. That end of the lake was, well, all drank up by a scanty little campground. But it was a different kind of campground.

You wouldn't see fathers in weekend polo shirts with smoke in their face and spatula in hand; nor would you see mothers drying off their lake-wetted children with towels; nor would you find nieces and nephews asking their uncle for his stories. It wasn't a campground for families, rather, a campground for those without them. It was home to those who had none. Mayhaw hadn't passed some stupid legislation making it an official homeless encampment park or anything. It just happened to be where maybe a dozen or so tired bodies would pause their long treks to nowhere, coming and going with the weather.

The first time I'd heard about the homeless there was in the eighth grade. We were studying local ecology and the whole class took a little by-bus fieldtrip out there. Our teacher wanted all of us to look at plant life and measure out pH levels in the water, and I guess we'd be butted up against the Northern Park. We were given permission slips that said we'd be working by the bridge that connected the two parks together. Most parents were fine with it because there'd be other teachers and parents there. It had never been deemed a *dangerous* place anyway; I just think we often make the mistake of associating the unknown with the dangerous. Perhaps humans—parents especially—tend to grow out of curiosity and into fear. Like my mother, who, upon seeing that permission slip, put on a face that told me I'd have to find out about the field trip from Dillon.

She was always strangely eerie about the homeless, my mother. Kind of an extremist with it. Even hitch-hikers out by the highway made her uneasy, vagabonds too, tucked back in the corners of town, cups filled halfway with nickels and dimes. She'd turn her head at them. I'd wonder where her sympathy was. I mean, it's not like people *choose* to become homeless. It made me wonder how my mother acted during holidays like Thanksgiving and Christmas, when she'd join her coworkers and visit the local shelters and serve food.

That day, my run to nowhere sort of dead-ended at the lake.

I never intended on making *that* far outside of what was familiar to me. Slowing to a walk, my panting thinned out as I moved heavily past a knotted wooden sign with LAKE WISLEY carved into it. I entered there, at the Southern Park, and followed the curvy smile of the dirt trail, trodden with lazy pine needles and lifeless leaves from earlier that Fall. Crunches and snaps under me, I looked up at the tall, old-friend-looking pine trees as the muted light flicked itself down on my hair and face.

Three older women walked past me in shorts and visors, exiting the park. Their chatter fell muffled, only to die off in the distance behind me. I walked on with the same easy pace, further into the Southern Park. Off to the right, a teenage couple was lying on a blanket by some bushes, laughing lightly and taking turns pointing up at the clouds through the trees. Walking on with a smile, I thought of Dillon and his girlfriend.

I reached out to skim my fingertips along the forgiving tree bark to my sides, walking on, deeper and deeper into it all. The silence was so thick, and the crunching sound under me was so earthy and real, like it was the only sound I ever needed to hear for the rest of my life. And then, before I could really notice, I'd been swallowed in all directions by the tall, confident trunks around me. It was like being in a crowded room of unconditionally-loving mothers. The nectar-like stillness of things hummed softly.

Without knowing it, I'd walked off the path, and I'd been off it for some time. As I looked up and out and saw what was ahead of me, I met an involuntary halt, leaning my shoulder against some warm bark.

It was the lake, out in front of me, the surface glistening and everything. Like wet glass, it sparkled for nobody else but me. The sun was sitting cross-legged above the horizon, moving lower and lower. Closer and closer I found myself footing through the rough of things, trunks my only guide, toward the water. Stepping across mostly pine needles that were huddled together by the winds, I made it to the shore, to a little inlet where a thin channel whispered its way under a graying wooden bridge.

I approached it, thinking of grandpas and grandsons and hotdog bait and makeshift fishing poles. The water underneath it had this clarity to it as it cascaded over shy rocks. The bridge was old and squat, but it had this personality to it, like it was inviting me to walk across into its untapped and seasoned wisdom.

I looked behind me and all around and found nobody but silence herself. And that once-warm quiet turned to a thin chill just then as a few curled and cracked-dry leaves danced in circles on the bridge's planks. I could've just stopped there and looked at the sun peek in through trees over that inlet of water and then turn around and walk back home through the Southern Park. But I didn't. For some reason, I wasn't supposed to.

◊

At my end of the bridge—jetting up out of the earth where the dirt met the wood planks—was a wooden sign atop a post. It had a large and red N painted on it. I'd reached the Northern Park.

I stepped over in front of a stone-covered drinking fountain and pulled the handle, washing away the dryness in my throat. The water felt good. Cold and wet. Drinking water in the shade is always a good feeling. I stood up and wiped my lips with the back of my arm, and then started to foot slowly onto and across the bridge, looking down in between the planks of wood at the water as it smoothed over itself. The sun kept its muted warmth at the right side of my face as the trees opened up to the lake.

My feet hit dirt once more as I stepped off the other side of the bridge, standing small in a good-sized clearing. For the first time, and not for the last time, I was in the Northern Park.

Twenty yards out began the scattering of tents, all backed by a green wall of shady pines. Gray tents, green tents, maybe old army tents. Some were small and others square and a couple were real pathetic looking, and there was one off to the right that was a dark red canvas tent, closest one to the shore.

It was all so new and different, but it had been there all along. It was so damn deserted and quiet, and that's the thing with quiet: some days it relaxes you; other days it'll frighten you right out of your pulled-tight shoelaces.

The last thing I wanted was for any of them to hear me and come out of their tent and shoot their eye contact at me. So with my head down, I walked off to my right, where a few feet from the shore sat a sun-grayed and wooden bench. It seemed harmless enough—crossing a bridge quietly to sit on a public bench. I dusted off a palette of dirt and pine needles and sat down on the right side of the bench, right in front of the lake. It was like nothing I'd seen before. But then again, Nature is always like nothing you've seen before.

I sat there with my jaw in my hands, elbows on my knees, letting the sun tint the sky a muted pink. I felt some leftover sweat adhere my t-shirt to my lower back. I closed my eyes for however long it was, just breathing for the sake of breathing. A warmth numbed the front of me. I knew time was passing only by the changing orange color on the insides of my eyelids.

And that's when it happened.

Pine needles and dry leaves began their crunch from behind me, slowly approaching, and with direction. The warmth across my legs and face emptied into a hollowness as my eyes shot open in front of me at an angled glare of setting sun. The crunching inched nearer, coming right at the back of me. My chest got tight in the dizziness of it, and as hard as I tried, I couldn't twist around to look. I couldn't move *anything*.

19

The sound weaved over to my left side, halting itself right behind me. I kept my focus forward, letting the sun streak my eyes with a hot burn, my peripherals screaming.

I felt the presence make its way around the front of the bench. And, without a sound or a look over, it sat down next to me. Seconds that felt like long and thin hours passed, and without revealing how much it had startled me, I turned my head an inch in the thick of the air, with sideways eyes, to study whatever it was.

It was a man, his shoulders sagging forward as he leaned in toward the lake, the sun distributing itself on the east side of his face. A few wrinkles hugged the corner of his right eye. He had a good head of hair, blonde and gray, dirty, pulled back into a thin ponytail. The lower half of his face was blanketed with a matching beard, short and tattered, like he'd been twisting at it. He wore a khaki jacket that had to be older than I was, green cargo pants, too, like you'd see soldiers in. The ones with all the pockets down the legs.

He said nothing. He just held a long squint out over the water, the silence making the air even heavier. I didn't know what to make of it; silence has so many damn connotations. And then, just as abruptly as he'd approached the bench to sit down, he began to speak. I can still hear his velvet-textured voice rubbing itself against the air between us for the first time.

"Somethin' about the way they dance...always changin' color, always shiftin' their direction. None of 'em content to stick around in one place long enough...always lookin' for somewhere different, somewhere better."

He stretched his jacketed arm out and pointed to the sparkling surface of the lake.

"The diamonds, you see 'em? Out there, dancin' along the ripples. The offspring of the sun."

I remained still as hell, squinting a bit myself. Terrified. Curious.

"It's like bein' in a museum after hours," he went on. "No one else around; it's all yours."

He looked over at me for the first time and must've seen that I didn't understand.

"Nature," he said a little louder, "it's right here to look at, all the time. Always open, always free admission. And you can just look at it, be in it and with it and part of it. It'll give you back the freedom you forgot you had."

My eyes were stuck on the blinking lake as the horizon nearly disappeared into the sky.

He went on with that voice of his, "I've been out here for a few weeks now, just puttin' my tent down for a little while, and you're the *first* person I've seen cross that bridge and find this view and sit down to watch; the *first* young kid I've seen that's wandered under these trees into somethin' great—into the stillness and silence and lightness of things. You see, kid, life's our time to witness what's beautiful and what's not. And once you start seein' what's beautiful, you just can't stop your lookin' for more. There's more out there than any one soul can ever know. But some of us are seekers, extremists; we need to keep findin' more magic that hides itself in Nature's inflatin' and deflatin' lungs. Seekers need to keep seekin', no matter the consequences. For me, it's a mentality I'll never escape—a mentality that moves me to move and keep movin' so that I feel alive. Perhaps this is my work, my blessing, not my doom."

I wanted to understand or smile or nod or say even five words.

But I didn't. I couldn't. Instead, the weaker self inside of me made me uneasy. Questions of *why* were pounding hard in my chest, but I couldn't find words, much less the right ones. How could he have *work*? He was homeless. And he used the word *blessing*. A homeless man. What was *this* all about? I thought of my mother and her wariness about the homeless and how she might've been onto something after all. My curiosity and fear quickly became only fear. It was all just a lot at once.

The early evening was tapping its fingers on the lake, and with each silent second, I felt further and further away from home. I offered him a stupid head-nod to show that I agreed with whatever he was getting at. I felt like such a little boy. Scared, my legs stood me up to leave and some words pushed themselves out of my mouth crookedly, "W-well, yes. Mhmm. Beautiful lake," I said as awkwardly as I possibly could have. "Have a nice…night…sir."

He smiled up at me, returning the head-nod. It was the first time we made eye contact, the first time I saw that he had two different colored eyes.

My feet throbbed in my sneakers as they took on the weight of me again. I rounded the bench and walked away, crunching over the same ground he'd approached me on. After crossing the bridge back into the Southern Park, bent down, I took a fake drink from the water fountain and looked across the distance at him. He just sat there, facing the lake. Still. Not a care in the world, or, perhaps every care in the world. He wasn't a big man. He had a little frame to him; his posture was humble. Not a day over 40 years old.

I couldn't decide where my fear had come from. Was I *that* startled by meeting a stranger? Wasn't I a stranger myself? Maybe I was just scared like a lot of other kids would've been. But, bent over the drinking fountain like that, looking at the distant back of him—his thin ponytail—I didn't want to be scared. More importantly, I didn't have reason to be—he hadn't asked for my name or for money or what part of town I called home. He didn't even try to shake my hand. Hell, he kept his distance on the bench and barely even looked at me.

All he did was share something he'd learned. That was all.

Once it all fell a good distance behind me, and the sound of my feet were lost in the endless trees, I kicked into a deer-like run along the dirt trail that thinned out and fattened up as it wound back through the Southern Park. Once I reached that knotty, old, wooden sign at the entrance, I stopped.

I didn't know what time it was, or how long I'd been gone. I didn't know what to think about anything. To the soundtrack of no more than a thudding heartbeat, I began my walk home on the opposite sidewalk. I unwrapped the granola bar I'd brought along, and chewing on it unconsciously, I looked up at each star poke its nose through the early evening sky, noticing how badly each one of them wanted to be the brightest one. The stretch of sky above my head perfectly mimicked the color of my mood—dull and quiet and maroon-yellow and alone.

I could feel the coolness of the evening crawl across my back as the sun set behind me. Once I reached that big hill in the road, however long it took me, I turned around in the direction of the lake, seeing last-minute colors collide in the sky as the sun flirted with the moon. I thought about the words *blessing* and *doom* but couldn't make any sense of them.

Walking on in that bubble of muted thought, before reaching my high school, a car puttered by with a vibrating hum, the headlights near blinding me. One of those little Volkswagens. I recognized the driver immediately, dark brown eyes behind glasses all under a red beret.

When I made it home and shut and locked the front door behind me, I felt the silence of an empty house. My mother must've been out doing whatever it was she did. So, with nothing else to do and barely an appetite, I climbed up into my bunk, exhausted. I rolled over to look out the window at the street below. I didn't understand why, but I felt like throwing up.

It was November. Still no snow. Not even genuine rain. Instead, the sun lingered on contentedly, and I didn't think anybody but the plants really minded. I rolled back over and closed my eyes under the white ceiling. I fell asleep heavy up there on my top bunk, my running sneakers untied and asleep as well somewhere on the floor below. My chest rose and fell as I slipped into dreams I won't remember, with the words *blessing* and *doom* floating somewhere in between my ears. Breathing long breaths, I lied on my back, my fingers laced together on my belly. I slept long and good, unlearned on how significant that day would be.

20

No more than two weeks passed by, and every day I thought about what that man had said.

It would all become clear, only to be muddled all over again, transforming itself from poetry to bullshit to transcendental forest talk to nonsense. At seventeen, what are you supposed to do with what adults say anyway?—especially an adult that was a stranger, an adult you'd met on a strange bench in a strange part of town, an adult that might've actually been onto something.

One late-November afternoon in Kristiansen's class, a hell of a coincidence fell heavy into my lap. You see, Kristiansen didn't issue us thirty-pound textbooks. Instead, he had us work from paperback titles you'd probably recognize, and of course he'd shell out his own handouts with excerpts of this or that all stapled together. The way we read what we were reading was pretty scattered in genre and time period, but Kristiansen somehow made it work. He'd pull stacks of paper out from his attaché like a magician does with his rabbit, and we'd give them a go as a class for however long it took—short stories and poems and essays and excerpts from books that I'd promise myself to read all the way through one day. People always make promises like that, and then, sometimes, life happens instead.

On the day of this *coincidence*—or whatever you'd like to call it, I was sitting in my left-handed desk along the wall with the windows, waiting for the shrinking stack of single white-page handouts to reach me. Warm sun came in through the yellowed windows onto my knees. I got the stack and took one and passed what was left back behind me. On the white page was a single poem.

When you're a senior in high school, you still believe that poetry was written for the sole reason of making you feel hard-headed rather than soft-minded. But it was different in that class. For some reason, we all trusted Kristiansen. You see, he demonstrated this difference between *knowing* and *understanding*. He had knowledge about so damn much, sure, but he really understood it all too. Don't teach what you don't understand, I guess; don't say what you don't believe. Kristiansen believed in what he taught, believed in the truth of it. There's something to be said about believers. Believers may not have *built* the wheel, but they sure as hell keep it turning.

One of the many things that's stayed with me from that English class was this: Knowledge is but the body, while wisdom the soul. If you're going to learn anything worth knowing, you have to be able to harness it and make it yours. Knowledge must flower into a silent and instinctual wisdom. You see, with knowledge, you're simply on the *ledge* of knowing. It isn't until you practice what you know that it can become understanding—or, *wisdom* for that matter. Thus, knowledge is but the body, while wisdom the soul.

Perhaps Kristiansen had us on our toes because he never forgot to *why* us. Eternal *whys*. Child-like, but more essential than you'd think. *Whys* that really dug, and not just deeper into holes that already existed, but into holes that weren't holes yet. Socrates did something like that, but was eventually put to death for it. And I'll always feel bad about that; I'll always wonder if Plato cried about Socrates as heavily as Nietzsche later would about a horse being callously whipped out on the street.

Kristiansen cleared his throat and adjusted his glasses. He lifted his beret off and put it back on again. We sat waiting for the words on the page in front of us to materialize into his voice. Looking down at the poet's name, some of us wondered who the hell Henry Van Dyke was, because unless he had a brother named Dick, we were out of ideas. The poem was called *Work*. It was the poem that would teach me that words can change everything. These fourteen lines would test my belief once more about coincidences and magic.

Let me but do my work from day to day,
In field or forest, at the desk or loom,
In roaring market-place or tranquil room;
Let me but find it in my heart to say,
When vagrant wishes beckon me astray,
This is my work; my blessing, not my doom;
Of all who live, I am the one by whom
This work can best be done in the right way.
Then shall I see it not too great, nor small,

To suit my spirit and to prove my powers;

Then shall I cheerful greet the labouring hours,
And cheerful turn, when the long shadows fall
At eventide, to play and love and rest,
Because I know for me my work is best.

○

That *one* line, buried in a poem from nearly a century ago.
This is my work, my blessing, not my doom.
Blessing! Doom! The man from the Northern Park!

Benumbed, with a burning glaze leaking itself across my eyes, I looked out the yellowing window to my left, wishing I could see the lake out of it, the bench, the man on it—the homeless man who'd spoken to me in *poetry*!

I knew right then that I wouldn't be learning about that poem in a left-handed school desk. It would have to be somewhere else, from someone else. After all, Coach Fischer *had* said most of our learning would take place outside of the classroom.

The sound of Kristiansen talking back and forth with students faded easily into a low hum. I wanted to listen. I just couldn't. I was crowded with images and what-ifs. I closed my eyes and, with the sun still coming in and landing on the tops of my thighs, I pretended I was, instead, sitting on the right side of a bench, under tall and noble pines. I could hear the water, the tide. And the warmth from the left was no longer the sun coming through the classroom window, but rather the presence of a man: a man who I would meet and befriend at the perfect time in my life.

PART TWO

1

That poem really hit me good and hard in my gut, and there was no sense in taking the bus home after school. The bell rang in Kristiansen's class, which always meant freedom for the day. I'd gathered my things quicker than everyone else, speeding toward the door, backpack slung over one arm. I made it out just a few steps before Kristiansen as he was putting the red beret back up on his head. He was always trying to get out just as quickly as the students. It was bizarre and refreshing and human and very much Mr. Kristiansen. I didn't cut him off or anything, but I got some sort of look from him I'm sure. I never knew what his looks meant. Since that semester had started, he'd yet to address me about my poem or the little yellow note he'd sent to me. He didn't make a big deal of me at all, really. But every now and again, I'd look at him and find that he'd already been looking at me. It was a look like *he* was trying to figure *me* out. But then of course, he'd look away.

I dashed across campus to the gym, backpack swinging, making my way into the boy's locker room. The football team was putting on all their stuff like they always did, and it always took them a good while. They laughed and hollered and swore and talked about things that may or may not have mattered. But when they got out into the green of the field, it was all different. They'd play like hell—rain, snow, twisted ankle, a coughing-up-green kind of cold—because they loved the sport. It was football, and it was theirs. I admired them for that.

After squeezing past a wide group of them on the way to my P.E. locker, getting stares and heads tilts of acknowledgement, I spun my lock open and hurriedly got out of jeans and into gym shorts. I footed into my running shoes too, pulling at the laces. I stuffed my backpack and whatever else wasn't coming with me to Lake Wisley back into my locker. I slammed my locker and spun the lock again. Click. I squeezed back through troops of shoulder pads and armpits and good profanity. I made it back to the exiting door, wondering what it would be like to be on a team like that.

I had the poem from class in my hand, so I stopped in the doorway to fold it into halves, then fourths, then eighths. Poem clutched in hand again, and taking my first rushed step, I nearly smacked right into someone: Coach Fischer, in all his roundness, sporting that dark blue jumpsuit. He didn't say anything. No need, I guess. He just kind of smiled and backed up a step and extended his hand to signal me out first.

◊

Panting like a wet dog, feet throbbing complainingly, I stood once more at the entrance to Lake Wisley. The wooden sign, the beginning of the path that ran through the Southern Park littered with pine needles—it all looked untouched since my last visit. With a single image painted across the wall of mind, I jetted onto the curvy path with a momentum you only get every now and then.

It was nearing four o'clock that Wednesday.

Heart pumping, I could feel the folded paper poem's dampness as I clutched it tighter in my hand. It was too much of a damn coincidence for Kristiansen to pull out *that* poem, of all poems, of all poets. But then again, I was becoming more and more inclined to take a thick black pen and cross out the word *coincidence* in our dictionary at home.

I got closer to the lake as it was glistening patiently. It slowed me down a good deal. It was like the lake wasn't allowing me to just pass by. It was like the painting of my grandmother's in our living room at home—the one of the evening ocean, right above our couch. The painting and the lake alike asked for your complete focus. Perhaps water just does that to people. And you should take more than a strand of seconds to look at it. Let it look at you, because if you don't, you'll get that guilty feeling that accumulates and makes you sick by the time you're forty.

At the bridge, I could hear the softness rolling in the water below. I took an inhaling drink from the fountain that was underneath the signpost with the big red N on it. I bent back up and wiped my lips with the back of my arm, still breathing a little irregularly. I footed onto the bridge, a little more confident this time. My hard breathing was still dancing around all over the place, and I could've sworn I saw a lizard scurry away just then into the in-betweens of the wooden planks I was walking across.

The Northern Park met the end of the bridge just like last time. I squinted out at everything. It looked about the same, but you could tell a handful of tents had been uprooted and moved along, and maybe some new ones had even arrived. What a weird freedom there was in that. It had only been a few weeks since I'd last been there.

The fourteen or so tents in front of me were muted gray or green canvas colors. Some had a rusted chair or two just outside;

some had little tables; all of them had small, round fire pits dug out with rocks or stones. The dark red tent from last time was still there. Standing out like a fire in a field, it had since been moved a little closer to the shore. It was on the incline of a small, dirt hill, a good twenty steps away from the bench we'd met on.

The pines above waved at me in the wind, inviting me to come closer. I sauntered over the dusty dirt clearing that opened into the park like a foyer. Before I could even make it to the bench, the flaps of that dark red tent flew open. Out came a head covered in blondish-gray hair, a beard to match, then a khaki jacket and green cargo pants.

He came out in a hurry, flustered. It was him. Making his way to the water's edge, he was nervously tucking what looked like an ink pen back into the breast pocket of his jacket. It wasn't unreasonably cold out, so I could understand why he was barefoot. He barefooted over to the bench, past the bench, onto the little shore, and stepped shin-deep right into the water, splashing. Hands on his hips and eyes on the diamonds of the water's surface, he let an exhale escape that made his shoulders fall. I looked out right along with him. The Northern Park was so damn beautiful, that raw kind of beautiful. There's such a difference when something is kept up by people and it's nice, and when something is kept up by Nature and it's beautiful. The park had that rustic face to it—that natural, five-o-clock-shadow look—that reminds you of how everything used to be, and it makes you happy but sad at the same time. It's a strange feeling—you're happy you're there to see it and you feel so privileged, but at the same time, you're sad that not *everything* is like that, and that not *everyone* knows about it. But I guess only a select few are meant to know about Nature's secrets like that. Perhaps that's what makes them secrets in the first place. And perhaps having that happy-sad feeling is a *blessing* rather than a *doom.*

I quietly made it to a standing position just in front of the bench. Even if he did hear me or the pine needles breaking in half underneath my feet, he didn't turn around.

How do you just approach a person when they're like that? The water splashed around his calves, reminding him it was there and alive. From about fifteen feet behind him, I noticed he was shorter, like me. It was the first time I'd seen him standing up. His size made him a lot more approachable, but even then, I couldn't just holler out at him and disrupt everything. I'm sure he was wearing that squint of his, peering out into the tired blue and yellow horizon. It wasn't a squint to block *out* light; it was a squint let it *in*. It was the kind of squint you'd have while looking up at white stars from Dillon's roof.

Just then, I did all I could do, really, and unfolded the sweat-licked poem from my fist. Ignoring the hot, swollen ball of nerves in my throat, I filled my chest with confident air and, nice and loud, read the first line that jumped out at me:

Of all who live, I am the one by whom this work can best be done.

2

The words cut through any breeze present.

They came out louder than planned, but perhaps they were supposed to. After all, maybe important things *should* be shouted. I caught the twitch in his shoulders. It read like a hiccup of laughter. He took a long second to turn around, and I just stood there, cemented into foreign ground. Looking down at the water, he turned and stepped back up onto the dry earth just a few paces in front of me. I could hear my heart pounding in my ears and its pulse swarmed my whole face. He halted there, facing me, and his bare feet glistened in their wetness. His pants were rolled up shin-high, and for a moment, he looked more like one for adventure than one who was homeless. Tom-Sawyer like, just older. He was still wearing that old jacket, and his hair and face weren't the cleanest, but you should've seen his eyes.

He looked into me.

I'd never seen eyes like his before—in person at least. Sure,

I'd seen other eyes: eyes that shake you; eyes like the Middle-Eastern girl in red on the cover of that magazine. But this man's eyes were right in front of me, real, and really something. His left one was a perfectly gentle blue; his right, a shade of green I'd never really seen before. Two different-colored eyes.

We stood there and stared at each other without context. He had the exact face I remembered, the same look about him that'd been crowding my consciousness ever since Kristiansen had read that same line of poetry. His face was like a painting, come to think of it. The beard with those eyes. The kind of painting where the artist washes out the foreground with muddy gray, melancholic hues, only to splash the background with never-before-seen greens and blues and pinks and yellows that he or she mixed together while listening to some sort of classical piano. It was just everything about his face and eyes—the combination of blue and that energetic green in such a subtle environment of grays. And the way he'd look into you, it made me feel like he had some sort of story to share, like he'd seen something that really mattered, something that I, too, needed to know.

Time stood soldier-still. Without words, he motioned to the bench. It was so simple. I sat down, telling myself I wouldn't be the same nervous Aydenn as last time. Hell, *I* was the one who'd come all the way out there after all, bellowing out lines of poetry to a man I knew only by face and jacket. He found the bench as well. With our hips situated closer together than last time, it didn't take him very long to speak.

"So you figured me out." He gave a healthy chuckle. "Weren't my words after all. Van Dyke's all along. Blessin' and doom. Hell of a poem. I really took it to heart when *I* first heard it myself…so many years ago."

I looked up from the poem I was holding in my lap, catching him just as he started squinting out again, peering far out into the lake like he was maybe looking for something he'd lost. He went on about poetry and what it can do to people and said something about me taking a liking to it at a young age.

"Yeah, it's...waking me up I think," I agreed, "you start to see things like...they're new or something. And it's all written really simply. Never knew how much weight a few words could carry. But the bit about *blessing* and *doom*. It's really...I..." I trailed off, waiting for him to see his cue to elaborate on what they meant."

Nothing.

I went on, fighting the ball of nerves expanding in my throat. "My English teacher over at Texana Hills High School...it's um...back a ways and down the road...he shared the poem with us in class...today actually." I looked at the poem in my lap again, the creases begging for a good flattening out.

I didn't understand why he wouldn't look over at me or the paper I was holding. Why wouldn't he ask me anything? He just looked out at the water changing directions. And he'd made no fuss over the coincidence; I mean *that* poem, of *all* poems! But maybe this man, whoever he was, was smart enough to see the whole idea of *coincidence* as nonexistent, and that all along it's been nothing more than a term used by nonbelievers of fate or magic. Perhaps this man knew that in a world like ours, coincidences were never the case, and everything was just as remarkable as it seemed.

He went on spreading his meditation across the water like marmalade, not taking the poem from me, but perhaps taking a lot more. Perhaps it was just nice for him to have company. Everyone needs someone to talk to. Everyone.

◊

The sun hadn't begun seducing the lake with its setting quite yet. The wind was awfully light, but I was still some sort of nervous sitting there in that quiet. Rubbing the paper creases flat against the top of my thigh, I thought to myself, *Who is this man next to me, and why the hell am I even out here?*

I wouldn't just up and leave again though. I knew I had to stay. My hands found the bench to both my sides, and I pressed down into the wood with the tips of my fingers, much like I'd done on the bleachers that first morning in P.E. with Coach Fischer.

The wood was warm and dry. I looked down at the man's wet feet, and then at my own, my running shoes still pulled decently tight. Right when I thought to bend forward and loosen them up, he started to talk; I mean *really* talk. With each couple of words, he became less and less a stranger and more the mentor that I never knew I needed. I guess that's how it is with mentors—you won't realize how much you needed them until they're right there spilling it all out in front of you. He spoke with his velvet-textured voice, and I did all that I'd come to do that day; I listened.

◊

"Nice a-you comin' back."

He licked his bottom lip. "You found your way back here by followin' a few lines of poetry…from that I think I might know some of the things goin' on in your head. Was in the same place maybe when I was your age, maybe a little older. But somethin' up front, kid. If you wanna know about some of these things, like this poem and what it really means and why the hell I sit at this lake and do nothin' but sit…let me tell you without you attemptin' to learn me. *Me* ain't very important with any of it, it's *you*; whether you realize it or not, you're the reason we're sittin' here today." The glaze on my eyes heated up. I suddenly felt the warm and quiet shelter of being under a large bird's wing.

"I got nothin' to hide, kid…I just see much of my own reality as futile to others. And you can probably see why," he

133

said, motioning behind him at his dark red tent that neighbored the others. "My physical travels won't explain much more than the dirt on my jacket or the sunburn on my face and hands. You see…when I was younger like yourself, I started to notice the world openin' up. Just readin' certain books, real good ones, the quiet things started gettin' louder as the loud things were hushin' up. I felt different, alone. But my aloneness didn't feel wrong or nothin'. I felt good about seein' things differently and slower than I'd ever seen 'em. It's a hell of a time relearnin' everythin' from the ground up with new eyes."

He paused and looked up, "Like this," he motioned out to the lake. "Everyone's got some idea about what beauty is and what freedom is and what the sun looks like on water, but ideas can be so damn skeptical, right? It's about experiences, kid. Bein' right there and seein' it and takin' it with you in your heart. Ideas are often just our attempts at feelin' like we've had the experience when we really haven't. You know how it gets…you see a photograph of this or that maybe, and it tricks you into thinkin' you've really seen what's in the photograph itself. It takes a good spendin' of patience to change your ways, to slow your pace, to be born again in between breaths just like that. And that's how I knew my life was going to be different when I was younger. I felt like I was onto somethin', somethin' big. I knew that if I just stayed awake to all that's unfoldin' in the background of things all the time, I'd see a hell of a lot more and maybe I'd even be happier."

He paused and got quiet, then trailed on again.

"But you see, the magic, the *real* magic isn't in the lake at all; it's in the lake's personality. Nature…she knows we're here, and she makes the subtlest attempts to say hello." The sun continued to descend invisibly in its perfect roundness. "It just takes some curiosity and a heapin' handful of patience. With them two, you'll never miss the hellos."

His left hand went up in front of him. He twisted his body to show me.

"You see?" he whispered.

My eyes quickly became glued to the murky gold wedding band that hugged his finger. It was curious as hell why he had it, but I wouldn't have time to think about it until later. And I sure wouldn't ask then and there like an idiot. He put his right hand up next to his left. They were both backed with hair, which was moving perfectly in the wind. "You see?" he said again, softer.

Nature was saying hello.

His hands found his lap as he went on.

"Seein' you back here today, seein' you on this bench again, it's somethin' special. A lot we can talk about, hell, maybe a lot we should talk about. A lot you're lookin' for and a lot I've found in lookin' for the same thing." He stopped and turned to his right to look at me. "I think we were brought together, somehow, by the winds. The wind knows everybody, after all."

He scratched his forehead with the tips of his fingers, and went on with words, soon quoting the poem that adhered our fates. "You seem like you're after somethin'. Perhaps you've been after it for a little while, and maybe you don't know why; perhaps you don't even know what it is you're after. But I'll lend what I can, *to suit my spirit and to prove my powers*, to anchor you somewhere safe."

Was this stranger offering, hell, *delegating* himself as my new teacher? Did people do this? How do you really trust a stranger anyway? Maybe you trust a stranger by not seeing him or her as a stranger in the first place, but rather a brother or sister. It was a strange situation. Why was I all the way out there anyway? Why didn't I just pull myself up off the wooden bench and walk back through the Southern Park and do normal things like the other senior boys at Texana Hills High School? For whatever reason, I didn't answer that question. Instead, I stayed sitting on that bench. And perhaps that was my answer in itself.

I squinted out at the lake, studying the distance between the sun and the horizon. I wouldn't have understood his eagerness to talk to me and teach me things if I hadn't seen the explanation written across the page I was still holding on my lap. It was two lines.

"Let me but do my work from day to day,
In field or forest, at the desk or loom."

He must have felt that it, whatever it was, was part of his duty, his journey, his purpose. Hell, maybe I needed him too. At the bare bones of it all, perhaps we both just needed someone, a stranger, to talk to about the nothings and everythings that spin around our uncharted minds.

And so I began, "That poem, *Work*, why that poem? Of all lines, why that one? Blessing...and doom." He crossed his left leg over his right, his ankle glistening wet, and he sat with folded, hairy hands in his lap. "Well...it's somethin' I read a long time ago. Somethin' that's kept findin' my thoughts one way or another over the years. Those are the important things," he paused and looked back up at the lake, "the things that never leave us and always remind us."

"What do you mean *remind* us?

Eyes out on the water, his brow was stern, contemplative. "The senses. Five of 'em. Five senses. Every day, whether we like it or not, we see them, hear them, touch them, taste and smell them."

"Them?"

"Distractions, kid," he declared. "We pick up the magazine instead of the book, gaze at reruns instead of out the window or into faces, take photographs of things instead of just lookin' at 'em, we run through parks like these to make our hearts pump, but we never slow down and walk through it, takin' it all in, lettin' our soul pump...we simply...forget."

A cold warmth ignited me. Cold warmths are what you feel

when you have an epiphany about something small or big. Other than those times, it's just an oxymoron.

"We forget about this." I exhaled, nodding to the water beyond us. "We forget about things like this." It was a sad, simple fact, and I could see it clear as day.

"We're all given things that we too often surrender," he breathed back. "We're born with these abilities to look around, to observe, to collect, to feel, to comprehend. And once we begin to really feel this thing we call life, we become responsible for explorin' it. Responsible." He scratched his forehead again in the same way, catalyzing his thoughts. "But it seems people forget that a little more each day...they walk around the world's library, blindfolded by their own lifestyles...not in love with the world or who they are or Nature or much at all. Maybe in love with ideas...and we know about bein' in love with ideas...all seems great 'til the wedding day...then we find out ideas ain't much after all. It's experience we wanna marry." I stole another glance at the ring on his finger just then. "And every day that I've been out here," he gestured all around with his arms up, "with it all, I've looked for understandin', for peace, for love...in Nature...and in myself. And once you learn how to love somethin', you can't ever forget about it...even through all the distractions."

It's strange how quickly we'd gotten into heavy talk. But perhaps that's how people *should* talk, even to strangers, *especially* to strangers, to cut out all the little talk that gets no one anywhere.

His left leg was still crossed over his right. He leaned his left elbow forward onto his left knee, resting his chin in the basket of his left hand. I could hear the scratch of his beard echo in his palm. A sigh escaped him. "Funny how it's called *homelessness*, isn't it?"

Before I could move my mouth, he went on.

"More like *house*less. Hell, *this* is a pretty good home," he said, pointing to the trees around him and the sky above us. Home is a very important thing. But, you see, we've been fooled, thinkin' that home is a physical place. Home, you see, if a feelin'. Big difference in sayin' *I am home* and *I feel at home*, you know? Eh, just thoughts," he trailed off.

I thought about my mother just then, and our living room, our kitchen, the bathroom we shared and the window in my bedroom. Was it really my home after all?

Forgetting boundaries, I really opened it up, displaying my true foolish-kid nature.

"How did you become home... well *houseless?*"

It was like I shattered his meditation into a thousand fragments. He looked at me so hard that I could tell he wanted me to *know* he was looking at me. I tried to apologize but my effort got lost somewhere on my tongue.

"I'm sorry, I..."

"You're smarter than that, kid."

Maybe I was. I'd tried to learn him, just like he'd said not to. I expected him to yell or swear or tell me off or something, like the average person will do. But he didn't. He was just as calm as the lake. "None of that's important, kid. None of it. So how about I stick to tellin' you only the things worth knowin'?"

I nodded, feeling lost as ever, guided by this shadow of a man.

He found his barren feet and stood up, turning around to me. I couldn't find any words. *Blessing* and *doom* were buried heavy somewhere underneath my tongue, and that's where they stayed. The sun was lower, the breeze heavier. I got those goddamn goosebumps on the backs of my arms and legs. Looking up at him from the bench, I tried my best not to shiver. Before I could form even a one-word apology, he let out an *It's been a long day* exhale, and stuck out his hairy hand.

"Name's Echo, by the way."

"Aydenn." I offered in my strongest tone, putting my hand

in his.

"Aydenn," he repeated back thoughtfully, still clutching my hand. "You know this bench *is* cemented in; it ain't goin' anywhere," he smiled. His words and his eyes softened everything. My goosebumps flattened out under the warmth between us. His blue eye nearly matched the tip of the blue ink pen jutting out of his jacket's breast pocket.

Time slowed as our eye contact broke and he turned to walk back in the direction of his dark red tent. I watched him do so, staring at that ponytail of his as if he were a horse riding off into the sunset at the end of an old movie. He threw wide the two tent flaps and disappeared inside.

I guess it was my time, too, to return home—or wherever it was I lived.

◊

I'd never met anyone like him before.

I felt bad for asking how he became homeless—houseless. I felt like I felt whenever I'd ask my mother about my father's death. It was all just insensitive, and maybe that's the worst thing you can be sometimes.

I walked home that evening, mind too busy for even a light jog. When I made it to the top of the hill on Main Street, I had a hell of a view of the sun saying its last 'hello' to Mayhaw. Into sight came a green square of grass in the distance. The football team had long finished practicing, and the field was empty. My feet took me all the way there as I looked up at the amaranth sky.

I thought about how the weather was so damn strange and that it was supposed to be snowing, at least raining. But all Mayhaw could cough up was some wind, maybe some of that morning mist, and a handful of clouds that threatened nobody. Walking closer to the edge of the field, the clouds were my only company—grey wisps on a purple background with smaller cirrus clouds that caught a hint of yellow from the setting sun.

It all made me feel small. I looked down at my bony knees and remembered that my blue jeans and backpack were still shoved into the boy's locker room. I couldn't just go home without them. It was Wednesday, and I had school in the morning.

I stood at the edge of the field, finding that there was quiet wind movement across each blade of grass. There it was. The subtle hello again. Echo was right.

Caught somewhere in the still of that early evening, I bent down and untied my shoes. I peeled them off along with my socks, stood back up, stuffed my socks into my pockets and hung my shoes—shoelaces tied together—around my neck, like kids do.

Echo said something about how people had *forgotten* what it was like to experience Nature, and I wanted to see if I was one of them. I stepped out onto the grass, barefoot. I can't remember if the grass was wet or not.

Looking up again, I walked aimlessly, backwards and in zigzags. I eventually made it up to a steady run, painting every inch of that field. My shoes clapped together under my chin. My breaths were cool and I felt light as hell, and I didn't care what I looked like. It's a hell of a feeling to be part of the evening like that.

I spread my arms out wide like wings, thinking of Jonathan Livingston Seagull, and ran to the end of the field in a perfect curve, looking up here and there at the stars as they poked holes in the sky.

3

Perhaps by now, some of you have raised your eyebrows at the fact that it wasn't yet *cold* in November. Sure, it was peculiar as hell, but only minuscule compared to what would happen a little over a month later. I never thought that the weather could be so damn poetic. Perhaps that's its personality. The sun would linger up there like it had forgotten to go home, but everyone was fine with it. The clouds tried their best to reclaim November, but the sun won every time.

My classes at Texana Hills had become just as colorful as the sky. P.E., Literature as Philosophy, and a History of Western Civilization are what I found soaking up most of my weekdays. P.E. made larger both my lungs and my mind. Coach Fischer hadn't talked any noticeable amount since the first day of class. But then again, I don't think he needed to. We all knew our duties after we'd gotten into our gym clothes. P.E. back then wasn't anywhere near what you're seeing today. Some days it was the pool, others the basketball gym, and some days, he only kept us half the period—he'd then point to the track and say, "It's optional...or perhaps it's not," and then he'd walk off somewhere. We respected the hell out of the guy, and no one ever really complained. Back then, I could never fully understand why he'd stayed so silent as the semester went on. I'd swim the laps or shoot the hoops or run the track, and I'd wait for him to say something, anything. His choice of words that first day of class had been a mind-full, and I wanted more. I guess that's why libraries are so vital. You can hear all the bold and brilliant voices you want, over and over again, and it's free and all you have to do is open a goddamn book. I kept at least one ear open whenever Coach Fischer was nearby, just in case he let some whispered profound words escape him. But all I ever heard was my own adrenaline—from running or something—kicking its bass onto my eardrums. Perhaps he helped me understand the power of silence altogether. Maybe it's characteristic of noble minds like his to sort of *graduate* into silence.

The history class I mentioned was, well, it was history, and it wasn't going anywhere anytime soon. That's the beauty of history: it waits there patiently for us to be interested. It's a beautiful, curious subject, really. You just have to be ready for it, really ready for it. And maybe it just wasn't my time to start looking back; I was just learning how to get my present time in order, and the past wouldn't be excusing itself from the table anytime soon.

◊

Kristiansen kept me busy in the best of ways; he was interesting as hell. He wasn't afraid of challenging us, and trying his hardest to make us understand things. He was always a bit off, and had his swings in mood, but was nonetheless passionate about it all; you could see it in his hands and his eyes. There was always a little bit of love to be found in a lot of what he said to us. It's a rare thing to find a teacher like that, but you'll know when you do, and you'll look back and be so grateful that it almost hurts. Perhaps I'm stretching it, but at times, he was the closest thing I'd ever known to a father—in terms of being told things that really help you grow up. I just looked up to him like that, and took a lot of his words to heart.

Outside of school, I barely had the time to just lie on my top bunk like I used to. Senior year homework had lived up to its bad reputation. I took to the sidewalk or the school track whenever I had a fistful of minutes of daylight to spare, but other than that, homework had forced me to be the homebody I hated being. I thought about Echo all the time, dreaming up when I would visit him next. It was a hell of a ways out there, and I'd been using up my legs in morning P.E. class. And I would never ride a bicycle or take the bus because then I'd miss it all; I'd miss the during-ness of the journey there. You'll hear the cliché about how *it's not the destination; it's the journey*, and you'll be so quick to stuff it away as common sense, but if you sit on it long enough, it's more than common sense, but *great* sense. And that's why clichés exist: they have such truth to them—truth that is somehow diluted in the waters of repetition. But diluted or not, it's still truth nonetheless.

One night, just before Thanksgiving break, I was home reading a pile of pages Kristiansen had handed out. He had us read all sorts of things. He must've felt responsible to show us things that we might not have ever come across otherwise. And perhaps it was just what we needed before we'd trek out onto the avenues of being with nothing more than a high school diploma rolled up in our hands. It must've been a hell of a time for him to parent our higher intellectual abilities like that, and he seemed flustered a good deal of the time, but preparing us for this big post-high school mystery of life and coming of age had to be a blessing for him, not a doom at all.

It was mature into the night, and I was situated underneath my bunk, hunched over my desk, ruminating over paperclipped pages that Kristiansen felt should be part of our lives. A whole bundle of what he called Romantic poetry was spread out, sunbathing under my desk lamp. He didn't tell us how to read it or anything, but perhaps direction on how to read poetry is the silliest idea ever. All he said was to read it slowly and in private.

Before reading a single word, I lit a thin, red candle and shut off my desk lamp, leaving the room darker than the inside of a closed dresser drawer. One of the pages was especially illuminated in the candlelight. I stumbled over a few of the words and images because I'd never really been in love, nor had I received much of it. Thus, romance was as unfamiliar a territory as the Northern Park of Lake Wisley had been. And whenever I stumbled through the poem, I'd secretly wish that Kristiansen were right by my side, underneath my bunk, to talk with his hands and point at certain words and guide me through. Dillon's father would help him with homework like that, and that's something I was always envious of.

My mother opened the door to my room. She must've just finished the dishes after dinner, or maybe the news, or hell, even her second or third glass of red wine. She didn't knock; the door was pushed open at a reasonable speed, lending a slight wind over to the candle that lit up my desk. I watched the flame dance for a second before turning around to see her leaning there, like that, with one hand still on the knob. She had a good grip on the glass in her hand. She looked around my room confusedly, as if I'd painted my walls pink or something.

She began quickly, "Aydenn, have you seen my...what's with the lights?" she said as her hand came off the knob to wave around the room. Though her countenance was so dimly lit, it managed to somehow look disapproving. "Ah, just reading some poetry, Mom." Her eyebrows went stern I think. "You've been awfully busy this month, Aydenn; I can't say that I even see you out of this room more than once a day."

I was as honest as I could be in my reply. "Just...school, Mom. Homework like I never would've guessed. Just part of senior year. Everyone's tearing their hair out over their textbooks. Perhaps teachers like to fill up our heads to the brim with this stuff just before the New Year can pollute it all over again."

She gave a little laugh. It was the only laugh she really had, except on the rare occasion where she was with her sister and they brought up some one-eyed dog named Pirate that they had when they were girls. That was a laugh I never really heard otherwise.

"What are you reading there?" she said, as she put down her glass on my dresser. She began to walk towards the back of my chair, briefly looking at my father's fire helmet on the way. The paper glowing in the candlelight was a poem by Pablo Neruda, one of Kristiansen's favorites. Perhaps my mother read the first two lines over my shoulder, enough for her to react.

"You said that this is for school?"

"Yeah." I paused. "It's this English class. Our teacher is really great, and...he's not like any other teacher I've..."

"Just don't be getting yourself shoulder deep in all this poetry stuff. All these big ideas, philosophies. You gotta be careful with some of it. A lotta stuff...a lotta heavy stuff in there sometimes." I felt her uneasiness, her almost-anger, spread across my shoulder blades with a dull warmth. She went on, "Some of it'll drive you mad...confuse you in ways that you might just regret one day. Reading is good, of course. Just be mindful of what you're exposing yourself to. Heavy reading can change people, Aydenn. Change them forever."

I hated her disinterest, her cautionary ways with me. She would've called me a damn fool or would've been embarrassed as hell had she seen me running around on the sports field barefoot with my arms stretched wide. We were so different, and it killed me. She'd never understand. I fought back as much as a son can fight back to a mother like that. "Oh, I know, but some of this stuff is really...."

She cut me off again. "You been preparing for your fire academy exam in the Spring?" Valid question. Wrong timing. She was dismissing my route of learning from Kristiansen just like that: writing it off as insignificant, unimportant, hell, pointless. I didn't know why she was acting like that. Perhaps she just got that way around anything romantic; reading about love would've surely made her think of my dead father. So I carried on with her direction. "Yes, Mom. Slowly and surely."

"Well keep me updated, okay? I want to see some progress, Aydenn. You know this is the only reason I'm okay with you not going to college like your friend Dillon and so many others." She paused. "Because I can call your aunt tomorrow and have her talk to your uncle and I'm sure he can pull some sort of strings up at the college out there. I wonder..."

It was my turn to cut *her* off. "I'll keep you updated, okay?" I turned around and looked at her. "I will."

She always did that. She made it seem like she was doing me a favor by not pressuring me to apply to schools like everyone else. But the truth is, she always left it at just words. She could've pushed me to go to college, and I knew she had some money in savings, but she never made the action toward it. Part of me thought that, deep down, it was because she didn't want me to leave home. She didn't want to be left a second time by a man she loved.

She backed out of the room, draining her glass. I could almost hear the wine glide over her front teeth. Before closing the door behind her, she motioned with her other hand, "Put on some of these lights, I know you don't wanna see yourself in glasses any more than I do." She shut the door just as casually as

146

she'd opened it. I heard her fingernail tinkering on the wineglass as she walked down the hall. I reflected on God-knows-what as I stared almost vulnerably at the candle on my desk. The flame was dancing like hell.

My attention was back on the pages in front of me.

I made two stacks on my desk. One was the poems that gave me a tugging feeling; the other was the what-the-hell-were-*they*-in-love-with poems.

I continued to read as if my mother had never interrupted. I planted my elbows on my desk, and with fists in cheeks, I squinted at random beautiful words—the ones that make you want to live a bigger life. The flame crackled at its own discretion. I read until I understood. I walked barefoot along the top of each line of poetry, feeling the contours underneath my feet. I didn't rush to finish the poems. It was never the bigger picture or the didactic message that mattered; what mattered was always the footprints you left in the sand between the poem's lines, the moments of transformation that happened in between reading the lines. That's how it's always been with poetry.

My goodnight to it all came soon thereafter. I stacked up the pages in order of my favorites, blew out the flame and watched the smoke rise in thin curls. I liked to think that, at that precise moment, someone else—somewhere else—was just lighting a candle of their, and our flames were the same. And, like the soul, my flame had merely transmigrated to another wick when I blew it out.

I did the nightly things that, over the years, we learn to do unconsciously, and with a clean face and clean teeth, I ambled up into my bunk, pulling only a corner of the bed sheet over my waist. It wasn't unreasonably cold, and we had the heater running, and heat rises of course. I was plenty warm up there, which felt good in a childlike way.

With my head on the pillow, just before I fell into some dream that I'll never remember, I thought about how incredible romantic love must be. I didn't think about Dillon or any of the other relationships at school. I thought about love between a man and woman, *real* love.

All those poets wrote a similar song, and it sounded like love could hurt like hell. But perhaps it needs to hurt. It's just like the seasons, really. You see, the Winter must happen before the Spring can come rolling along. And the Spring and all its greens and yellows and blues would never be as bright as they are without the preceding gray rains and hollow winds of Winter. What I'm really getting at is that perhaps the longing for something—the nostalgia, the heartbreak—must *all* happen in order to really understand the storm of love. A lot of romantic notions evolve during the in-between times of love anyway—pre and post relations. We learn a lot in the directionless in-betweens. And the pain behind this *love*, whatever it may be or feel like, can't be *all* that bad. You see, people say that when it rains it pours—and it does. And that's another cliché, but there's such truth in it. And it goes even further if you keep digging; the cliché shouldn't ever stop there, you see, people always seem to forget how the nature of things works; they forget about what happens next.

Sure, the rain pours and pours, and then it really starts to come down hard, but then, just like that, it all stops. When it rains, it pours. But then it stops.

It stops.

And you don't need *me* to tell you that; it's written in the personality of Nature. She's telling us secrets all the time, and like Echo had said, all we have to do is listen. And pretty soon, life becomes much lighter than you thought it could ever be because it's all so much simpler than we make it.

4

As you know, Thanksgiving was a holiday I usually spent with the Rubensons.

And I was more and more thankful for every year I sat at their table. Dillon's mother had called my house at one point to remind me that I was invited as usual and how, no matter what, she'd set a place for me at their table. She was kind like that. There's a mother like her maybe once every five years. However, nothing anywhere in my intuition told me to join them that year.

Sure, we remained best friends at heart, but Dillon had a girlfriend now. She drove Dillon to and from school and held his hand in the hallways and looked at him with big eyes. I'm sure she'd laughingly help Mrs. Rubenson fold Dillon's laundry, and surely she had a girly connection with little Arietta. In truth, she was sweet; she was good for Dillon. And I wasn't jealous. How *could* I be jealous after Dillon had introduced her to me as his *best friend since childhood?*

I'd see them both at school and they'd wave and I'd wave back. They were no strangers to public displays of affection, the progression of which always baffled me in high school. One week it was the exchange of those smiles that only meant one thing; the next: maybe a talk by the girl's locker after school—the boy leans on the locker next to hers; he looks confident like a man, but is really nervous as hell like a boy; then maybe a week or two later, after a date or a front porch canoodle, their hands have this magnetism to them; no more than a month wanders by and you witness the routine goodbye kiss in front of the girl's classroom— she walks in as light as a feather, and he continues down the hall, trying so hard to suppress a giddy smile that would only threaten his male friendships. And then it happens, just like that—necking like it was the new tobacco. And you always knew when the couples first had sex too. You'd never see two individuals so damn happy on a Monday morning. Because unless they were drinking the wine twice at church the day before, they'd definitely been up to *something* over the weekend. But then again, what the hell did I know? I'd been listening to what a *seagull* had to say, hell, and befriending the homeless too.

The Rubensons had Thanksgiving without me, and perhaps they all silently understood why. Maybe Dillon even respected my decision. It's not like it distanced us. We'd always be best friends because he'd always remember. He'd always remember how we'd look up at the stars together, smoking cigars and talking about the things boys have always talked about. And the stars would always hang overhead to remind him of that. My mother would ask about him and his mother, and I'd say they were fine and that Dillon was busy as hell with college applications, and that Mr. Rubenson was really on him to be *proactive*. Fathers use words like that.

I didn't tell her about Dillon's girlfriend. I didn't tell her because then she'd ask why I didn't have a girlfriend, and then I'd have to explain to her how I was busy in other parts of my life, more important ones. And then she'd ask me to elaborate, and at that point I'd be telling her about an eccentric literature teacher in a cherry red beret who taught us things that we could never forget even if we tried. And I'd also end up telling her about Echo. Imagine that: "Yeah Mom, he's this really interesting homeless guy I met. He's sort of mentoring me on things." She'd love that.

She never got too involved, which made it easy to keep secrets.

But that's how families are. Kids have their secrets, and the parents have theirs. If there's only one thing that keeps us independent and unique and individuals, perhaps it is our secrets.

My mother and I had Thanksgiving together that year.

I told her the day before that I wouldn't be going to Dillon's, and sure enough, the next morning she was up early as hell, cooking. There was her display of love, right there in the kitchen. It turned out to be more of a late lunch than a dinner, because she'd still have to go and serve the homeless food with her coworkers, the same way they did on every Christmas Eve. I'd always wonder how she felt about that, and why she never tried to back out of doing it. Like I said, she had this unmistakable eeriness about the homeless.

That morning, before I'd even lifted my eyelids a millimeter, the slight smell of homemade gravy found its way into my room from the kitchen and right up into my nostrils. That'll get you up. It was about eleven o'clock. Thursday, like Thanksgiving always is.

Sooner than later, we ate. I did what I could do to help, but you have to be careful helping people who already know exactly what they're doing. Just work in any kind of kitchen for even a day and you'll know what I mean. Distancing myself from everything edible, I set the table. Forks and knives and plates and spoons and harvest-themed cloth napkins. I even put out two wine glasses to show her I was growing up.

After setting up, I retreated to the living room off the kitchen and laid down half way on the couch with my legs dangling over the arm. It's the preferred way to sit on a couch as a kid or whatever I was. Overhead, I stretched out my arms, holding a piece of paper up in the yellow light that came down thick from the skylight—a decent-sized square cut out of the ceiling in the middle of our living room. You couldn't see the sky out of it. It was fogged glass or something. But you felt it, especially if the sun was lined up with it, beating down. Must've been how the blind feel when they stand out in the sun. Around that time of year, you'd usually hear the rain tapping on it like an anxious neighbor at the door. But the rain had missed the bus, then the train, then its flight, and we were all still waiting for it, people and plants together.

I was holding the same piece of paper that I'd brought out to the park to show Echo. I was looking at the words without actually reading them, which is only possible on rare occasion. Those two in particular—*blessing* and *doom*—were like fish that couldn't be caught. I could watch them swim all I wanted, but when I wanted to put a hook in their mouth and pull them in and gut them for their meanings, I realized I wasn't a fisherman at all. Echo hadn't even told me much about the poem itself. When I brought it up, he came back with talk about the lake and how it's easy to forget important things.

I lied there on the couch for however long it was, feet still dangling and starting to tingle. Those two words, along with the smell of balsamic turkey marinade, hypnotized me as I fell somewhere in between meditation and soft, accidental sleep.

My mother's head was poked out of the kitchen doorway, steam behind her. She was calling my name to stir something or other.

A few more things done and then we got seated. Through a smile she told me how she'd mixed Mayhaw's local honey with the cranberry sauce for the turkey. She got excited about little things like that, tastes and smells in the kitchen. I think I loved her for it.

She looked sideways at me briefly as I popped the cork and poured the wine. She could've taken it from me and done it herself; she could've been silently wishing I'd never drink like her. But she said nothing.

Any conversation we had was in between chews.

There are two signs of food being really delicious: one, little to no conversation in the first couple minutes of jaw work; two, you nearly forget to drink you water or your wine.

School was brought up because that's all she really knew about me. It wasn't long before my Literature as Philosophy class surfaced into the conversation. She was oddly curious about it— what we were reading and talking about, our teacher too.

Our living room wasn't one of those living rooms with oak bookshelves, vertical spines with tiny letters; hell, my mother never read. Maybe that's why I'd never read anything big before that semester.

If she wanted to know about it all, then I'd tell her. If I was old enough to have a glass of wine with her, perhaps I was old enough to tell her things without fearing judgment. I spilled words about the poetry competition and what I wrote and why I wrote it and how I didn't win; about the little yellow note from the runner; about the man in the red beret who, just by looking at you and talking about things, made you want to try your best, to live your best. I left out the part about the Van Dyke poem and how it had brought me to Echo. I kept it to what I'd been learning in a school desk, not on a park bench.

She had her opinion of course, but she listened. When I said how Kristiansen had read so many books and has so much wisdom about him, she came back with, "That's nice, Aydenn, but you don't want to be one of those kinds of people forever chasing answers that don't exist." She said it kindly, genuinely, as if she really cared about me. But her saying it depressed me. She picked up her wine glass and nearly drained it. "God knows we need more depressed page-turners with coffee-stained teeth. You were born to be a fireman, Aydenn. Just like your father."

It hurt to have her put down what I'd learned to value. She should've been proud of me for taking an interest in school like that. She should've been so much more than she was. Stabbing at the same slice of turkey, I rationalized that it just wasn't worth it—she wasn't worth the words. Perhaps you just can't explain some things to people; perhaps you can't turn some people around from the gray wall they stubbornly face. I could've told her about how I felt when I ran across the sports field barefoot, and how people should do that more often. I could've talked about clouds being the world's most experienced travelers.

But then it hit me.

My mother was just one of those kinds of people. She was the kind of person Echo had talked about. Perhaps she hadn't always been like that though. Growing up by the ocean, I always thought she'd learned to see and feel things differently, with a little more freedom. But where was that freedom now? I guess you *can* forget some things that you think you never will, or you never want to. Perhaps something dislodged her, threw her off, made her one of the people that's existing and not living, one who'd forgotten. I know my father's death had put a hole in her heart and a cloud over her eyes. But would it be that way forever? What did she still hold onto so strongly that hindered her from changing, from growing? She was a beautiful lady, really—driven, worked hard. Why couldn't she just soften up to the art in life? Why couldn't she ever just stand out in the rain?

I wondered what she'd see from mine and Echo's bench if she sat between us.

She continued, softer, "You know that I just want you to be happy Aydenn, and please, find something that makes you happy. Just don't get all in over your head with all that literature, that philosophy. You don't want to find yourself underwater with it." She took a generous gulp from her glass, "It's known to create...distractions in your head...maybe set you back from a career...from joining the fire academy." She paused and looked right at me, "And I know how important that is to you, Aydenn."

Create distractions?

So I had Echo telling me that insight to life and reading and poetry steers you toward love and away from distractions, and then I had my own mother telling me that all that stuff *is* the distraction. It's a real coming of age when you realize that maybe your parents' answers aren't always the best ones for you.

It was after four o'clock, and my mother had just headed out to one of the churches or shelters to feed the homeless Thanksgiving dinner with a handful of her coworkers. She'd be out until late, and I had a decent-looking afternoon to myself. My stomach and mind were packed full of good things, and I needed movement. I couldn't just while away inside. Dillon and his family—and *her*—were probably just sitting down to dinner, and Emma's Café would've been closed for the holiday.

I gave a patient look out the big window above my bunk to find that November was just the same. A come-and-go chill in the air that had a bite as threatening as a newborn kitten. Without debate, I pulled tight the laces on my running shoes, and I was out the door.

()

The bridge to the Northern Park squeaked when I walked across its wooden planks. It was an achy, cold-outside squeak. Though breathing hard, I didn't even stop for a drink at the fountain. And I didn't bring the poem this time. All I brought were questions, curiosities and little ruminations you'll collect in between seeing the people who put seeds in your mind. It was colder out there, under the trees. I'd pulled on sweats and all that, and I even brought along an ugly ass scarf. Who runs in a scarf anyway?

It had only been a week or so since my last visit with him, but it felt much longer. There was the bench to my right, *cemented in the ground* as Echo had put it. The pine trees blew like hell in the wind off the lake. It wasn't the welcoming, waving kind of motion from the branches this time. This time, I didn't feel as invited. Nature's a real interesting girl like that. There's a whole lot stitched right into her. And it's important to be in touch with it. Because if you're not in touch with Nature, well, what are you in touch with?

I walked across the big clearing that opened up to the tents that sat cold, perched on their elbows. And of course, off to the right, near the bench, was Echo's. Dark red, sort of blushing at you. Feet crunching over the pine needles as I walked, I found myself just outside of it. *This is where he sleeps*, I thought. *This is where this man's life begins every day and ends every night.*

"*Hello?*" I whispered into the outside wall of his tent.

Nothing.

Another whispered hello. Nothing again.

I tapped on the dark red canvas with my fingernail and tried again.

"Hello. Echo? It's…Aydenn."

Silence.

I cleared my throat with decent volume. Twice. If he was

asleep, he'd surely wake up to that. Still, nothing. Not even the sound of breathing.

Biting my bottom lip in disappointment, I looked around at the other tents. Lifeless. Straight ahead in the distance there was a single fire. It wasn't much. Almost pathetic. It barely burned outside of a greenish tent that looked older than Mark Twain. Unconsciously, I walked toward it, toward the warmth. I got right up to the fire. A small hole dug out in the dirt, encircled by what looked like carefully picked out, beautifully shaped, gray stones. The heat hit me in the ankles. And then, from inside the tent came movement.

A leather-tan, bony hand made its way out of the two flaps of green canvas. It was followed by the long face of an old man. He looked tired, and more than that, heartbroken. You can always just tell when someone's heart is hurting. He looked up at me from his round, brown eyes. There were several wet drops on his collar, just below his chin. Tears. He'd been crying in there. But it wasn't the helpless wail kind of cry. It was the other kind, when the tears just kind of fall out into a gentle stream because you can't hold them in. You cry silently, and you can't hold the tears back because tears are words that can't be spoken but still need to come out somehow.

He was frail. Little. Hungry. I could've hugged him just then. He had long, stringy hair and the cheekbones of an old sculpture. As if cobwebs were in his throat, he began to speak to me through them. And he somehow knew what I wanted to know.

"They're all gone...they all took the bus to the church for Thanksgiving dinner. Together."

A stupid and simple "Oh" is all I could give, staring invasively at the wetness on his collar, right underneath his jaw line.

"I would've gone," he said as he sort of bit his lip and looked down, "but I always spend Thanksgiving alone with...*her*." He looked down at the little body of flames warming our legs. Over it was a small pot of black beans and a single cob of corn. Resting atop one of the gray stones was a small gold frame I hadn't noticed before. Fingerprints and lip marks smudged the glass. Inside it was a woman with a powder-soft face and one of those older hairstyles you don't see anymore. To ask who she was may not have been right. I smiled instead. You can never fail someone with a smile. The air felt like he wouldn't have minded if I stuck around, but I wanted him to spend Thanksgiving with *her*, like he'd said.

I wished him a nice day and nodded my head in some sort of understanding. I wished I would've touched his hand or said something warm, but I was still young and afraid, and turned around to walk away. A few steps back toward where I came from, I was flooded by the emptiness all around me. It felt cemetery-like. Unwelcomingly still. Behind me, I heard the man mumbling to himself, maybe to the frame.

The lake itself seemed bothered. I shivered even through the layers I was wrapped in. I pulled my fists into my sleeves, tightened my scarf and jerked over to the bench. I sat right where I would've sat had Echo been there to my left.

The sky on the horizon was confused and pretty washed out, but it had a harshly bright whitish tint that'll remind you why you have eyelids. I had to squint twice as hard because the wind right off the lake was so thin and stung like hell. I sat there, lost. Would I wait for him to come back? What if, for some reason, he never did? There's no schedule for men like him.

I got up off the bench, rubbing my arms quickly with my hands for heat, and wheeled around, seeing the fire in the distance again, the old man with that frame on his knee. He sat there, behind the fire, staring deeply into the flames as if he was asleep with his eyes open. "Maybe *that's* what love is like," I thought, "staring into a flame with open, calm eyes."

It was my intention to cross back over the bridge—to cut

through the Southern Park, back to the street, up the hill, past Texana Hills, and eventually back home, where I'd throw a match in the fireplace and have a fire of my own and maybe have a raspberry tea right in front of it.

But as I took one last look at the grounds, that dark red tent stuck out like an important line in a poem. I looked to my right and left, and off into the distance, and then back over the bridge into the Southern Park. The wind was the only thing moving. I walked quickly, in a straight line, right over to the dark red tent. I was standing at the entrance. One last look out over the top of the tent and through the grounds. Nothing. With my hands together like in prayer, I stuck them into the crack of the two canvas flaps and spread my arms open. Two small steps forward and the flaps fell behind me. I stood there, bent down and squinting, swallowed in the quiet darkness of Echo's tent.

5

It was quiet as hell, squatting there, my eyes tripping over themselves in the dark.

A small tear in the top of the tent toward the back let a slant of light in. I'd kind of forgotten I was trespassing so heavily like that. But I'd come too far. Couldn't go back now. Who *was* this man? I wanted to know. I had to know.

The slant of light came down on a crooked tree stump parked there in the back corner. Sitting atop was a stout, red candle. Ducking my head, I footed closer. A book of matches too, right there. I stopped to listen once more for sounds outside the tent. The air was naked. Still. Unbothered. I lit the candle almost unconsciously. It cracked violently, soon finding a stable waltz there on the wick. A brilliant red glow warmed the four walls of what Echo had called home for God knows how long. The tent was longer than it was wide. Along one wall was some sort of bed that I didn't even get near; along the other wall leaned a crippled-looking bookshelf—some planks of wood and some mason jars stacked up to hold what looked like seven or eight hardcover books. Who knew the homeless—*houseless*—could live like this?

I crawled over, on my knees now, and tilted my head to read the titles carved into the book spines. Jack London and *Siddhartha* and *Walden* and some strange-looking book about motorcycle maintenance and...and *Jonathan Livingston Seagull*!

I couldn't believe it! But, at the same time, I guess I could. You sort of become more of a believer when things like that happen to you. And I think that's a very good thing. We need a world of more believers.

I flipped through every one of those books. Small, quick notes filled up the margins in blue ink and with really nice handwriting, calligraphy-like. Each book had a different smell, some of oak, some of sea salt.

I snapped back into reality, remembering how wrong I was just going through his things like that. My heart fluttered at the thought of him finding out, hell, catching me in the act. I didn't know how long I'd been in there for, or when they'd all return from dinner at the church. I didn't want to lose my new friend's trust. He'd said to not try and *learn* him, and right then and there, that's exactly what I was doing.

I stood up into a squat and footed back to blow out the candle and make everything how it was before I'd been there. But in those few steps, I managed to accidentally kick something, and I heard it slide across the canvas floor of the tent, into a dark corner. I'd find out later that accidents are never really accidents.

I grabbed the candle—still lit—and held it down to the ground to investigate.

Back in that dark corner, under the wide glow of the candle, sat a thick stack of pages, wrapped tightly together vertically and horizontally with tattered hemp string. I should've left right then. I should've blown out the candle and gotten the hell out of there.

It was all wrong, being inside his tent. But of course, curiosity always wins when you're young.

The bundle of pages was kept warm in between two thick pieces of cardboard. I turned to look at the entrance of the tent. The two flaps blew strangely in the wind as if they knew something I didn't.

In my hands, the stack of pages felt heavy, important. Perhaps words do carry weight after all. I unraveled the hemp slowly—vertically, then horizontally, then vertically again. I set the stack down on the canvas floor in front of me, carefully, like I was putting it to bed. I got to my knees, hovering over it. On the first page was only one handwritten line. Blue ink, and that calligraphy again. It read: *Standing Out In the Rain: An Autobiography.*

I flipped through the pages with my thumb. There were scratch-outs and underlines and arrows and more scratch-outs. All sorts of dates were scribbled throughout. Dates all that way back to 1974, the same year I was born.

How long had he been out here? I thought.

How long had he been alone like this, houseless?

Just then, I remembered Echo having that blue pen tucked into his breast pocket the last time I'd seen him. Whatever this was, it was real. Perhaps it was his story, the same story that was still being written that very moment. I planted my hands down in front of me on both sides of the stack. I turned the cover page and began to read.

Perhaps it is now that my life truly begins.

There was a big scratch out that went for about eight lines under this. So scratched out you couldn't read through it. Then, the lines continued in blue.

I left because I had to; I left because I was supposed to.

No stars can reveal if or when I'll make it back to her, but that's nothing I can control. It was my time to go. I felt it so deeply. It was just my time. We're all, at some point, summoned by the greater parts of ourselves to take some sort of journey—be it mental or physical—and I knew that this was mine. I knew it for long enough, couldn't ignore the call any longer.

And now, living like this, with nothing in the way, I hope to find the things that have been buried only in my imaginings, my dreams—the fullness of life. The less you have, the less can get in your way. And out here, living homeless, I hope to find the something in the nothing. Like the transcendentalists or even the existentialists. Perhaps out here I will become my own 'ist'. And maybe, in time, I'll understand just what it was that impeded me from letting go of boyish curiosities and just settling into loving her, my wife. Why couldn't I just be her husband and love her and stay put? What itched so badly at my spirit that made me abandon it all? Perhaps it was the need to experience momentum, flight, the primal freedom that we're all born into and can so easily forget. Perhaps I needed to feel what it feels like to just go.

Or it could've had to do with love. Maybe I didn't have enough love for myself. Maybe that's it. Maybe love must first germinate within, only to later blossom outward. Like I said, perhaps it is now that my life truly begins.

I thought about the ring on Echo's finger, taking its shelter from the hair on the back of his left hand.

The self is a delicate, delicate thing. And if left undeveloped, ungardened, and unrecognized, it is only a hindrance to any kind of relationship we might ever embrace. Far too few of us truly become something; instead, many of us fall into something. And it's too often that one settles for whatever falls into his or her lap. The self goes undiscovered, and distractions pull us away from ever understanding anything about our inner lives, our childhood-dream echoing self. The self waits for our attention. I'm talking about the real, look-in-the-mirror-and-look-about-your-face-and-into-the-deep-black-of-your-pupils self; that little seed inside of us all which we have abundant—perhaps endless—potential to water if we just remember it's there. And once that seed roots itself within us, this great self can begin to grow tall toward the sun.

THEN can it become a tree and bear fruit.

THEN can we can love things freely, because we will have inner fruit for sustenance. We won't need to fear loss or loneliness when something we love departs from us. We will have gardened the independence, individuality, and love for the self that resides within us. And that very self will help us along the rusted-steel railroad tracks of life.

I read on, confused and intrigued, sensing life becoming more and more important and sacred with each calligraphic word.

Love is perhaps the single thing one ever really desires—consciously or unconsciously. It is perhaps the only thing that one ever needs. And like any alcohol or hallucinogen or glass of wine, once we have our first taste of it, we only want more. It's a simple truth that, at their most primal core, people want to be in love. But like any experience worth having, you must be patient. You must wait, prepare yourself for it, prepare your SELF for it.

This term is used—"fall" in love—and that just can't be right. Love between two people is never as accidental as a fall. It's all been written out somewhere, somehow.

Romantic love is entertained since early on in life. I've even read a novel about an eight-year-old, Tereza, who'd fall asleep at night holding her own hand, pretending it was that of the man she'd love when she was older. We are all, by nature, romantic.

But love is like art. It should be treated delicately, like one would catch a butterfly by its wings. You can't just sneak up and pounce on it, because even if you do catch the butterfly that way, it'll be weakened by your grip, startled, uneasy. It will feel imprisoned, and love can only exist in some sort of freedom.

Everybody wants to be in love, but you must tiptoe toward it. Perhaps this tiptoeing is the journey—the journey of the self, the footsteps you take as an individual to garden that inner seed and learn to love within.

I felt empty inside. Empty. Not a whole lot of love for my life. And I couldn't have that. How could I love her and be with her and stay with her if my own heart was rotting inside of me. It's not that her love wasn't enough, it's that my own heart wasn't pumping enough for the both of us.

Forgetting where I was again, I kept reading as my eyes got warm with something.

Love must come, and it will.

We must experience romantic love, and we will.

But never should we fall or jump into it. Humans have voids. Many voids. Some are filled by children, God, animals, spouses, passions. But there's one that can't be filled by anything other than gardening that internal seed—taking the journey of the self. This is what I've come to believe.

Perhaps I'll find her again someday, and love her with all I'll be. But for now, my life truly begins here, on this journey. What I'm looking for is unknown. What I'll find, unknown too. I'll travel on, searching and resting and living in between the minutes that nobody ever sees. Sure I'll be lonely, anxious, terrified. I'm sure the journey will be cold and dark, brilliant and liberating, dizzy, beautiful. Maybe she'll read this one day and be able to understand. But for now, and for however long 'now' is going to be, I have to say 'until then' to it all.

Here he was, saying it all—all that ran from his mind to his heart. Everything someone could want to know about a person. Except for, who was *she*?

I flipped a couple pages. Another date was scribed above the body of words that might've meant more than the sun and the moon that day.

Romantic love adds color to our palettes and reminds us why life is so charming.

It livens our senses and lets us see, once again, the beauty in everything: flower petals and words and voices and clouds. But you have to be ready, really awake, prepared to take it on.

And the self is so important in all of this—in love, romantic love, life.

In the end, we are all quite alone. Really sit on that. We are quite alone. In our heads, in our bodies, we are quite alone. We enter this world the same way as we exit it—alone. And this is the far from a bad thing if we just learn to understand the self that we are coming and going with. This journey to understand the self—truly becoming the individual—is written from sources borrowed from our childhood dreams. Whether we're aware of it, we're always dreaming of a life that we wish we were living, or had lived. These dreams map out our truest desires, and it's too often that we let them slip away, treating them as simply imaginative. But where does this disconnect happen? Why does it happen? Where does our childhood curiosity meet our adult practicality? When do we stop living and start dying?

Only a brave few rake up the needed courage to confront the scariest people of all—ourselves.

Somehow, a single, warm tear began to push itself out of me.

By birth, we are committed to the self. We are thrown into our freedom, and we must act. We must sow that seed as much as our gardening abilities allow us before we can open up to love another deeply and fully and with awareness and intention. It's that simple! It's a matter of, first, satisfying the me. Satisfying the me! It may sound selfish, but it's true!

Love with another shouldn't be an escape from the self. That is weakness, and we aren't born humans to be weak! We are individuals; we are responsible for becoming, for taking the journey toward wisdom, toward love, no matter the circumstance.

This is a truth that one may be able to ignore on a conscious level, but it buries itself somewhere in the subconscious, perhaps even deeper, in the unconscious, as we get older. Because those dreams we had as children—to see things and touch them and wander along paths asking a million WHYs—are very similar to boomerangs, you see: cast them off somewhere in your dizzy slumber of life, and one day, they come back, and they come hard. They come back and knock at the door of the self, and no one answers.

There was an obsessive tone in his writing that I couldn't ignore. The *self*, the *self*, the *self*. Some sort of conflict wept quietly in between his words. But perhaps he was onto something.

I read on.

Life is short—yes, this is true.

So I'll take my small rowboat of hope, of chance, of curiosity, and I'll paddle out somewhere and search for a type of peace that can only be found by he who ventures alone—that ineffable intrigue in your abdominals; the feeling in your feet that makes all ground you walk on feel like sacred ground.

On I'll travel.

Through beaches and ridges and valleys and bridges, lakes and seas and in every breeze.

To satisfy the me, and return to maybe find her again.

And if there are answers somewhere along this journey, perhaps they are not objective ones; perhaps they will be just as subjective as the bird that sings not because he has an answer, but simply because he has a song.

And perhaps—

"Hey! What the...!"

My arms collapsed under the quick and crooked jolt of my elbows. One of the tent flaps flung open, a harsh jet of light hitting my guilty face. A cold breeze flooded in as two different colored eyes met mine. My bones froze.

I barely got the words out, choking on them. "Echo, I...I..."

"What the hell do you think you're doin' in my...."

He saw what was on the ground below me.

His eyes opened more like big green and blue balls of glass.

"Get out! Get out!" he shouted.

I shot to my feet with a gasp and was clumsily out of the open flap before I could exhale.

He backed up, watching me with anger and fear. I was scared as hell.

The second I expected redness to flood the whites of his eyes, those blue and green balls of glass got smaller, softer. I didn't even know this man, let alone what he would do to me.

As if everything had slowed down, he spoke calmly, his hair blowing softly in the lake's breath. "Why kid? You don't do that. You don't go through people's lives like that."

"I know...I, I'm sorry...I just came all the way out here to talk to y——"

"You're smarter than that kid."

There, he'd said it again. It was either a compliment or it was his way of telling me when I was being an idiot. Either way, the words stung. He wasn't angry; worse, he was disappointed. My shaky hands were stuffed into my sweatpants pockets, and my throat expanded hotly underneath my scarf.

"Did you read?" he said, looking at me in a way to make sure I was looking back at him.

"No, I just...." I hated lying.

"Did you read?" he said a bit louder.

"No. Honest. I just came across it and opened it up...only saw the title page by the time...by the time you found me, and I'm sorry, I really am."

He studied me up and down for the truth.

"I got nothin' to hide, kid. I told you that. I said to not try and learn me. Didn't I say that? I said that. That's why the tent's got flaps," he looked back at it, "so you can shut 'em."

He gave a long exhale out over the lake. It was stronger than the breeze. Looking out, squintedly, he softly said, "Come back Saturday. There're some things we should talk about, Aydenn."

I felt his eyes on me as I walked back across the bridge.

Perhaps he knew I'd read.

Stepping off into the Southern Park, I noticed a slight movement up ahead on the thin, dirt path. It was a lizard. It had jetted out from a bush and stopped right there in the trail, looking up at me. The sun was almost done setting, and I could barely see it. I walked right past it, and I swear that its little head with its big eyes turned, following me.

I walked on, heavy in the head, with not only one, but *two* pairs of eyes at my back.

○

Evening matured into night on that long walk home.

Who was this man named Echo?

What was he?

Homeless? A vagabond? A writer? A husband to some long lost woman?

Whatever he was, he was on some sort of journey. And perhaps I'd become part of it.

Walking home, all I knew was that he wanted to show me something, on Saturday.

6

Like what most seventeen-year-olds do after Thanksgiving and before Christmas, I came down with the flu. A jumpy fever and a sore throat that makes you not want to eat food or even swallow your own warm spit. It stretched only as far as the weekend did, and I was back to normal temperatures by Monday. But of course, it cost me my Saturday.

Twice in a row now, I'd disappointed Echo.

Lying on my top bunk—on my side with a cool, wet washcloth balanced on my forehead—I looked out my window past the street, out at that big oak tree. It stood strong. Permanent. It would never go anywhere. It wouldn't just get up and move one day. It wasn't like people. It wasn't like Echo.

I had time to think about what I'd read in his tent.

His ideas about love were like nothing I'd ever heard. It wasn't that I thought they were right or wrong. Hell, what would I know? But they seemed very carefully thought out. And maybe

TO PASS IT ON

love can be technical like that. Or maybe not; maybe it's random as hell. Who really knows? Perhaps that was just *his* route to love, wherever it would lie for him. Perhaps that's how love works—millions of crooked and random and lengthy and accidental routes all to the same place.

Usually by then—the tail end of November—that big oak tree was as naked as a girl in the shower. Leafless. But not that November. Everything was different that Fall, you see. Even the air felt different, thinner and excited, like something was coming. Something big.

So maybe that's where my life really began—weighing down a fever and aches with too many blankets, looking out the window crookedly from underneath a damp washcloth, thinking about what some blue, calligraphic words had said. Words like *self* and *internal fruits* and *romantic love* and *satisfying the me* are a mouthful and mindful when you're just seventeen. Or perhaps it has nothing to do with age; perhaps it all has to do with experience.

Sunday was another slow day. Fever gone, but aches still hanging around.

I dangled my legs over the arm of the couch in the living room, staring up at the skylight. I waited for the dance of rain, but I knew it wouldn't come. I wondered if *I* had a journey, and how you know when to take it, or where it starts, or if someone older would tell you, or if you had to pray to God about it. Or maybe we're the ones responsible for recognizing it, embracing it, taking the first steps, no matter the consequences. Maybe we have a responsibility to stand out in the rain sometimes, out in the wild wetness of things.

I walked to the bus stop slowly Monday morning, a dozen little *hellos* from Nature happening right under my nose—sounds and smells; quiet, invisible moisture painting the air. It's amazing, the difference in being asleep and being awake.

I plopped into my window seat at the back of the bus; the seat to my left was vacant. I filled it with my tired backpack. The engine kicked along, past 13th street, and you could always see a good chunk of Dillon's house from the corner there. I wondered if his front door had been repainted yet, red. It had looked awful last time I'd seen it, like someone who'd lost a good amount of blood.

Looking out the window at time smear by, I'd think about my own life moving by just as fast. I was already seventeen. I'd be eighteen in the Spring, and soon enough, twenty-five. The thought of time passing us by without our permission would scare the hell out of me and remind me to slow things down and take smaller steps through prettier places.

The ride to school was no more than twenty minutes, what with the few stops along the way. But for some reason, that early morning, it was enough for me to fall back asleep, cheek against the cold glass. I don't remember intending to fall asleep, but I do remember the dream I had.

◊

There I was, standing on broken glass, jackets and backpacks in disarray. The school bus was tilted on its side, seats above us, windows facing the sky. There was smoke and soot everywhere and everyone inside was screaming or crying or both. Legs trampled over legs, looking for an exit. Movement was everywhere, everyone trying to get out.

But not me.

I just stood there. My feet weighed more than the whole

dream. I was much more calm than I should've been. By some ambiguous dream logic, I could also see directly outside from where I stood. I saw parents, everyone's parents. They stood with weak legs on the nearest curb. Mothers stood in sweatshirts with their hands cupped over their swollen faces. Fathers who hadn't already left for work stood next to their wives like tall, cold statues. Neither of them seemed to know what'd happened or how it happened. They all took turns looking upward into the grayness for an answer, a reason, a prayer. It took a second to realize why the fathers remained on the curb, a good thirty feet away, and weren't running toward us with their strong and willing arms. It's because the bus was ablaze and smoking at the front end. The red-hot, unforgiving flames danced recklessly, keeping everyone away.

Well, not everyone.

Sirens cried in the distance. Someone was on the way.

I heard a kid's voice yell that the bus driver was unconscious, maybe dead. There were freshmen on the bus. They were the ones crying. It's the worst hearing kids cry like that; they're meant to be heard laughing.

Next came that loud silence of uncertainty that always sneaks in at some point between moments of chaos. Everything hushes down and slows down and you really see the emotion in the people around you. I saw saliva stretch from one girl's bottom lip to her top lip as she let out a wail. She was hugging her backpack as if it was her only rescue, her leg stuck in between the seats, broken. And yet, I was as still as ever.

With legs of lead, I started to believe that I wasn't supposed to be the one to help; I wasn't supposed to be the hero. Whatever had happened, the bus must've, at some point, hit a fire hydrant dead on. Everything was wet, bursts of water raining down on and into the spiral-cracked windows above.

Just then, the truck arrived. A smear of red flooded into view, blocking my ambiguous sight outside at the curbed parents.

A shadow fell down onto us from above, the fire escape window unlatched with a slam. It flew open violently, as if God Himself were entering Hell to save the ones that weren't supposed to be there.

A young girl I hadn't noticed before laid limp across the seats at my feet, her head resting on the toe of my shoe. She was so small. But I couldn't do anything. I couldn't move. It was like I was put in the dream specifically to watch. The first thing I saw come down from the fire escape window was the orange gloves—dusty and used and filled with unimaginable strength; then, the helmet—a familiar-looking one. Heavy legs swung in next, and the man dropped down and landed right in front of me. His presence was thick. The smoke and water were married in a terrible haze, and I couldn't see his face, just his big, red helmet.

He immediately reached down and swooped up the girl as if it were a child of his own. The other firefighters found their way into the bus as well; I heard glass shatter towards the front—one of them cracking his ax at the door, by the bus driver.

More water came at the bus from hoses. Kids rushed toward the front of the bus, where the other firefighters were signaling at them through the opaque-grey shapes of smoke. The kids looked at the firefighters the way they would their own parents.

The firefighter in front of me hoisted the limp girl up over his shoulder, her two long pigtails following lifelessly. Just before he turned around to follow the others out, he stopped and looked at me. His face was masked by those same shapes of smoke that plundered the bus's insides. More water started to rain down on us from outside the bus. Fire hoses drenched my hair and face ruthlessly. I struggled to squint through it, struggled to see this man's face.

But then I realized something. I didn't have to see his face. I knew exactly who it was. And right there, stitched on the breast of his jacket, was the word PRICE in capital letters.

I woke up with a fierce jerk, hitting my head against the same glass I'd fallen asleep against. The bus driver was leaned over me. A necklace of cold sweat hung around my neck.

It was a dream.

I looked at him, head to toe. He was alive, not dead. I could've jumped up and hugged him. I got to my feet slowly, grabbing my backpack and hugging it as he backed up. Concern painted his face. I walked down past the rows of cushioned, empty seats and stepped off the bus, through the glass door that hadn't been shattered by an ax after all.

7

Everybody had already begun their circling around the track by the time I got into my gym clothes and made it over. Hopping on one foot while tying the laces on the other, I saw Coach Fischer sitting on the bleachers underneath the big oak tree. Just him and his clipboard. I jumped right into stretching, and before I'd really gotten into my hamstrings, he looked up at me.

"Morning Aydenn...good to see ya."

Just as soon as he'd looked up, he was already back down at his clipboard.

There was so much more he could've said. There was so much more I wanted him to say. It made me think about how people tend to say too much when they only need to say a little, and not enough when they should be saying a whole lot more.

I did my laps, making it through P.E. and onto my other classes, and through lunch, and soon enough, I found myself sitting tiredly in my left-handed desk, waiting for the man in the red beret to walk in the door somewhere between three and five minutes late.

Just as soon as I started to replay the dream I had on the bus, the classroom door was sucked in by the outside and Kristiansen appeared there in front of us. His routine tardiness was nothing of conversation between any of us. We all noticed it. But teachers will just have little idiosyncrasies like that, and that's what we usually remember most about them.

His attaché—buckles unclasped—dropped down next to the podium where it leaned the same way I leaned my elbow on my desk. He set his coffee on the podium. He always walked in gripping his coffee with a beige napkin. He'd put the coffee down on top of the napkin, remove the lid, drop the lid in the trash can, pick the cup back up, wrap the napkin around it again, and take his first sip. He'd take a head count from behind the steam and over the rim of the white, paper cup. Class was always pretty full, pretty quiet; no one ever really missed it, at least not on purpose. For one reason or another, I think we all felt responsible for being there. We never really knew what to expect; his only reliable routine in class was the coffee thing. Other than that, every day was, well, different. He'd been teaching at Texana Hills for a couple years. I'd heard he'd been to other high schools before ours. I'd also heard that *Literature as Philosophy* was all his idea; he'd made up the class and was the only English teacher who taught it. Perhaps he was the only one who could. And it's funny, because none of us students really talked about him or the class much when we were outside of class. It was like we all went in there for our own, quiet, personal experiences. It was like church I guess.

He began that afternoon with heavy stuff, only to get

heavier.

Origins of philosophy and who said what, and how they died, and who we should listen to and who we shouldn't waste our ears on; oh, and that we should never read Nietzsche at night, whatever that meant.

Aristotle started us off; his name always sounded the most interesting anyway.

A messy page full of notes later—notes that I *still* have, folded up somewhere in something—Kristiansen threw this Greek word at us, turning around to scribble it up on the blackboard. The chalk sounded like a storm. He wrote in all capitals, his Es looking more like backwards 3s. Soon, his elbows were back up on the podium as he began his talking with his hands like he always did. Sitting in the second row, I always noticed the back of one of his hands and how it looked like it had been burnt or something.

"*Entelechy*," we heard echo from inside his coffee cup as he near-disappeared behind the rim again. He put the cup down and licked his top lip, where a mustache was trying its hardest to push through. He didn't reach down for his attaché or anything. That word just sat up there in the air, waiting for someone to aim and shoot at it or something. Entelechy. He made that general eye contact with all of us.

It's going to be one of those days, I thought to myself—a day where we'd all just kind of talk and listen to him or to each other. I feel like they need these kinds of days more in every classroom. Everyone opens up like flowers and by the end of class, a whole garden has just bloomed that you never would've seen otherwise.

A brave hand went up.

He nodded at the girl.

"Does it mean *intellect*?"

He inhaled through his nose as he looked into the air at the word still hanging there.

Another hand.

Soldiers these kids were, real lionhearts.

He nodded over at this student as well.

"The study of wisdom? Or um, the study of...intelligence?"

Kristiansen's look didn't change; instead, his hands rose up into action as he began.

"It's more than that. It's a lot more than that."

The two wounded soldiers slumped in their seats, defeated.

"But it's a start," he reinforced with the little smile that we only saw a handful of times.

The soldiers sat back up straight again.

"It's a type of intellect. It's a form of wisdom. Something one should always try and hold onto. And before..." he said, scratching his head under his beret, "...before you take your final exams, and start a new year...and graduate, and fall into your new lives, it's something I think you should all know about. I feel...responsible to, to pass it on."

We waited the same way a dog waits at the ankles of his owner for his food bowl to be filled. And we didn't have to wait very long.

"What am I?" he didn't wait for a response this time; "a human." He continued, "And why is that a good thing? Why is being one of our species a 'good' thing?" This time he did wait. A boy way in the back put up his hand like the question was meant for him, like it was his day. He was a boy I'd seen around since freshman year, and I'd sort of forgotten he was in the class. He was painfully quiet, really, and always wore a rosary around his neck. He'd tuck it in down the front of his shirt for whatever reason, but you could still see the little black beads curve around the sides of his neck. I guess I admired him for that; he had the ounce of character we're always looking for in people.

"It's a good thing that you're human," he stumbled a bit, "because humans can think, and they...they can reason."

"A start!" Kristiansen sent a cheerful yell back at him. "Humans can think! Humans can reason!" he repeated

179

energetically. "And what else?"

His eyes darted around the room for the next voice that wanted to be heard. His glasses were thick as hell, making it appear as though he was looking at you twice as hard. Usually I'd avoid eye contact with teachers, but when those two eyes made their way to the left side of the classroom and on to my own face, I responded without even raising my hand.

"Humans have a *self*."

I didn't know what I'd said or why I'd said it. It just came out. Perhaps that's the difference between knowledge and wisdom. Perhaps knowledge is engineered, while wisdom just comes out—from its cave, smoking its pipe—when it needs to.

It took him a few seconds that felt like a few hours. And then he did it; he finally gave me the look I'd been waiting for all semester.

"We have a *self*! Yes, we do! Yes we do, Aydenn!"

He looked back at me, and with his hands opening up toward me with stiff fingers, he begged, "And what is this *self*; who is this *self*?" It was then that I felt the raw pressure on my knees, as if I was kneeling inside a dark red tent, reading all about such a word.

"Well…" I started, "you said we can think. And that makes us more powerful than any other species, right? It's…it's like you just mentioned at the beginning of class, with that Descartes guy. We think, therefore, we…*are*, right?" He nodded. "And by that, we know that we…exist, and…as we live our lives, we…we learn about how opportunities and…and *journeys* can make up…*us*…the individual. We're always developing…becoming this or that…growing by choice…and whatever the result…well…that's the…the *self*."

I ended on an inquisitive pitch, which always makes it better if you're wrong. He stared at me just for just a half-second longer, and then focused his attention back on the class.

"Right…Aydenn's right! We're all *becoming* something. One

way or another. Evolving…on an individual basis. Every day."

He stepped back from the podium for more elbowroom.

"And it's often the case that we're *choosing* what we become. And once we realize we have this *choice*, well, perhaps that's when life becomes life."

I could feel heads around me tilting at his words.

He walked across the front of the classroom, back and forth and back again.

"Why am I here?" he said with an inquisitive demand.

A thick silence saturated the room again. He bit his lip in hope that someone might know—either for the sake of the topic, or perhaps for his own. Was the question rhetorical, or wasn't it?

"Why are *you* here?" he pointed to the girl in the front row—the initial soldier who'd entered battle in the fields of entelechy. She froze. He moved on right away. "Why are *you* here?" he said to the same boy in back. He fuddled with the beads around his neck. He almost answered, but then a third time, "Why are *you* here?" he said, pointing to the girl next to me. His aim was getting closer. He went on like that, pacing in between rows, asking perhaps the most difficult question to answer. But nobody's voice made it past his or her lips. Perhaps no one knew the answer, including the one asking the question.

"Why are *any* of us here?" he begged. It *was* all rhetorical. He was setting the stage, not casting characters. We were all humans and we knew our names, and by that, we knew *what* we were and *who* we were. The classroom we were in and the clock on the wall told us the *where* and *when* we were. But nothing could tell us *why* we were.

"Who looked into the mirror this morning?" he went on.

Hands went up at a stupid rate, as if no one could remember if they'd seen themselves yet that day. "Not 'Who looked *in* the mirror this morning'." Hands went down at the same pace they went up. "*INTO* the mirror," he emphasized.

Hands were then half up, half down, sideways, fingers

spread apart, wrists bent, elbows confused as hell. Nobody knew *what* to do.

"And what'd you see?"

He waited.

Nothing.

Then, he went for it himself: "Perhaps...you saw that your hair looked good today, or maybe just okay. Maybe you stressed over the acne blemish that no one but yourself could ever notice. Maybe you even saw that your clothes are fitting better, after all those laps Fischer's making you do. Maybe you saw a lot of different things. But I know that all of you, when you looked in the mirror this morning, saw a person there, in the reflection. A body, arms, legs, a head, a face, eyes, a mouth. And maybe you noticed that this same person is reaching the end of this long stint of high school and maturity and whatever else you're involved in at this point. Here you are, a few months from graduation. Some of you will leave this little town...maybe forever. Some of you will stay because...well you haven't figured it out yet. Some of you will stay because, well, this is the place you're supposed to be."

He was right.

"You're all in the first stage of deciding—really *choosing*— what you're going to become. It's this kind of...freedom that you're handed. A freedom that's...yours. And it can be a tough thing to manage. You see, freedom surrounds you, and demands nothing. *You* decide what to do with it."

He'd made it back to the front of the classroom and was looking down into his coffee cup as he picked it up for another long sip. A stiff silence stung the walls of the classroom, a type of quiet that could make Gandhi look like a football-game cheerleader.

"It's like...it's like you're all standing in front of this door," he started back up, "standing there, waiting for it open; or maybe *you're* waiting to open *it*. It's in a hallway. A long hallway, with other doors. A bunch of other doors. But you stare only at the one right in front of you. Behind it lies...your future, the next *you*. You look down at your feet. The toe of your shoes is kissed by the light coming out from the bottom of this door."

That's the beautiful thing about painting with words. Everyone can see them, even the blind.

"You turn the knob and push, and the light floods your face and chest all the way down to your legs. You walk in at whatever pace is right for you. But! Don't close the door behind you, at least not all the way. Leave it open a crack...you must do this."

He was over by the same door he'd crossed in through at the beginning of class, talking at it. Then he turned back around again.

"Explore the room and all the walls and textures and people in it and the furniture and the picture frames hung around and the smells and the way the ground feels underneath you. But don't forget to leave that door cracked. This...this will let the light from the room sneak its way out into the hallway and give it a glow. This way you'll remember that the hallway is there, glowing quietly, its other doors still there, unopened."

In a couple good-sized steps, he was at the back of the classroom. He sat himself in one of the empty desks. He was on our level now; he was us. Each and every one of us was as quiet as a church mouse.

"Once our time begins to feel thin in that first room...once we know or feel or guess that it's time to leave, we can. We can easily peel that cracked door back open, and cross over the threshold and into the softly lit hallway once more. We can walk up to another door...we can open it...we can become something else."

A weird air spun around our classroom—in between desks and over heads. No one turned around to look at him back there. No one raised their hand. And subtly as ever, he'd changed from saying *you* to saying *we*.

183

"We're humans...and we can think. If we think long enough and hard enough and openly enough and fearlessly enough, we'll learn why we're here...to experience things...to grow and evolve and put weight into our potential. We're here to blossom...to grow taller and faster and leaner in mind and in body. We're here to *become*. *That's* what we do with our freedom...we *become*."

I noticed the clock's ticking just then. It was loud as hell. I heard him at the back of the classroom as he took one last drawn out sip, and he walked back up to the front and threw away his coffee cup and the napkin hugging it.

He lifted his beret from off his head and set it on the podium. God knew how long he'd had it, or why he'd had it. His hair was thin-blonde and perspiration lightly dressed his forehead. But his eyes were the same as they were at the beginning of class, magnified behind the lenses from which he saw the world so differently, so much bigger.

"Entelechy."

The word floated into the air again, this time a little thicker, and it traced over the initial one that was still floating up there like an exhalation of smoke.

"It's the quality that allows the acorn to become the oak tree...the fundamental truth that allows us to...improve...through an increased awareness of this world around us. Aristotle came up with it." He said the name like it was an old college buddy. "He might've described it as some...natural energy out there that motivates something toward its fulfillment."

He wiped the perspiration away with the back of his burnt-looking hand.

"But always just try to...to remember that hallway...the doors...the unopened ones. Another life waits for you on the other side of the door you've already entered. It's simple to understand...a whole 'nother thing to live by. Takes impatient curiosity maybe, and courage...definitely courage. And faith. You see, that hallway is our infinite potential...our innate ability to become—to become anything...anything new...at any moment."

I noticed that I'd only taken four or five breaths in the last four or five minutes.

He went on like a one-way flight.

"Here you sit; here you've been sitting...in these desks...these classrooms. And soon enough you'll get your diploma...and walk off that stage...accomplished. Some off to college, some off to begin whatever destiny hands you...or even whatever you choose to hand destiny."

He looked down at his feet as if his shoelaces gave him a pang of nostalgia.

"And then you begin your life." He paused. "Years unfurl, and perhaps you wore the right tie or said the right words and you got the job...maybe one you always wanted, maybe one that always wanted you, or maybe just one that found you before you could find it. Soon enough, rent and bills are in your name, and even though you have to pay them yourself, there's an odd, good-and-warm feeling at the pit of your stomach every time you do. It's the feeling of responsibility. And then slowly, you begin to see that school was the study guide...maybe it wasn't real life at all, but perhaps preparation for it instead. And more years unfurl as you put into practice just what you'd learned in the same desks you couldn't wait to get out of. Perhaps then, a significant other finds you sooner than later; or maybe you're quite alone. Somehow, you don't realize it, but you're busy...all the time. But maybe busy is good. Or maybe it's not good, because suddenly you don't have time to reread those books you'd once held dear during high school summers. They sit there up on the shelf, collecting dust, much like yourself. You feel a small bee sting of guilt every time you walk by the shelf and read the titles, vertically frowning at you from the book spines. But then marriage may come along and everything changes; everything's different...or maybe it's not. Maybe deep down at the pit of it all...at the pit of your life...it's still all the same." He gazed toward the windows next to me. "Yeah. Time moves along without your permission. That acrylic paint set mailed to you as a nineteenth-birthday gift in college has long dried up, much like your ambition to paint that mural in the living room of your first home."

Whatever life this was, whoever or whatever he was illustrating, it made me hurt just hearing about it. But maybe it was true. Maybe it was a lot of people's lives.

"You run into the café on your way to work...looking only accidentally at the adjacent city library as you cross the street. You'd always had fantasies of being sprawled out on the floor in there...leaned on elbows that served as your anchor in an ocean of titles from *The Iliad* to *The Catcher in the Rye* to *The Old Man and The Sea*.

Maybe pregnancy comes next. A baby. The new cries and laughter replace those once-silent moments of the running kitchen sink water, rinsing silverware after a home-cooked dinner for only two. And it's all comfortable. It's all quite content. But there's an itch that won't go away. It won't go away because you don't know how to scratch it.

And then you wake up one day...you're grown up. Turns out you ended up looking more like your father than your mother. It's still early and the sun is barely awake. Kids are asleep downstairs. The sound of the unforgiving alarm clock shouts 6:*00* at you. You lie frozen there in bed. Three inches of blankets separate you and whoever lies next to you from the rest of the world. You slide out of bed anyway, unconsciously half-shimmying on those same slippers that sleep on the floor right next to you. You make your way over to the square window off to the left, the one you've been passing by on the way to the shower all those mornings...maybe all those years. You pull the curtain back three or four inches and find that the sun is still just as puffy-eyed as you are. You think about when days became measured by microwave clocks and wristwatches and not sunrises and sunsets."

He stopped to stroke the top of his beret down on the surface of the podium, making all the red, corduroy fabric lie in the same direction. Perhaps he was pulling these scenes from the reality of others—friends or family members or parents or lovers—or perhaps he was just making it all up like any author does when he or she sits behind twenty-six letters and a handful of crazy punctuation marks. He wasn't married himself. We knew that. What we didn't know was what the hell he was getting at. There had to be a greater intention than just depressing the hell out of us. He went on, talking fiction that perhaps wasn't fiction at all.

"From up there in that window, you look down at the gray driveway. The same crack runs through the middle. Maybe it's the crack that becomes the free throw line of the basketball court when your car isn't parked there, when you're not home to see it. You follow the crack from one side of the driveway to the other with your eyes, wishing you could understand again. You follow it invisibly as it extends itself upward, into the trees of the neighborhood. There's a morning-green tint to them all...and you notice each leaf moving at its own, unique rhythm. That line keeps extending upward, invisibly, up into sky. You don't see anything but clouds—you look for a dinosaur head, maybe an ice cream cone...but all you see are clouds. You lean a hand on the windowsill and press your face against the cold glass...."

Still quiet as parked cars, some of us were looking out the window or down at our hands or even up at the ceiling. Others might've taken the opportunity to put their heads in their arms on their desks and just kind of disappear. But I made sure to look at Kristiansen.

He'd walked over to the windows on my side of the

classroom by that point, and was leaning on the windowsill, looking up into the sky. His face was almost pressed up against the glass. He was ten feet from me, beret-less.

"Looking up there...you realize..." he started slowly, quietly, "that you'd never penetrated those clouds."

I noticed a strange moisture begin to glaze his eyeballs in the reflection of the overcast sunlight coming in from the outside. "...you never penetrated those clouds...sitting uncomfortably in some tiny airplane...heading toward Greece," he paused, as the smallest smile lifted the lower half of his face, "...Crete to be exact."

He talked softly, like no one was around, like he was talking to himself.

"...you'd always wanted to go there...you talked about it in college...wrote about it in that little black journal...but somewhere...somehow...that idea became just another...old pair of shoes...."

He turned around to find the podium again, his voice struggling to bounce back to its original volume.

"Old pairs of shoes...they're a funny thing...we never wear them anymore, but sentiment makes us keep them around...piled up in the corner of our closet next to some sepia-toned photo album.

"It's...it's easy, class, to forget about the hallway...and to go on living your life...a train with no conductor...but it's never too late to *become*," he said with yellow hope. "It's never too late to *become*." He said it again. "The important thing is that we *do* become. Not *becoming*...well...it only disappoints the philosopher inside of us...it buries our lives before we're even dead."

As soon as I noticed that it was definitely moisture welling up in the dark brown eyes behind his lenses, he bent down and picked up his attaché in one swoop. The top of his thin-haired, blonde head faced us only for a second. He reclined back up, gave us a *Good day* nod, shuffled over to the door, pushed it open softly, and disappeared into the outside.

Class wouldn't be out for another twenty minutes.

It was strange, even for him—a kind of strange that wouldn't make sense until later. There was a minute of stiff silence, then crooked waves of chatter. Before long, everyone must've reasoned he wasn't coming back. Backpack zippers and squeaking legs of chairs became louder than the chatter. And then, just like that, one after another, the classroom emptied itself of students. All except for one.

I sat, looking out the window, thinking of everything and thinking of nothing. I was so in between time that I barely reacted to what I saw next.

Right there, on the other side of the yellowed window, little droplets began to collect, tapping on the window diagonally in the wind, only to roll down like tears. I watched it for some time. It was finally here. The rain. The rain we'd needed. The rain that brings life.

From that left-handed desk, leaned back into my seat, slouched, I started to replay the words Kristiansen had just let escape from underneath his red, corduroy beret.

The beret!

It was still there up there! On the podium!

I jolted up and unconsciously grabbed my backpack. Making room for it between books, I pulled out my jacket as I walked over. I threw my arms into the elephant trunk sleeves, flipped my hood over and, walking, lifted the beret off the podium. Into my backpack it went, safe.

I got out of the classroom, and the minute I thought to bring the beret to his office, I realized that if I did that, we'd both be in trouble for being out of class early. *I'll just give it to him tomorrow*, I reasoned. *I'm sure he can go a day without it.*

I made it across campus, jogging against the drizzle to the bus stop. Sure I was early—school hadn't gotten out yet. I got on my bus anyway with the few others who'd been in my class. No words. Just looks of understanding. It smelled like wet grass on rubber shoes. The bus driver was a woman this time.

Soon enough, the bus's heart pumped underneath me in the back and it pulled out onto Main Street. I looked out the window at every house we passed by in a wet blur. I wondered who lived in them, and if they knew about this word, this idea, this *entelechy*.

Droplets continued to stick onto the bus windows as we cut through the curtain of new rain. Looking at the droplets, and then through them, I noticed how everything appeared upside down. Must've been one of Nature's secrets, like it was reminding us to look at things differently in the rain, because if we do, maybe we'll see things better.

Almost home, the bus neared the corner by Dillon's.

I looked down 13th Street, seeing the nose of his porch through the persistent wet blur of rain. Something had been put up, affixed to the pillars, blocking his porch. It was strange. Some sort of tarp, maybe. More houses passed over my window in a smear. I held my damp backpack on my two knees, hugging it tighter and tighter.

8

The next day was even more peculiar.

It was a Tuesday, and perhaps it was the day it all really began.

I climbed aboard the bus like usual, the alive-and-well bus driver giving me a special little nod on my way up the three steps. I wondered how and why he'd ended up in that seat behind that big wheel. Perhaps he just loved kids; he didn't have a wedding ring or anything, and maybe that was the only way he could ever really be a father.

It had been raining nonstop since the day before, and with each second, I believed that the sun had gone back up to heaven, and Winter was finally here to stay. The bus passed 13th Street, and, looking down, I saw that it was still there—a tall, wide, gray tarp nailed up on the two pillars bookending the Rubenson's front porch.

191

◊

Raincoats and the sound of nylon rubbing against itself and umbrellas could be witnessed in all corners of school that day. I've learned to see umbrellas as sort of romantic. It's like you can be alone inside, but still be outside. What an intimate little space under there, especially if you're sharing it with someone. What's romantic about it is the little instances when everyone is scurrying around, trying to stay dry, and you see one person there—usually a young woman—underneath her umbrella, not minding the rain at all. You can't quite see her face, just her jacket, her legs. And in the spell of her walking, angling the umbrella to deflect the wind-born drizzle, you can sometimes catch a brief sight of her jaw line, her mouth. And maybe sometimes you even catch a smile. It's a type of smile that could make the puddles all dry up and the sun come back out forever. It's so damn beautiful and unexpected that you could just fall in love with her right there.

◊

After lunch, the sound of the bell vibrated the drizzle in the air and I found myself, once more, seated in the left-handed desk of my Literature as Philosophy class. Eye on the door, I waited for him to walk in. My right hand was in my backpack, thumb and index finger gently gripping the brim of his red beret. I wondered if I should give it to him before or after taking our exam that day.

The clock soon said that class should've started a couple minutes ago, but still no teacher behind the podium. But his tardiness was nothing new. And then, just like that, the door was pulled open.

But a different pair of feet crossed into the classroom. They were a woman's. She was holding a thin, black briefcase and had one of those concentrated looks on her face. Gradually, the room fell silent. She put her briefcase down on a table in the front corner of the room and turned to face us with her hands clasped together just underneath her abdomen. Some of the wet from outside had gotten into her straight, brown hair. She wore a red blazer, black slacks. She was pretty. But other than her rectangle glasses, she wasn't Kristiansen at all.

She told us who she was, where she came from, why she was there. She introduced herself as Miss May: a new substitute on campus. She told us the news of Kristiansen falling ill, and that he'd be out until further notice. It was hard to hear. But she moved on from his condition rather quickly, beginning to verbally outline the classroom direction he'd supposedly left for her.

We'd write a long essay as our midterm. The essay had only a short prompt, but it was a real mouthful of words.

She turned around, the curves in her black slacks facing us, and wrote the prompt up on the blackboard. She wrote it slowly, delicately. It's a weird meditation to watch people and how they write. While writing, over her shoulder she told us how we'd have the full class period and how grammar wouldn't be too important. Apparently, Kristiansen wanted us to *react* to a statement he'd composed for us, and we were to apply the philosophical principles we'd learned, making literary allusions as well to support our cases. Perhaps he felt that raw thought should take priority over the correct use of a dangling, little comma.

She put the chalk down in the tray just as softly as she'd entered the room. She moved out of the way so we could all see the blackboard clear as day. It read:

I know what I <u>can</u> know; therefore, I know everything.

193

My hand was off the beret.

It now held a blue ink pen instead, like Echo's.

Kristiansen had spent the first half of the previous class summing up all those different philosophers, what their general contributions were. But I knew that these words were his own. Where he'd come up with them, who knew? It wasn't *how* or *why* or *where* he'd come up with the aphorism that was important; it was *that* he did.

I know what I can know; therefore, I know everything.

Instantly, bells rang with the Cartesian: "I think; therefore, I am." Socrates came up too; he felt he was the brightest because he knew that he knew nothing. Without my complete awareness, my pen began its voyage across the page. I made as many references as I could, to Aristotle and a few others, even throwing in something about Henry Van Dyke and how his *work* must've given him some great knowledge or wisdom of everything. I used the letters s-e-l-f together so much that it became weird seeing them as part of other words. I talked about the hallway and how it's important to remember that it's there; how it's important to not close the door behind you after you enter the first room. I wrote how it's about being aware. It's about maintaining some sort of awareness that there's always possibility; there's always potential to *become*. And I added—as Kristiansen had ended class the day before—how it's never too late to become. It's entelechy. Our lives are designed to experience everything and anything, at any time. And those experiences are out there; we just have to remember they are; we just have to remember the doors that quietly align themselves along the hallway like trees lining a street in the Springtime. If we can remember this much, we have the secret to life. If we can remember this much, we know everything that is important to know. If we can remember this much, we will know what we *can* know; therefore, we will know everything.

As life changes, we can change with it.

We can always become something new.

It's like the cat I mentioned a long time ago. Curiosity never killed the cat, it only lead it out of that first room, back into the hallway.

As soon as the pen dropped and left my hand empty, a throbbing was quick to fill it again. I thought of Echo and all those pages *he'd* written, and how my writing was just slants of chicken scratch and his was so fluent and graceful. He'd wanted to show me something the Saturday before, when I was sick and never got to see it. I hated knowing I'd let him down.

Leaned back in my seat, slouching, I looked at the pen-dented essay pages in front of me. Perhaps Kristiansen's goal with us was to teach us—maybe re-teach us—how to *feel*, how to really be emotionally involved in our thoughts. And he did just that. Because when I turned to look at everyone else writing, there it was, written across each one of their brows. They all appeared to be somewhere else but that classroom. And that brief scene of them there, writing, is still one of the most beautiful things I've ever seen.

I was the second or third to finish the essay.

There were fifteen or so minutes left in class.

Just then, a strange slant of light came into the room.

I saw the substitute, Miss May, looking out the window too.

The drizzle was gone. The sun struggled to push its head through, as if the sky was nothing more than a gray t-shirt that'd been shrunk in the dryer.

The bell eventually rang, and I zipped my backpack shut, stood up and gave Miss May all my thoughts written down. I smiled at her because she was pretty and you just can't help some things. Out of the classroom and onto the school grounds, the wind had gone into hiding along with the wetness in the air. Umbrellas were now seen folded back up into thin sticks. I looked up into the sky as I passed by my bus; I wouldn't be it taking home that day.

With nothing on my mind but the single image of a bridge, I

made my way across the damp, squeaky-bladed sports fields and onto Main Street. No running shoes. I'd walk. If the weather was going to slow itself down for me, it wouldn't be fair to speed myself up and run. I had to see him; I had to talk to Echo. He wanted to show me something.

I found myself up at the top of that hill in the road, delicately stuffing my raincoat into my backpack as I looked out at the foreheads and eyebrows of the pine trees that garnished Lake Wisley. The words *blessing* and *doom* floated high up in the air where the rain had been just a few hours before.

9

It was like he'd been waiting for me.

From the bridge, I saw him sitting there on the bench. He faced the lake, perhaps his eyes were even closed. I leaned an elbow on the railing of the bridge just to stare at the back of his head, stuck between thinking that I knew him well and didn't really know him at all. It's a rare and beautiful thing to catch people like that—real natural, when they don't know anyone's watching them, when they're not acting for anyone's sake, when they're just simply being.

I remembered why I was there and footed forward off the bridge softly. Into the clearing and up to and around my side of the bench, I made eye contact with his dark red tent. It had been moved even closer to our bench. I didn't understand why he was doing it, moving it like that. I also noticed how its two flaps had been rope-tied shut.

It was odd approaching the bench like that—it was the

same way he'd approached me on our first meeting. And much like he'd done, I just kind of sat down and looked out, nothing more. I wiggled out of my backpack straps, plopping the weight of it all down on the ground, leaning it up against the bench's skinny leg. And just like that first day, the diamonds were there, dancing. It was beautiful, and the lake and the young breeze seemed all new underneath the returning sun. And perhaps that's how children see things: as new all the time; as if days aren't measured out by hours or accomplishments, but by the simple tint in the sky; as if the year isn't measured by the passing months or time off of school and work, but by the personality of the leaves up in the trees—changing their colors and disappearing and returning again.

Reading my very thoughts, he let out a soft, "Beautiful, ain't it?"

I nodded my head, thinking it was time to acknowledge each other, to look at each other. I looked at him and saw only two things—one, the fact that his eyes were still spread out across the water and in no rush to find my own; and two, that he had that same blue ink pen poking out from his breast pocket. Before time allowed me to blurt anything out about *self* or *entelechy* or *blessing and doom*, he stood straight up off the bench.

"Come on...somethin' to show ya...remember?"

Before I could even blink, he'd made it around the bench and halfway to the bridge, back into the Southern Park. Leaving my backpack, I followed the thin, blonde-with-gray ponytail that fell thin on his back like tired, old rope. Crossing the bridge, following his wood-thick footsteps, I stepped over that damn lizard again. I turned around and, sure enough, it was glaring back at me. I walked on, catching up to Echo just as he broke off from the winding path and stepped into the woods. Over twigs and in between trees, I followed loyally, mimicking his footsteps like a child might do on a fishing trip with his father.

Crunching along, not looking back, he paused and bent

down lieutenant-like. I stopped too. He picked up a medium-sized pinecone, examined it, and unfolded himself back up into a standing position. In that quick-yet-still moment, looking at the dirt on his khaki jacket, I wondered how my life had gotten me there, following a homeless man into the thin woods of Lake Wisley. It was something I never thought I'd be doing and something no one I knew would ever do themselves. But perhaps life begins right there, when we walk through woods not for the sake of going somewhere, but for the sake of going.

◌

After a while, we were greeted by the whispers of an obvious yet quaint inlet cutting into the woods at a sharp angle. No bridge over this one. On the other side of the gap was a small lawn in the shape of a heart. Every so often, I'd hear people talk about it—*Lover's Lawn*—in the halls at Texana Hills. A pretty self-explanatory place.

Nearing the water's edge, Echo held up the hand without the pinecone in it, halting both of us. Two tree stumps squatted right behind some young-looking pine trees that lined the shore. He looked back at me, smiled, and motioned his head over to one of them. It was odd how there were two stumps and two of us, but the minute the word *coincidence* floated into one ear, it was pushed immediately out of the other.

Sitting down, I think we both noticed the two teenagers through the feeble pine branches, lying next to one another on a black and red-checkered blanket. The boy was pointing up at something in the sky; she was lifting her eyes from his chest where she rested her head, listening to everything he was saying. There's something warm about youth and love—not good, not bad, not poetic or silly or existential; just warm.

Finding the flat stumps underneath us, Echo looked at me looking over at the couple on the lawn. He started, "In love yourself, Aydenn?" He began to pick at the ground in front of him. I looked at him as he went on, "I mean, ya ever been in love?" He smiled gently, clearing crunchy twigs and pines from the space below us. He took my silence as fuel, going on more, "That's alright...that's a good start."

Just flat dirt now between our two stumps, he picked up a thin stick no longer than a ruler that looked like an arm with its elbow bent. *How is never being in love a good start?*, I thought. He drew a triangle in the dirt and traced over it, carving in deeper and deeper three or four times. The pinecone was balancing on his knee.

"Good start?" I asked.

Not quite looking up yet, he began, "Well the thing about love, Aydenn...is...a lot of people don't see it for what it is. It's like any...art. Takes practice. Preparation. More than that, it's like a tree, really." He dropped the stick off to the side and dusted off his hands, pinecone shaking on his knee, barely hanging on. "It's the only thing anybody ever really wants. Love. The only thing anybody ever really needs. And in a lifetime, each one of us will find ourselves sittin' in front of this tree, waitin' for the fruit to appear. The right fruit. Once it appears, people don't think twice about who they are as individuals, and they just go ahead and pick it, snatch it right out of the tree, eat it up. They're hungry, of course. We all are. We all got that pit of hunger in our stomachs. But I think there's another tree we should be eatin' from first."

He scratched his beard, looking up now, maybe at me, maybe through my chest. My eyes were glued down on the cleared patch of dirt.

"There's another tree, you see. Well...it's a seed actually...it starts as a seed. Seed's in here," he pointed to his chest, "and it's us...it's the *self.*"

There it was: the four-letter word.

"It's about plantin' this seed, ya see? Water it...tree'll

grow...then fruit. Our own fruit, from...from inside." I was careful not to nod my head too much because then he might've thought I *had* read those pages in his tent. I tried my best to look big-eyed and new to it all.

"*That's* the fruit we gotta be eatin' first...to take care of our hunger...that initial hunger we get growin' up. And our initial hunger can't be fed by the fruit of the other tree—the fruit of a lover or a mate. Our initial hunger can only truly be satisfied by the fruit of our own tree...the tree of the self."

A breeze exhaled right between us.

"Garden the self...those other trees'll still be there by the time we got our very own green thumb. A whole grove of 'em'll be there! And it's *then* that we can walk on up and pick the fruit without feelin' vulnerable and hungry anymore. You see, when we're ready to pick from the trees that bear the fruits of lovers and of mates, it won't be to replace our hunger; instead, it'll be to merely replace the taste in our mouths."

He had a romantic way about him. His language could be hard to follow, but it was comprised of good and true and colorful and tangible words nonetheless. But how? I looked at the wedding band around his finger. It was dusty sitting there, tucked between his other fingers. Who was he, really, and what caused him to have eyes like this? A heart like this?

I looked up through the trees at Lover's Lawn. "So, younger couples don't have a damn clue what they're doing?" I thought of Dillon when I said it. "They're hungry as hell, and have no sense of self, so they grab the first fruit they see to quell their hunger...because they're young and don't know any better."

"No," he said firmly. "No...it's nothin' to do with age. It's never about age, Aydenn...it's about experience. It's that way with everything."

He went on. "Love ain't a science...ain't math...it ain't anything. It's *love*...and it's just as much of a blessing as it is a doom...which is why experience is needed. You see, Aydenn, people are fallin' in love all the time—lotta times it's with other people before it's with themselves." He paused with a tense mouth and picked the pinecone up off his knee, examining it. "Not in a narcissistic way of course, but there's this whole other aspect of love, and it starts with the self." I thought of Kristiansen, of his sudden absence, of his red beret that was at the bottom of my backpack—the backpack that I wasn't anywhere near.

"It's so important, Aydenn, to find love for yourself...to feel warm in your own body, your life." I crept in, "You mean people don't take the time to explore themselves...and find the love inside before they dive into a...romantic love with...with another."

"Exactly," he said, looking up at me with the same seriousness in both his green and blue eye. Who knew that two different colors could ever see the world the same way? He went on, "There's this whole journey, you see. A journey inward. A journey of the self. A journey *by* yourself. And you're responsible to do everythin' in your power to see it manifest."

There was a clear and undeniable obsession in his voice. The *self*, the *self*, the *self*. I couldn't look away from it. I struggled with it; it made me feel a new weight in my chest. And I looked at him and thought, *What did this way of thinking do for the man in front of me?* I'd wonder if thinking about this *self* too much would drive that same *self* crazy. It's a funny thing, obsession. Perhaps obsession is just part of learning balance.

He went on, his words in line with the breeze that came off the inlet. "It's a journey that begins with our childhood perhaps...with those dreams we dream up about who we see ourselves becomin' one day. Of course, those dreams are stretched...real imaginative...but, they still teach us *how* to dream...*how* to imagine ourselves anywhere else but *here*. And maybe we're onto somethin' with that as kids. Maybe kids hold the lesson within them of how one can dream his or herself out of discontent."

He paused to let the sun warm his beard as it came through the thin pines in speckles. "This whole idea, Aydenn, of the self embarkin' on somethin'...somethin' big, somethin' important, sacred even...it'll really ignite you. It's terrifyingly excitin' and, well, no one can really explain why. Have you ever...you ever picked up a book and just *really* fell into it? So close to the characters that you could even catch a cold from 'em?

I nodded as a bird glided by way overhead, its faint shadow briefly painting my shoes.

"Well, it's like that Aydenn...the journey...moments when you witness transformation happenin' right then and there...when truths come out from behind the trees, naked. Some of these things—these certain bits of magic—can only really happen like that if you're alone, isolated, open to them happenin'. It's the journey of the self...the first real steps toward bein' the us that we oughta be."

It had all been written out in those pages of his one way or another. It was the second time I was hearing these ideas. But there's something about written words being inflated with the author's voice. It's then that it becomes real; it's then that you feel the words tattoo themselves on your insides.

"This journey, Aydenn, it's no more than the chapter of life where we're *satisfyin' the me*."

"*Satisfying the me*," I repeated to myself in a whisper loud enough to hear.

"Precisely," he said through an inhale as he adjusted on his stump. He took the pinecone from his knee and placed it in the dirt, right in the middle of the triangle he'd drawn out. He gave it a few twists to make sure it was stuck in the ground good. With his stick in hand again, he pointed to the bottom, left corner of the triangle. "This...this is the self." He paused to look up at me briefly, and when he saw I understood, he pointed to the bottom, right corner. "This...romantic love...love between people. Life is all just one, big love story really, Aydenn…never forget that. It's why we're here. Even take out religion, philosophy, all that. Then anyone can see why we're here: to give meanin' to why our hearts beat in the first place. To love."

Perhaps it was the answer Kristiansen had been looking for when he asked us all *why* we were here. There he was, on my mind again. His beret, pathetically shrouded in my backpack, his intense stare through those thick-framed glasses, the way he'd tell stories with his hands. I wondered what he'd think of Echo.

Echo went on, "It's a matter of goin' up…to the summit. From the self to the summit, Aydenn. We can't just cut across the bottom, straight to romantic love. That ain't bein' fair to ourselves. People do it, sure, but those same people wipe out the whole journey of the self. And what kind of journey is any journey if you leave the self at home?

"Self to summit first," he said again. "That's how we see the view from the top…the clarity of it all under the sunlight."

I squinted at the dirt, listening with my ears. But I couldn't listen with my heart. I just couldn't. It was too busy booming with its own curiosities: *Why wasn't he married anymore or at least in love? Why didn't he have children of his own to teach this to? Why was this wisdom of his so unheard, quieted by the woods around us, and not shouted into the ears of the world? And lastly, How come this man was homeless instead of someone's husband, someone's father?*

He went on with his velvet voice, "But we can't just sit up there forever and ever, you see…" he went on, intrigued, "…at some point, when we're ready of course, we gotta make it back down the summit, on the other side of the hill…into this other kind of love…love with the *other*, romantic love."

He traced the triangle down to the bottom, right corner slowly, as if he was playing the closing note on a cello. It seemed simple enough—the self, up alone to the summit, and then after however long it was or needed to be, treading down the other side of the mountain into the warm arms of another. Really, it seemed simple as hell. But perhaps the things that seem simple turn out being the most difficult. And of course, those which seem difficult end up being simpler than a leaf floating on lakewater.

He continued, tapping his stick on that same corner, flustered, "But...but the journey as a whole, Aydenn...it doesn't end there....nor anywhere; there is no *end*." He traced the triangle over and over with the stick, the triangle growing disfigured. There was a new, panicky excitement that banged on the walls of his body. "It's a constant cycle, you see! We're constantly movin'...from one corner...to the next! The journey of the self just has to *begin* in isolation." He was heaving his breaths out. "After the summit...it's still a journey...but with a little more company...a little more freedom...maybe even a little less discipline!"

I was trying my best to keep up as he sped on, "From up on top of that summit, Aydenn, the sunlight comes down on us. And the fruits inside us begin to grow, plump, ready to eat. Our hunger...it dissipates. We can feed ourselves...our spirits...we've responded to our journey...took all the footsteps ourselves. Took 'em, no matter the consequence."

My voice met his in the air between us, "But this journey of the self...how do we...how do we know what it is, or when it is...how do we get on the path...what path is right?" I was growing worried about the same life that I was supposed to be growing intrigued by. I looked down at the pinecone with my jaw inside my hands, elbows on knees. I could feel him smile.

He tapped the pinecone gently on the head with his stick.

"This," he said, "this is how it's all made possible, Aydenn."

I waited for his words the same way I used to wait for Kristiansen to walk in the door five minutes after the bell rang.

"Passion," he said softly. "It's our passion, kid."

He leaned over on his stump, picked up the pinecone and handed it to me. Dirt fell into my hands along with it. "It's our passion that guides us...throughout the journey...throughout love... throughout life. It's our passion that lets us...become.

"You see, those dreams we have as children...they stay with us somehow as we grow up. And we're always, at least subconsciously, thinkin' of bein' somewhere else, someone else. It's just part of our imagination's personality that never seems to leave. And that's what gives us these initial ideas about this *journey*. We're a curious bunch, us humans.

"And what motivates this journey...what gives it meanin' and purpose and momentum...well, are our passions: the things that we do for no other reason than love; they're our little places in the world that bring us to and from love; they help hatch the self; they boost us toward love with others, most importantly, Aydenn, they teach us how to be *passionate*."

We both scratched our heads. I listened as he went on.

"That's why cuttin' across the bottom of the mountain from the self to romantic love ain't right...it's...incomplete. Instead, you learn to let your passions pull you up to the summit, kid. Either you find your passions or they find you, but either way, once you're together, you'll make it up and into the sunlight that warms the summit."

He looked to his right, at the water nodding its head between the branches of pine.

"If this journey of the self is neglected, well, you never quite learn how to be passionate. And what kind of love can be offered if the offerer knows not how to truly be passionate?"

Before I could ask, he answered.

"Passions are anythin'...artistic passions...literature or music or conversation or even cookin'. We're all, by nature, artists, Aydenn." He showed me the palms of his hands. "We're born to create things and foster passion in each one of our movements and really become the artists of our lives. Look at young kids, creatin' things all the time, doin' it just to do it. And you wonder, why does this stop? Passions are our work, Aydenn.

Perhaps Van Dyke's poem makes a little more sense to you now."

Work. I had work to do. My own work to do. Somewhere out there. Either I'd wait for my passions or they'd wait for me. But *there* was the answer—the answer to the void in the pit of my stomach. I'd always thought the void was created by the death of my father. But perhaps it wasn't. Perhaps it was created by the simple birth of myself. Perhaps, at birth, you're given a void to fill with this passionate energy.

Whether it was an accident or not, Echo switched his tone to a quietness that flirted with lonesomeness. I froze and listened with the same two ears I'd always had for him.

"Look, I'll be honest with you, because my journey of the self's almost up...the *me* is finally satisfied. Yes, I may seem pretty old to just be finishin' now, but as I said, it's never about age...."

I looked right into his eyes as I finished the sentence for him, "...it's about experience."

He smiled and then squinted off into the distance at the young couple still on the lawn. "I was like that once...I had that once. But maybe what I had wasn't all I could've had. And I knew one thing I did have...that void...eatin' at me. I had the seed of the self, but no tree, no fruit. I knew I still had work to do...still had this journey to go on. You can only fight with yourself for so long, then you gotta start doin' instead of thinkin' so much. It was terrifyin'...I was so young and couldn't escape the paranoia of it all. All I was readin'...the poets and philosophers and authors all pointed me in the same damn direction. What was I supposed to do? You can't just turn off your mind."

Water found his eyes, and for the first time, Echo became more than my mentor. He was someone I cared about. He was my friend.

"I didn't want to hurt her..." he went on quietly, brokenly, "but I couldn't take on this journey without startin' it alone. We were only just married. I…I didn't really want to leave her, but I knew I had to. I didn't feel alive anymore. And I couldn't be myself because…well, *myself* was waitin' for me at the top of the summit, gettin' sunburned."

Tears debated forming and rolling out of his eyes.

"I told her I'd come back…how much I wanted to love her the way I really could. I wasn't a husband; I was just a…kid…scared and curious. And now…now…so many years later…*so many* years later, I know I was right. And sometimes it hurts to be right. But I feel…good now. Whole. Warm. I feel…love, Aydenn."

I could've cried right there. For someone that was so alone to feel a warm love made me realize that life is just as we imagine it as children—limitless and un-impossible.

He leaned forward and, with his bare hand, wiped the triangle back into flat dirt. He looked at me, right into my pupils, and spoke one last time.

"Being conscious of this journey, Aydenn…it's a *blessin'*…not a *doom*."

I walked home that late afternoon with my head mostly down, focused on the feet that had brought me to where I was in life, the feet that would bring me to all the places I'd go.

There wasn't a whole lot to put together; not much to rethink, nothing to analyze.

It was all there.

Love starts in the self. There's this chamber inside us with big, heavy doors, but we're born with the strength to open them. This strength resides in the self, the true and discovered self. We're responsible to become; we're meant to grow, to have passions. Passions. Writing a book or teaching class or acting or dancing or sports or taking photographs or singing or painting or selling houses to families or drawing up blueprints or driving a bus or staring out at the lake or traveling to somewhere you've always wanted to go. Passions are the things responsible for the good twitches in our heart.

I thought about Echo—about who he was underneath his words, how strange his life must've been. He'd left a woman and ended up homeless. Homeless, but brilliant. Brilliant, but alone. Alone, but with love simmering on the inside. I couldn't decide how to feel, so I walked on, eyes on the cracks in the sidewalk.

A million and a half cracks later, the street sign on the corner of 13th and Main jumped right in front of me. Sitting atop an impulse, I walked down the street slowly. Approaching Dillon's house, I saw their big camper parked out on the street under that same tree. The streetlight was glowing dimly above. I wondered where they'd go next, or, if *where* they'd go didn't matter as much as going did.

No cars were in the driveway. I walked right up to the two front lawns and stopped. Up on the porch, you could see that the tarp had been removed. All that stood between the two pillars now was the view of the Rubenson's front door. My heart was having trouble deciding how much it should flutter at that moment. Looking up, between the pillars, their door had been painted the brightest red I'd ever seen.

10

The rest of that week passed by nearly unnoticed.

The rains appeared again, then disappeared, then came back again strong as ever.

Undoubtedly, people were skeptical of it sticking around for very long; it's a hard feat to trust the weather; it's even harder to trust God or other people or even yourself sometimes. But I just went along with whatever the sky coughed up. Sometimes that's all you can do.

There was still no sign of a returning Mr. Kristiansen. It made me despondent as hell. I hated just losing people like that. And from being apart from my father, then Dillon, and now Kristiansen, it all made me realize how important gardening the self really is. Because no matter who departs from your life, you'll always have yourself to rely on—this tree that grows inside of you, this tree that started from a seed; its fruits'll get you by until you meet the next person who's going to change your life somehow.

Kristiansen had been a hell of a lot for me that semester. He'd taught me things no one else could've taught me. Losing him was like losing a father for the second time or something. And while the substitute would do her best, it wasn't quite enough to keep my eyes from floating out the window and listening to words in my head like *hallway, become, entelechy*. The rain would pound down on the school grounds, making up for its absence. Some days, I could almost see Kristiansen standing right there, in front of that same window, staring upward into the sky, talking about being on some sort of airplane, going somewhere, mentioning Greece, *Crete to be exact*.

◊

P.E. class took a turn right along with the weather.

Coach Fischer got his voice back, though it was softer than before.

The rain kept us inside the gym like it always did. Early one morning that December, we all stood in the gym, our cold P.E. clothes pulled over our growing bodies. The rain danced clumsily on the roof way overhead. We filled the entire sideline of the basketball court, standing shoulder to shoulder, as we waited for Fischer's word.

All the padded wrestling mats had been laid out across the hardwood floor. The basketball court nearly disappeared underneath them. Maybe we were moving into a wrestling unit; it seemed primal enough to fit Fischer's curriculum. He even made us take our shoes off and stand there in socks. But it all changed the minute he took off his shoes as well and walked to where half-court would've been, sitting down cross-legged, both of his feet pulled up onto the tops of his thighs.

Maybe it was only me, or maybe we *all* noticed that he didn't even have his usual whistle dangling down in front of his chest. He sat there, still as ever, with some object wrapped up in his grip. He looked down at it, down toward his lap. Under his instruction—his voice softer than the mats our walking feet pressed across—we all spread out and found a place to lie down on our backs. I saw the ceiling of the gym like I'd never seen it before. Strange how we can forget to look completely upward at the ceilings of familiar buildings.

Necks craned and bodies propped up on our elbows, we watched him unwrap a medium-sized brass bowl. From inside the bowl, he pulled out a round, wooden stick no bigger than a toothbrush.

"This here's a singing bowl," he said, his voice barely sneaking in between the intervals of raindrops above. "Perhaps some of you have meditated before. Perhaps some of you think you have. Much different than a daydream. Much different than relaxation." He went on, tracing the outer lip of the bowl carefully. "The thing about meditation is…it's voluntary…you *mean* to do it. Not like sleep…sleep happens when it wants to. Meditation is intentional…happens when *you* want it to." Certain notes of breathing made it into the air close to me and I could tell a few kids had fallen asleep. But I guess that's just how it goes. There'll always be one or two who are asleep right next to you when you're awake as hell.

The bowl began its high and deeply resounding hum as he went on. "We do it to…to figure things out. Isolate our minds. Trace things. Examine the world inside us. It's still exercise of course…exercise of the mind."

He went on about *mental terrain* and walking barefoot through your thoughts and treating moods like weather. He said that as long as the rain kept up inside, we'd work on our stretching, our breathing; we'd hold some poses borrowed from the practice of yoga, and then we'd meditate at the end of every class. In the last fifteen minutes, we'd all sink our backs into the big mats and close our eyes. He'd sit there at half-court, cross-legged, with the bowl sitting in his flat, open palm. He'd softly strike into it with the round, wooden stick. He'd then guide us through with words, telling us to imagine we were breathing in through the pores of our body, telling us to *arrive* into ourselves. We'd start breathing in through the soles of our feet and slowly make it up to our thighs and hips and lower back and abdominals and rib cage and chest, and we even reached our cheekbones and the hair follicles atop our head.

That first day of it was the turning over of a new leaf—a leaf I didn't even know existed. I thought about Echo and the two trees he'd mentioned, and that maybe the first tree was the one that produced such a leaf.

Coach Fischer was a man of patience, a man of practice. You'd think practices like that are a whole lot at once, but the truth is, they're quite simple. Turns out a lot of seemingly complex things are simple if you're patient and open and you show up a hundred percent to move through them. At the end of that class, in the middle of our closing meditation, my body fell away, leaving only my mind to vibrate along with the singing bowl. Just my thoughts and I, and for the first time in my life, it was a good thing. Face to face with myself—my *self*. Coach Fischer had tattooed on my mind that very first day of class not to run from our problems, but to run *with* them. And there I was, confronting it all: the problems, the wonders, the worries, the wounds, the *passing idea*, the faceless fireman, Dillon, my mother, Kristiansen, a bench just off the lake, and of course, Echo. You wouldn't believe how much you can see into your mind when your body isn't there. Lying there breathing, we were doing nothing, but we were doing everything.

()

I went to bed later that night thinking that perhaps meditation is the first step in *satisfying the me*.

Satisfying the me was about the journey, the journey of the self. It was about making sure you revisited that childhood need to imagine, and more than that, that you believed in those imaginings; it was remembering the hallway, and remembering to leave that first door slightly open; it was making sure that the true *you* would evolve and blossom no matter the amount of time it would take. *Satisfying the me* meant having enough gumption to abandon any state of discontent to become whatever it is you're supposed to become, no matter the consequence. Consequence can be a real villain if you let it. Consequence had left Echo homeless in the woods with a tarnished wedding band clinging onto his finger. But he wasn't weakened by any of it. Whatever it was that Echo had found out there in the woods, it had strengthened every ounce of him, maybe forever.

11

When you're in high school, the second week of December usually always means the same thing. I was busy as hell studying for those final exams, and it turned out that Coach Fischer was going to make us write a paper on what we'd learned in his class that semester—everything from running, to how your heart beats, to why it beats, to lying-flat-on-your-back meditation. It wasn't the kind of paper you could just do the night before. Funny how paper is so simple when it's just flimsy and white and blank, but once you put a handful of words you care about on it, you realize that even something so light can have so much weight to it.

A whole other story was the final exam for my History of Western Civilization class.

I haven't mentioned it much because it doesn't hold much significance to this particular story. But I *will* say that the final exam was tough as hell. It was what I'd studied for the most, but got the worst grade on. Some things will never make sense about school; we learn that as we move through the system of it. I went into that test thinking how there were just so many dates and names and timelines and fast forwards and rewinds, and if this moment *now* is the only time that ever truly exists, how can we really remember all those dates and names, and better yet, give significance to them?

The questions never stop.

But perhaps they mustn't.

Perhaps it's questions that breathe life into us; perhaps it's the inquisitive nature of humans that has kept things moving— and we know by now how essential movement is. In the end, we're no different than the diamonds dancing on the lake really, always going here and there, looking for something, something else. Perhaps each beat of our heart represents a new question forming somewhere in our consciousness. And maybe the heart and mind *do* work together after all.

◊

The rain stayed with us.

Umbrellas stretched their arms out again, ready for battle, and while there seemed to be a struggle with the wetness, we all secretly knew we needed it. Rain brings life, you see. It's a fact you can't ignore, no matter how much you love the sun.

It was Friday of that last real week of school.

It was on that day that I saw something from my bus window that I never thought I'd see.

I'd taken Kristiansen's beret with me to school again, being the last day and all, but he didn't show up; it was just the substitute again, with her thin arms and long eyelashes.

The red beret hid from the rain in my backpack all day, until that bus ride home. The seat next to me was empty as usual, so I took out the beret and put it right down on the seat next to me. The bus got warmer when I did it, and it almost felt like if I looked out the window just then, I'd see sunlight instead of rain. For the flash of a second, I even thought I *did* see a burst of sun in the distance behind some houses just before Dillon's. But driving down Main Street into the mirage, I, along with everyone else, saw that it wasn't sunlight at all.

Flames reached their hands high into the air as if hell were trying to choke heaven.

In the jump of a moment, faces were pressing themselves against the cold, glass windows on my side of the bus. It was chaos alright, especially for a sleepy place like Mayhaw. But at the same time, it was all very poetic—a house catching fire in the rain. It was as if Nature herself were trying to help. And then, a large red truck with a ladder on the side pulled up next to us. It was strangely echoic of the dream I'd had in that same seat. The fire truck was neck and neck with us just for a crack of a moment, but it was long enough for me to see the firefighter's hands strongly wrapped on the steering wheel.

I couldn't help but think of my father.

That evening I was particularly pensive, maybe even down.

It could've been from a lot of things.

Normally, I wouldn't have thought twice and thrown on a jacket and stuffed my hands deep into its pockets and walked down to Emma's Café. But I didn't want to deal with the rain. Sometimes it's just easier to stay inside.

I cleaned my room to busy myself because you can't always just be lazy when it's raining outside; it makes you feel like life is happening without you if you just spend all the time inside looking out the window waiting for the clouds to yawn. I folded and dusted and washed and dried and vacuumed and made my bed, wrestling with that one, far corner of my fitted bed sheet. Of course, I still felt a heaviness doing all of it, and thoughts of my father didn't stray too far. Those kind of thoughts always came around that time of the year. The frown of the clouds and the supposed-to-be, family-themed holidays could always get me down, no matter what. Unintentionally, that night, at dinner, after my room was dead spotless, I brought up my father. Of course I knew it was hard for my mother to talk about him, but sometimes emotion has no manners.

Earlier in life, when I first began asking about him, she'd always tell me softly, "Just know that he loves you, Aydenn...just always know that. And he's always here with you." I never knew exactly what she meant or how spiritual she was, but those words were always comforting, and at times, I *did* feel him right there with me like he'd never died at all. But that night at dinner, I just had to ask; I had to hear her talk about him. I told you before that I was always a curious young man, and in life, you have to let birds fly.

"Mom...um...about Dad...."

A lump punched itself into my throat.

"How...how did he die again, Mom? How did it...happen again?"

I knew all the details already, but sometimes hearing a sad story more than once somehow makes it less sad.

"Aydenn..." she breathed, somewhere between broken and disappointed. She'd always kept anything about him very brief. And over the years, I made myself okay with that. Maybe I had to. But that night, she went ahead and recounted the story anyway, as lightly as she could, but not putting her hand on top of mine or hugging me afterward or anything.

"It was his first call into the station. Middle of the night." She moved the food around on her plate, eyes transparent, more miles away than Main Street was long. "We were living together a few hours South of here, recently married, as you know; we were new parents as well."

She sipped on her wine, putting her glass back down close by.

"He shouldn't have gone back into it...that's what the lieutenant told me. He shouldn't have. He didn't have to. The whole place was on fire...the whole thing was going down...it was so dark out and the old, lonely man who owned it was standing outside on the street in his bathrobe, whaling the repeated words, "My book! My book! My manuscript! It's all in there! My life! It's all in there!" She shook her head in disappointment. "He shouldn't have gone back in, your father. Not for a stack of pages. He abandoned everything he had for a stack of damn pages."

She picked up her glass one last time and drained it. From inside the crystal, her voice was foggy. "But that was your father...driven by romantic ideas. And God only knows where that book is now."

Sleep just wouldn't find me that night.

There was just something about the way my mother talked about my father; it made it all worse. It made me more sad about him being gone and all. It was hard for me to understand, as much as I wanted to, that it was all for a lonely old man's manuscript. A book. My father risked everything—his life—over a book. He left my mother's side to go into that fire, into that unknown. And he died doing it.

To new ears, it would've seemed petty as hell. But that was *my* father, and such a simple act warmed the parts of my heart that you almost forget are there. And there was something curious about a helpless, lonely, old man and his handwritten manuscript that makes me want to cry in a good way—like life is beautiful as hell and we're all such romantics in the end.

I clambered down from my bed after lying there awake for

however long it was.

It was somewhere between the late p.m. and the early a.m. when I tiptoed into the kitchen and put water on for tea. The water took its time to get hot like it always does. Waiting, I poured into the living room, but didn't turn on the lights. I fetched a book of matches from the drawer in the end table by the couch and threw the damper of the fireplace open. A coolness descended down onto my hand from our chimney's tall throat. With soot smeared on my fingers, I struck a match and kissed it to the few pieces of thin firewood that were leaning on each other in the fireplace—apparently they couldn't sleep either.

I waited for the flames to wink at me. Sitting there, I looked to my left at my grandmother's painting up on the wall. It had a lot of weight to it, there, above the couch. That night, for the first time, I really saw the painting for what it was, for what it had been all along. And it had almost nothing to do with *what* was painted. It was the texture.

The flickering, infant fire breathed an easy orange glow up onto it, as the brushstrokes became the fingerprints of my grandmother herself. To do something with such intimacy as painting—such passion was there, and I could finally see it. Her little place in the world had been right in front of a canvas, her little place of freedom. All that I knew about her, and everything I didn't know about her, had been carefully placed in between the grooves of brushstrokes.

I saw her there. Perhaps when you die, you simply become whatever it was you created while you were alive.

Back in the kitchen, I was greeted with a rolling boil of water. I flicked off the stovetop and poured the water over a raspberry teabag that was fastened to my favorite mug. It was a turquoise, ceramic mug. Nothing like Dillon's, which, might I remind you, read: *It's always Summertime in here!* across its side. It's stupid things like that that dementia couldn't even make you forget.

Back into the living room, the fire was quiet. I fetched the wool blanket from off the back of the couch and folded it in half, placing it a few feet in front of the fireplace. I sat down and waited for my tea to cool. The rain knocked on the skylight directly above me as I watched the fire change shape. There was an unbeatable warmth at my chest and knees.

I thought about my father.

As if rain had leaked in and dripped down from the skylight, I soon found my cheek wet. A tear pushed its way out, forming the path for others to follow. You'll hear people talk about emotional moments as the ones that *get you*. The voice of a man in a coffee shop will grow raspy as you hear him talk to a friend about how a certain Joni Mitchell song *gets* him every time he hears it. Or you'll hear the girls in homeroom talk about the film they all saw over the weekend with their parents' money and how the ending really *got* them.

But this isn't the case at all, I've found. One doesn't get emotional about something because *it* gets *them*. The real reason why we cry isn't because we are *gotten* by something. No, you see, the tears come when *we* get *it*. And right there, sitting in front of that warmth, I *got* it.

It was a simple and painful truth: the presence of my mother worsened the absence of my father, and it finally made sense, as if my tears had washed my perception clean.

Through wet eyes, I watched the flames rise and fall like somber music and thought about the whole idea of *passions* and *becoming*, and how they're just like fire. They warm you up and hypnotize you and engage you like hell, all the while never taking one, true shape. They're always changing.

Mug in lap, the steam flirted with the raspberry scent as it rose up into my nostrils. It helped me fight back the quiet tears. The tea was too hot to drink, so I waited for it to cool. And it's moments like that, perhaps, when you realize how simple life can be. We all get caught up in this or that and we get ourselves so busy and we make things so damn complicated all the time. We do. But sometimes it just takes something small and insignificant, like waiting for tea to cool, to lesson us on things like patience. Things come if you let them. The flower of our enjoyment blossoms from the stem of our patience. You see, Nature's always hinting with little metaphors like that. It's a damn shame we don't listen more.

My eyelids were heavy. From a lot of things.

It just killed me that I would never get a chance to meet my father; it wasn't fair that I'd never even seen the man who'd helped create me.

A small noise, big enough to hear, clicked from back in the hallway behind me. Perhaps houses snore at night as well. Turning around to examine it, my small and squat shadow danced against the cold, back wall. The philosopher Plato came to mind.

Kristiansen had said something about him. Something about a cave with people sitting in it and how *they should just get the hell up already*. I sure missed him, Kristiansen—his eccentricities and his intense stares out of brown eyes through thick glasses. In truth, I didn't know *why* I was still carrying that damned beret around with me. By that time, it was just strange. Weird. I should've just forked it over to the front office the day I found it and turned around and walked away.

The mug-born heat in my hands grew comfortable. I took a long sip of tea and laid back, flat. I noticed how I was breathing, and thought of Coach Fischer. I sank into the wool blanket as the clock tapped its fingers on one of the a.m. hours. I slipped into something. Not thought. Not meditation. But something. And I forgot about the tea, and I'm sure it got cold as hell. I forgot about the painting and my shadow on the back wall. My mind was off my father, and off father figures, and even off the fire in front of me.

I thought of nothing.

Nothing mattered.

The *nothingness* of that moment mattered.

But surely, all moments meet their end, and then a new image is painted across your mind. For me, it was the image of a hair-backed hand, holding a stick and pointing down at a triangle drawn out in the dirt.

12

As the story goes, the final week of school found us.

Kids bustled in and out of classroom doors, defeating and being defeated by final exams, slamming lockers shut with unreasonable amounts of strength. They all acted like kids *should* act before they get to leave school for nearly a month straight. But me being me, I couldn't help but feel strange. Sure, a break from school *is* the greatest luxury when you're not eighteen yet. But I think that some small, nearly invisible part of everyone begins to really like school once it starts coming to a close. You realize stupid, little things that you're going to miss one way or another. Bells that tell you where and when to go; moments when teachers suddenly become real people; strategically placed scribbles inside bathroom stalls—the ones written in places janitors can never quite get to, the ones that hark some Bob Dylan lyric or tell you to call some number for a promising *good time*. There was just something sad and lonely about leaving the school halls cold like that in the silent deadness of Winter. Perhaps I'd begun to understand Texana Hills as some sort of home. Perhaps home can exist in more than one place, or perhaps home is not an actual place at all. Perhaps it's simply wherever there is love—the kind of love that you don't have to analyze or dissect or manipulate to make it real; a home is somewhere where love simply *is*.

There was a sense of home like I'd never known in Kristiansen, in Coach Fischer. Kristiansen had made sure we did more than *listen* in his class. He'd made sure we *heard*. When you *hear*, when you really *hear* something, it's much more than sound; it's a brief kind of symphony and you'll never understand how it was written, but you'll always remember the music.

Coach Fischer gave a kind of warmth to everything; it was something you don't just find in teachers. He pushed us, only to watch us the same way a father watches his son pedal away without the help of training wheels.

Perhaps the sense of home I got from these two men was nothing more than the product of my desperate longing for a father figure—someone to look at and see his strength and want so badly to emulate it. Truth is, finding one had always been so difficult in a small plot of land like Mayhaw. The older men I'd see situated in the corners of Emma's Café were always so distant, inaccessible, too into their Hemingway or daily papers. They'd recede into the dark, cozy corners of the café with their cork pipes poking out just above their breast pockets. You could feel it: they wanted to be bothered by nothing more than the words they were reading.

Coach Fischer and Kristiansen were two in a million.

And then there was Mr. Rubenson, of course; Dillon's father. He was always nice to me. He was an architect. Busiest guy I knew. But he always found the time to grip my hand a little tighter and hold it a little longer when greeting me. He was Dillon and Arietta's father, not mine, and I never wanted it to feel different than that. But that didn't mean I wouldn't listen to his stories—sometimes with more ear than his own two children. The more you listen to older people tell stories, the less frightening growing up becomes. Perhaps we don't have to grow *up*; perhaps, if we do it right, we simply grow *outward* instead. He'd talk with his hands just like Kristiansen, and I began to think that all important men did this.

And with that, of course, I wondered if my father had done the same.

〇

We finished out P.E. that semester with our stretching and yoga and meditation.

It doesn't seem like much, but you wouldn't believe the intensity involved in fine movement. And we had to turn in that paper of course. It was an artsy topic to write about, with a lot of room for air, but writing is almost as easy as breathing if you really believe what you're writing.

Coach Fischer had tried a number of things with us toward the end of that semester—things you don't usually see kids doing in P.E. class. Perhaps he'd been a late-blooming hippie. Perhaps hippies were onto something and they weren't crazy after all. Or even if they were crazy, perhaps all ideas timeless and brilliant and poetic have blossomed from some bit of craziness. Whatever he was, he was in touch with something bigger than any of us, and he tried with an unforgettable vigor to pass it on. It must take a whole lot of vitality to have *that* much faith in the spirits of seventeen and eighteen-year-olds.

In those final weeks, under his whistle-less direction, we sat down in foldout chairs or lied down barefooted and meditated. We stretched and bent our bodies in ways we never thought we could—some of us giggling, some of us really giggling, some of us just breathing with our eyes closed. Then there was the day we all tried to sit cross-legged on the wrestling mats and fold our feet into our laps. He called it the Lotus position. More like *Lo-duh shit*. No one had that flexibility, not even the gymnast kids.

All the meditation-themed fluff sounded easy as hell. But when you commit yourself to these simple, barely-moving practices, you realize how difficult they really are. It took me one particular day to really get it all.

The rain had been holding its breath all morning, so he led us outside in single file. He was quick to point to the track and trace its shape in the air in front of him. We stood there as our bony knees did their best to hide underneath our gym shorts. The last thing any of us wanted to do was run. Even me.

His voice spread itself out thick into the dry, morning air.

"You're gonna pick a spot out here...anywhere," he started. "Lay down some place that ain't too damp. The dirt's soft enough." He looked over at two kids kicking powdered dirt on each other's feet, "And SPREAD OUT," he emphasized. "Isolate yourselves. Sometimes you can get more out of something if you're on your own."

Barely-there specs of wetness began to fall from the sky. It was angels blowing kisses. Tiny angels. Maybe the angels of infants and children who'd died too early.

As soon as I thought he'd turn us loose and quietly walk off, he did just the opposite.

I hadn't really expected any more words from him that semester. He had this silence about him, this simplicity, this minimalism. It in itself said enough. I assumed I'd end that Fall semester and just kind of walk away, in silence as well, always knowing that I once knew the guy. The smartest thing you can do in life is to let go of someone once you've gotten all you were supposed get from them—once they've fulfilled their role in your life. Perhaps some people are only supposed to be in your life for a short period of time. It's a hell of a truth to swallow, but truths always digest somehow. Like my father—the passing idea.

Perhaps that's how it was supposed to be. And who will ever win the fight against what was supposed to be?

You see, the passing idea had gotten in the way of my blossoming. I thought *it* was damaging me, but it was *me* who was damaging me. The nighttime longing for him and the begging of the eternal *why* had placed such a thick, dusty curtain over the whole concept of *entelechy* for long enough, and I had to learn to let go. Perhaps we waste time making big ideas out of relationships with people. Perhaps we spend more time thinking about and assessing relationships than we do actually having them. So maybe we should live for the chain of singular moments in which you know people. You'll gain a lot more than you lose that way. Like Echo and I—eventually he'd move along and stick his tent down in dirt somewhere else, and I'd move on, remembering what he'd taught me, and I'd grow up and join the academy and *satisfy the me*. And that would be it for us. It was sad if you looked at it through sad eyes. But through honest eyes, it was as natural as leaves falling in Fall.

At that point in my life, the only thing I was really making an effort to hold onto was Kristiansen's beret. Or perhaps it was holding onto me.

We stood in our P.E. clothes, in a tired semicircle, around the portly man in the navy blue tracksuit. He began, "People lose something in their lives that I don't want any of you to lose. We've come a long way this semester. Together. Alone. But there's something small I think we should all explore today." He bit his bottom lip as he looked down at the dirt in front of him. "You see, this big blue or gray or black or white sky above us…the older we get, it seems to become just another sort of ceiling. And not everyone pays attentions to ceilings much unless they're in some sort of chapel.

Sure, we see the sky. But do we really see it like it is every day? Do we really see it as *new* every day? Sure, we see storms coming and the sunset rehearsing and birds flying southward. We see all that. But that's because we don't have a problem looking *out* at the sky. Our problem is looking *up* at it."

We listened with arms crossed, like boys trying to be men. Whatever we were, we were becoming perplexed by his words.

"When you're kids," he went on, "I mean real young kids, you're always looking up...you're looking up at the sky from on your backs. The world's still so new, and you haven't gotten used to much of anything yet. In a three-foot-eight timber, you fall to your backs on grass, and you take turns opening and closing your eyes. You see the sky from a view that you'll spend your whole adult life trying to see again. You lie there, thinking of not much more than why the clouds are acting the way they are. You see the sky from directly underneath it, lying extra still to see if the Earth has a pulse just like you."

As the morning got more still, he went on for just a little longer. He sat down on the track in front of our half-circle of teenage bodies. With a craned neck and squinted eyes, he looked up over our heads and into the sky he was talking about.

"Nature's all we really got. It's all that's ever been. All that'll ever be." He chuckled, "The philosopher Thoreau said it himself: *Let us first be as simple and well as Nature ourselves.*" I admired how lightly he chose to see the things that other people would fall into a heaviness of a million words over. His eyes down from over our heads, and now upon our faces, he spoke one last time.

"Spread out. Have a lay. Isolate yourselves from everything except your senses. Be like children under the sky. But remember to breathe big and round and full breaths. You'll know you've got it right when you're still enough to see the clouds moving."

Every single color of gray was up there that day.

Interesting what Coach Fischer had said, as if our perspectives become more and more limited as we get older. It's a real wonder when you think about how knowledge and wisdom correlate with adults and children—who has which and who the real teachers are. I found a spot to lay down right on the shoulder of the track by the school's biggest oak tree. Perhaps it was related to the one out my bedroom window. I kicked the dirt around to dry out the surface dampness. I lied down with all my weight and emptied my lungs. Before I could take in air again, soft steps in the dirt crunched from behind me.

It reminded me of the day I met Echo.

Once the crunching ceased, I turned up and saw that it was Coach Fischer. No more than fifteen feet from me, he'd found *his* place to lie down. All I could see was the rubber bottoms of his shoes along with his belly rising and falling like the cusp of sun on the horizon.

The best teachers are the ones who aren't afraid to become students like that. The best teachers know that learning, just like any art, is never finished. There's always more you can learn, and knowing that is a treasure for life. *I know what I can know; therefore, I know everything.*

Looking up at the sky—a moving view you can never see the same way twice—I was able to see its raw beauty rather than its lack of color. There was a good marriage between self and Nature just then; just the clouds and I. Or perhaps I didn't exist at all. They say your body is made up of so much water, you know. Perhaps, in that moment, I had evaporated into the clouds myself. Perhaps it wasn't me and Nature anymore; perhaps we were Nature together.

Just then, like a beautiful sentence written across a page, a bird crossed over the sky, flying perfectly underneath the gray and white tufts. Everything else, even the wind, fell off the Earth. I recognized the bird. Somehow, it was a seagull.

The ocean wasn't in close proximity to us. Maybe the seagull was terribly lost. Or maybe it was right where it was supposed to be. Some things we'll never know for sure.

13

Nonchalantly, with no expression on its face, the last day of school arrived.

It had been my longest semester at Texana Hills High School. I'm sure it had been the same amount of weekdays and weekends and school bells and alarm clock sounds as all the previous semesters, but sometimes, certain people and experiences can bring a new depth to time.

It was the 14th of December. A whole 'nother year had wiped its mouth and gotten up from the table. Perhaps what they say is true. Perhaps time does fly: it flies with light, easy wings when you yourself decide to fly right along with it. The passing of time is natural as hell, beautiful even, when you're busy *becoming*—when you're onto something good.

Time ticked its way into the early afternoon that Friday. I walked down the hall to my last final exam. You guessed it: Literature as Philosophy. Closer and closer to the door, scratching the side of my pencil with my thumbnail, I had one last crumb of hope that he'd be behind his podium, waiting on us, hatless. I'd brought his beret with me one last time. If he wasn't there, I'd get rid of it. I was tired of having it. Ten feet from grabbing and turning the brass doorknob and finding out if Kristiansen was inside the classroom, I heard my name hollered from back behind me, echoing off the lockers. A familiar voice. Not Kristiansen; that would've been too perfect.

"Aydenn! Hey man, wait up!"

It was Dillon.

"Dillon? Wh-what's going on?"

I wanted to say more, to tell the guy that I missed him and his family, and his sarcasm, and even the way his little sister Arietta would run to the door when she knew it was me. I wanted to tell him about Coach Fischer and how Kristiansen had just disappeared after that one day, and that I saw how his dad had repainted their front door. I wanted to tell him about Echo—meeting him and going back to the park and sneaking into his tent and talking with him under the trees about important things. I hadn't told anybody about Echo. I knew Dillon would give me both ears. Perhaps I could explain it all to him up on his roof.

He caught up to me and gave me a *hey buddy* slap on the arm. "Kinda in a rush, man…just finished my last test. Gotta scoot outta here quick. Girlfriend's waiting for me. Me, ma, dad, Arietta and her are leaving for my grandparents' tonight. Taking the camper up there for a bit. Then we're gonna take everyone up north and stay with my dad's brother. My uncle said it's snowing like hell up there. Arietta's on edge with this undecided weather, not being able to make her snow angels and all." He took a much-needed breath in. "I won't be back 'til January, man." He looked down at his hands, "…I know I haven't been seeing much of ya at all these past few months. We gotta get on my roof again next semester, man. Like old times. Won't have to steal smokes from my dad anymore, eh?"

He saw that I didn't really know what to say. Could you really be mad at a guy for spending his time with a girl he liked?

"Well shit," he reached into the lumpy pocket in the front of his hooded sweatshirt. "Merry Christmas, man." He held out a small box wrapped in red. "Ain't much," he said, "but you'll like it. Knew you'd wanna have it."

I thanked him in a couple words. We got the closest that high school guys get to hugging, and we bumped fists. "Don't open it 'til Christmas, man!" he shouted over his shoulder as he trotted off back down the hall.

I swung my backpack around to put the present inside just as a girl from Kristiansen's class breezed by me. The perfume that breathed from her hair made me turn on point and follow her into the classroom. Girls do things like that to boys.

The door shut behind us. I placed the present in my backpack, just on top of the red beret, and looked up. It was the substitute.

I sat down, filled up with frustration. Kristiansen was supposed to bookend everything he'd started with us! He'd left us hanging with questions that'd take years to answer! But I couldn't blame him for being ill; I just wanted that sense of closure. But perhaps, too often, we search for closure from other people that we need to find on our own.

He'd given our eyes some great literature to look at; he talked about his summers in Norway and even spoke Spanish to us sometimes—*Spain* Spanish, of course. He'd even brought me and Echo together with that Van Dyke poem. Kristiansen was the kind of person you don't meet again; all you can really do is be glad that you *did* meet him. The gladness simply came from the fact that he searched for wisdom in people with such honesty, such simplicity.

The substitute quietly passed out our final exams, and after filling in the 127 bubbles of multiple choice questions, I dropped my warm and tired pencil down on my desk, and read the essay portion on the wide-open back page.

It read: *Discuss the necessity of responding to the call of the self and how one may go about harnessing this idea of 'becoming'. Apply your reasoning both contextually and personally. No more than eight pages. Use as many allusions to authors, philosophers and bodies of work as you can. Give a good introduction. No need for a concluding paragraph, for we should be arriving at conclusions all throughout the essay. Staple your work together.*

I wrote for one hour.

I can't remember everything that came out of the tip of my pencil, but I knew it was all there. Over time, I think you forget what you write, much like with journals and diaries. But maybe it's not what you write than matters in the end; in the end, it's *that* you wrote.

I'm sure I wrote about how neglecting the call of the self would result in two great tragedies. One, the more obvious, that you'll arise one morning and realize that you never really became the *you* that you'd always dreamed about. Maybe you became someone else that isn't that bad, but you ask anyway, "What happened to chasing down a *great* life? When and why did I stop at *good?*"

The second tragedy would be that it hinders you from experiencing the great capacity of love. Neglecting the call of the self, you simply sidestep the fullness of the journey. You never dunk your head in your passions. Perhaps you only dabble in them, and what great life can a dabbler really live? And because of this, you can't possibly learn what it means to be *passionate*. And thus, you're less aware of the capacity of love. Love is the only reason we're here, and to know not its capacity is to know not much at all.

I even talked about *satisfying the me*, realizing even more how much Kristiansen and Echo paralleled each other. I really pushed my pencil down hard as I wrote, concluding the paper with, "However, no matter how long one may neglect the call of the self and its journey, the beautiful truth that saves us in the end is that it is never too late to become something else, something new." I dropped down a line and finished with all caps:

IT IS NEVER TOO LATE TO BECOME.

I was one of the last ones writing. I stapled my pages twice so they'd be together forever. Placing them on the podium up front, a curiosity and stubbornness teamed up inside me and forced me to ask about Kristiansen. The substitute went on lightly with her blinking eyelashes and small lips that he'd fallen very ill, and while he was going to be okay, they weren't sure when he'd return to Texana Hills.

I hated hearing it. I hated that I hated him for being sick. But that was just the way it was, and I wouldn't be stupid enough to deny my real feelings. There was, however, no way in hell I'd bring that beret back home with me.

I pushed the classroom door open, filling the hall that was supposed to feel like freedom. But it didn't. I was out of school for Winter break; I could have done *anything* just then; I was free until *January*. But before I could feel that way, there was something I had to do.

I made it outside, under hues of yellow, gray, pink and white. I marched across campus to the faculty offices. Light rain fell soft and quiet on everything. I felt the weight in my backpack as I wrenched the aluminum door open and entered the small wing that held the English and Art teacher offices. I was met with the front side of a large desk, and behind it sat a middle-aged, unmarried woman who had eyebrows like Audrey Hepburn.

Before she could ask, I answered.

"I have something of Mr. Kristiansen's." She looked at me like she didn't speak my language. "It needs to be returned," I went on. "Today."

Yeah, yeah, I know he's ill, I thought. I just needed to have it put in his office or even hung on his doorknob. She didn't speak at first. She just looked at me, maybe reading how genuine I was. Still, without words, she looked around behind her, then got up from her desk and began to walk down the hall. I followed her close. We passed all the other doors; they were all shut tight.

She looked back at me a couple of times, the way a mother looks at her son before she tells him bad news. Before reaching the small, brown wall plaque engraved with *Jay Kristiansen*, she whispered back, "No one really knows what...what to do about him being gone." Her stumble of words scared the hell out of me and I thought maybe he'd died or something.

Her heels quit their click-clack as we got to his door.

It wasn't shut tightly like the others. It was just barely cracked open, leaning on the door frame, a little bit of light leaking out into the hallway we'd just walked down. She looked over my head, back down the hall, then pushed the office door open. She moved back a few feet and nodded down at me. We had brief eye contact before I took my first step across the doorway. There was a thin layer of dust lying down, sleeping on everything—the desks and bookshelves, computer and telephone. A good deal of papers, binders and books were lodged into a narrow bookshelf, barely able to breathe. I caught sight of a strange word on one of the book spines; it read: *Zorba.*

Then I noticed something.

It was what I was supposed to notice.

It was a piece of torn out notebook paper, folded in half and taped up on the computer screen. I turned around to look at the woman behind me. She gave another nod, her eyes nervous under her thick eyebrows. I got the feeling that I wasn't supposed to be in there, that she wasn't supposed to let students in teachers' offices like that.

I inched forward anyway, further into the quiet space of my English teacher's office, reaching to pull the tape off of the peculiar, folded piece of paper. I did so, and the paper opened itself flat against the gray computer screen, right in front of my face. My feet got heavy. My spine shot a new temperature down my back. The words were written in all capitals. I read them twice, my eyes getting warmer and warmer as I did. I dropped my head down afterward, feeling the moisture burn behind my eyelids as they closed.

But I didn't drop my head down to cry; I did it to hide a smile from the woman behind me. I stood there, just like that, doing my best to tuck that little smile down into my neck.

I was smiling because I understood.

In his scribbled handwriting, with Es that looked like backwards 3s, the paper read:

GONE TO CRETE!
THANK YOU!

That's all it said.
Five words. Nineteen letters. That was all.
And somehow, I understood.

14

I said goodbye to Kristiansen that day.

I let him go. Perhaps it's goodbyes that bring us closer to people than hellos.

He'd gone to Crete, to Greece, just like that. That's why the bit about the airplane and penetrating the clouds and traveling had fallen clumsily into that final lecture of his. He hadn't been ill at all. Farthest thing from it. It was the first time I'd really see gumption in someone: the gumption to *go* because *going* was no longer an option, but an obligation—an obligation to the self. Perhaps all we ever need is a drop of gumption like that. In one drop, all of life waits for us.

I've never been certain who he was thanking in that farewell note. Perhaps he was thanking the hallway for never closing its walls up on him; perhaps Aristotle; perhaps Texana Hills for reminding him of where he was only supposed to be for a little while, not forever. Whatever they meant—those two words,

THANK YOU—they were as perfect as anything can be perfect.

I never saw him again, except for in memories. So much of what he'd said in class would go on to echo down the hallways of my mind—at random times, stupid times, desperate times. And that's what's great about an echo: it can never fully disappear.

It's never too late to become. He showed us that. He showed me that. Perhaps he was the best teacher ever; perhaps just the most human.

And for that, I loved him.

○

Thoughts, days and clouds passed.

It was just about Christmas Eve.

My mother got a call from my Aunt Jodie and Uncle Lou. She always said *Hello* a second time once she knew it was them. She said it with a sweetness I didn't hear very often. My aunt and uncle would always *both* be on the phone—they had two phones and would each pick one up and talk on them from different rooms. It made them *them*.

In the living room, where my mother had recently woken up the fireplace, I was glued to both the couch and to *The Brady Bunch*. It was my show. From the kitchen, my mother hollered over the running sink water to me. Her sister and Uncle Lou would be coming down on Christmas like usual, but this time they'd stay the night. Then of course, they'd be off again, maybe downstate, hitting their favorite Winter spots. Places to read and take photographs and rest and look at each other like old lovers.

Christmas was already looking different that year—good and bad different. Overnight guests, extra decorating, and the absence of sitting and drinking hot cocoa with Dillon in his living room. The absence of his stupid mug.

Still, my mother and I had the tradition of watching *A Christmas Story* on the couch together—a movie that I'd gotten so damn tired of. But by the time December came around every year, I just *had* to see it. Maybe it wasn't the movie I had to see at all. Maybe it was the tradition. Traditions can be awfully stupid, a seeming waste of time, a sure way to make life feel like it may never get exciting again like it once was. But traditions are, and will continue to be, the loyal four walls of night-black rooms— the walls we reach out and feel for when we're lost and dizzy somewhere and can't see a thing.

Up until lunch, and then a little after, I helped my mother with the house.

Cleaning floors and window sills and stitching the perimeter of our living room with little white lights, and dragging our five-foot-three artificial tree up from the basement and then going back down to pull up the guest bed and make an Aunt Jodie and Uncle Lou-like abode on the floor in my room for, well, Aunt Jodie and Uncle Lou. My mother wouldn't let them sleep out in their camper. And I'd sleep on the couch so they could have my room.

With the television talking to nobody, I overheard the weatherman say calmly the uncalm news that a blizzard was expected tomorrow. A blizzard on Christmas Eve. Poor Santa. Poor Mrs. Clause.

I straightened out the tree near the fireplace, stacking the humble pile of envelopes and colorfully wrapped shapes underneath it. I put Dillon's on top. A red, perfect box. It wasn't really the shake-and-listen type. I'd find out why on Christmas Eve.

My mother and I always opened one present on Christmas Eve.

She'd unwrap a bottle of this or that, or even gourmet chocolates. A card would always be attached. She'd smile at it like a little girl. They were gifts from coworkers or old clients or recent homebuyers. She helped a lot of people find homes. People retiring, people just getting started, new lovers even. Perhaps realtors aren't that bad. Perhaps realtors sometimes pick up where Cupid leaves off. Who knows?

As the opening-one-gift tradition followed, before I'd open my gift, I'd open the card from the Rubensons. Mrs. Rubenson always mailed it to us. She wrote both of our names on the back in tall and neat cursive: *Emily & Aydenn Price*. Though different words were written on the inside each year, they always meant the same thing, retaining the same warmth. It was a foot-in-a-thick-sock warmth. And the last line always read *Love—Jane, Carl, Dillon & Arietta*. Arietta always wrote her own name in. It got a little neater every year, and it would remind me that I wanted kids some day.

In truth, Christmas Eve had always been normal as hell. Up until that Christmas Eve, there were never any surprises, never anything to think twice about. A quiet Christmas warmed up by some cards and a living-room fire. And for years, nothing really changed that.

But perhaps we know by now that change is a hell of a traveler. Change is always on the road. Sometimes it's late; sometimes it's early. It comes when we're *not* waiting for it at the train station; and it *doesn't* come when we are.

◊

All things done—for me at least—I squinted up and out the window in my room.

The big oak tree across the street danced drunkenly in the wind, its half-naked branches waving at me. It's funny how you never know if trees are waving you hello or waving you goodbye—it's like they know when you're coming and going. It did this under a patchy sky. You see, there was a black-gray in the far, far distance, way over the tree's head. But when I went outside and looked directly up, the sky smiled a milky gray that I could trust. I thought of Coach Fischer.

The distant blackness in the sky was *then*. I went along with the milky gray *nowness* right overhead instead. I double knotted my laces from the sidewalk there, and with an easiness and a quietness, I took off for Lake Wisley. Little did I know it would be my last visit. Well, at least my last visit before the night everything happened.

◊

The lines in the sidewalk passed under my feet one after the other. My pace quickened; more strides per second; more heartbeats per minute. The lake was pulling me closer and closer. It did that to me. It was as if the lake had, on my first visit, threaded a needle and poked it through my heart, and now each time I was supposed to go back, it just gave the string a little tug with its current, and there I'd be.

But then, of course I'd wonder what'd even brought me out there, all that way, the first time. Was it fate? The simple idea that Echo and I were destined to meet? Was it all just a consequence of me needing to get out of the house that day, away from my mother, away from my life? Echo was the last kind of person I'd have ever expected to become important in my life. But he did. He became important. Sometimes, you don't exactly get a say on who the significant people in your life are. Sometimes they just walk out from behind the trees and sit down next to you. And maybe it was just that that'd brought me back—the warmth of another; the warmth of sitting down next to someone, with someone. That's what'd made Dillon and I best friends. And at times, when I'd think that maybe Echo had replaced Dillon, I'd realize that no one person can replace another. People can't replace people; they can only show up when others leave. And it's not the people that come in and out of our lives that matter; it's the moments with those people that do.

Shoulders stacked above the balls of my feet, I ran on with a straight back. My backpack bounced up and down, just enough to feel it there. I'd tightened the straps as tight as they'd go. It felt secure, and it needed to be, for what was inside.

Eventually up and down the big hill past Texana Hills, I had a feeling like warm wind in my chest. It was the kind of lightness you'll get when there's no past or future. I barely caught the tips of pine trees in the far distance as the weather went on being weather.

A million and two strides later, I winded past the sign that familiarly read LAKE WISLEY. The trail bent its body around the trees and lawns of the Southern Park. I slowed, jogging down the trail like blood through a small vein. A slowed blur of tree trunks and water reflections sparkling through the gaps, and there I was, in front of the bridge again—the tall sign with the N painted on it in red; the squat, stone-covered drinking fountain. But no lizard. It wasn't that I necessarily *wanted* to see the lizard there; it's just that it—much like Echo—had added to the sense of home I'd found in that forgotten, little corner of Mayhaw.

I crossed the bridge, the wide planks of wood feeling thick under my feet. That bridge would probably be there forever. Shallow water swept gently in and out of the inlet below me, with nowhere to go and nowhere it had to be. Into the clearing, I halted to set my eyes wide on the Northern Park. It was the last time I'd ever see it like that—undisturbed, patient, honest. It was still as hell; any breeze must've passed right through me. In the distance was someone I recognized. It was the frail, old man, sitting by a pathetic fire that wasn't pathetic at all. It was the greatest fire I'd ever seen.

He sat there and looked into it the same way a child might—he was content as hell just because the wonder of color and movement was manifesting right in front of him. And that similarity—him with a child—is one of the things that makes me sure there's a God. You see, you hear the doorknockers and churchgoers talk about how we are God's children. And seeing that we become just like children again as we slip into old age, it seems only right that there *is* a God. Perhaps whenever we are with him—before and after our lives—we are with him as children. And getting older isn't getting older at all, but is instead a returning to the state of childhood. That way, when we die, we don't die at all. We simply return to God as the children he remembers us as.

◊

I looked from the lake to the bench and then on to the dark red, canvas tent. It was even *closer* to the bench now. Only one of the flaps was drawn shut.

I walked toward the tent. Though Echo was assuredly inside, I was hesitant walking up because of that one day. I felt the weight of something round in my backpack as I crunched along on fallen pines. Making sure not to step on any pinecones, I tiptoed closer and closer, drumming my fingers along the back of our wooden bench as I passed behind it.

I bent forward to see in through the open flap. He didn't notice me at first. Hundreds of pages seemed to litter the floor around where he sat. He had a look on his face that I'd never seen on him, much less anybody else. It was a look that conveyed a marriage of fear and excitement.

The books from his shelf were scattered about the same way. Some papers laid tired in his lap, some in his hands, some balancing on his knees. Just as I saw the one with that title written in the blue calligraphy of his—*Standing Out In the Rain: An Autobiography*—his eyes met mine. At that eerily beautiful moment, I couldn't decide if I liked his green or blue eye more. It isn't often that you meet people with two different colored eyes. Maybe each eye saw the world differently, in its own way. They were equally beautiful, and I decided right then that choosing between two beautiful things is perhaps the ugliest thing a person can do.

Echo looked different, too. His ponytail had been snipped off, his hair hanging just above his ears, blondish-gray. His beard was gone, and there was a boyish paleness in the skin where it had been. His clothes were different too. Cleaner.

As if a bee had stung him into action, he lunged out of his sitting position, hug-sweeping all the papers around him, knocking over the stout, red candle that sat lit by his feet. It bled hot wax onto one of the pages and hardened before Echo could do anything about it.

I stepped backwards toward the lake, toward the bench. I was nervous, but I couldn't leave. I turned around from him, giving him space as I waited there, looking out at the lake with my fingers laced together on top of my head. I felt the weight of my backpack again. I couldn't leave just yet. I had something to give him.

15

Eyes out on the lake, eased by the rolling underneath its glass surface, I heard the tent flaps flip open. A crunching sound—made only by feet—approached me from behind. I was still nervous, from my fingertips all the way down to my ankle bones. The sound soon fell into only my right ear. He'd gone right passed me, right for the bench. I watched him sit down and let out all the air in his lungs. It was so odd not seeing that thin pony tail hanging behind him anymore.

I followed suit, walking over and sitting down myself.

When I looked up and over at him to maybe say something, anything, I couldn't. He had that squint across his eyes. It was the kind of squint that quiets everything around it. Through those narrow eyelids, he looked out over the water like he'd done so many times. Maybe the goal in life is to learn how to look at the same beautiful things over and over, only to see them—each time—as new again.

The same words that I thought should come out of my mouth thought themselves that they should stay *in* my mouth. I resorted to peeling my backpack off and placing it in the dirt at my feet.

With not much else to do, I looked at the backs of his hands. They lied flat on the tops of his knees. Blonde and gray hairs danced just like the diamonds on the water, under the smudge of sun. He finally let a sigh escape him, a deep sigh, following it with, "No...this won't do." He paused. His lips got stiff. "Follow me," he said while easing up off the bench. I obeyed, puppy-like, and followed suit again, snatching my backpack with his gift inside. I wouldn't give it to him just yet.

We made our way back across the clearing, onto the bridge; with two clean hops, Echo planted a foot and jumped and swung his legs over the side of the bridge, landing a nice sit-down, facing the lake with his legs dangling down insouciantly over the inlet.

With less finesse, I copied him.

It was the most serene view of the lake. There was something about sitting there on that bridge; perhaps it was more than the view; perhaps it was that it connected the Southern Park to the Northern Park, the familiar to the strange, the known to the unknown, me to Echo.

We dangled our legs like fishing lines right over the inlet below, which lined up perfectly with an opening in the pine trees. It was a view I'd always walked by, and somehow, one I'd never really taken the time to see. Funny how our *own* movements can steal our attention away from Nature's. It was like Coach Fischer had said, "You'll know you've got it right when you're still enough to see the clouds moving."

()

With nowhere else to look, our focus narrowed through the

tall, skinny-standing pines and out onto the water. I'm sure we both thought about the threatening grayness that flirted a little too much with the horizon. I thought about if I'd make it home dry that day; I thought about how I'd go about fishing his gift out of my backpack, and if he'd even like it; I thought about the next time I'd see Echo, and if there'd even be a next time. And I'm sure he had thoughts of his own, buzzing along the walls of his mind. It's funny how thought can be the loudest sound you've ever heard. But as you learn to meditate on it, run *with* it and not *from* it, you eventually find the volume knob.

With his legs swinging in small circles, he breathed words into the air with that unfailing velvet voice of his.

"There's somethin' I forgot, Aydenn...about...about the journey...the satisfying the me...heck, about all of life." His face couldn't decide whether to be stone serious or smile-ridden. He scratched at where his beard would've been.

"It can be a bit of a hell at first, but it'll become a heaven if you tame it...give it some direction. It's...*curiosity*, Aydenn. Curiosity." He looked at me the second time he said it. "It's the gasoline. It's the wind behind us, the hot-white sun that waits outside for us to stand in. It gives us reason for the journey. It's...it's our justification for goin' just for the sake of goin'."

I thought of Kristiansen.

"You see, we're always wonderin' about things, ever since we're young children. And that's just part of bein' human. You *wonder*. And that's a damn good thing. Perhaps a lifetime of curiosity is the only justice to our imaginations. The question is, what do we do with all that wonderin', all that dreamin', all that thinkin'?"

I bent down to loosen my laces, keeping my eyes up on him.

"There's just so much damn freedom in human thought," he continued, "and once you *understand* that freedom, your curiosity can shoot you into anythin'...euphoria, anxiety, paranoia, momentum, obsession, depression. Curiosity will introduce you to some awful and beautiful avenues. It's just a matter of knowin' that gettin' lost is okay. Gettin' lost is part of it. How do you ever expect to be *found* if you don't get a little lost first? You'll find your way with a good heart…an honest heart. A good head and a good faith about you. Curiosity…it's a garden, Aydenn. A matter of knowin' when to water it and when to just let it grow…how much sunlight it needs and when you oughta prune it."

It's a hell of a thing meeting people who talk in ways where you know that they not only understand what they're saying, but they mean it too.

"Curiosity puts you on the doormat of where passion lives. To be a lifelong dreamer or wonderer…to never settle for any old path you end up on…well, that's the wisest path of all. Or perhaps it's not a *path* at all. Maybe, just maybe, Aydenn, we oughta live our lives not searchin' for which *paths* to take, but looking for which *fields* to run through instead. More room that way"

He dropped his head, facing now the inlet below, where a blanket of water glided over smooth, round stones.

"Best words I ever heard: *Be curious.* I was eighteen. Twenty years later, I finally understand 'em. I mean," he smiled, "you gotta be *interested* before you can be *interestin'*, right?"

We've all heard somewhere about the importance in being earnest, but I'd never heard about the importance in being curious. But like many things that are unfamiliar, not well-known or oft-said, it sounded right.

"It's about askin' questions that build bridges between things like *Who am I?* and *Who can I be?*" Something came together just then. *I know what I can know; therefore, I know everything.* There lied the face of curiosity! It all started with questioning! When you question what you *can* know, you can answer that you *can* know everything.

At that moment, I wished more than ever that the man to

my right could've met the man who'd just arrived in Greece—
Crete to be exact. And that's when he said it. "Curiosity,
Aydenn...it's got two faces...no matter what kind of binds it gets
us in...or how alone it can make us feel...how many rivers it can
leave us nearly drownin' in...in the long run...it too, is a blessin',
not a doom."

Minutes, maybe hours, maybe only a few breaths passed
between us in silence. Then he went on. "Twenty or so years
ago, I left. I just...went." His voice changed to a soft, carpet-like
texture. I immediately felt sympathy—as much sympathy as you
can feel when you're seventeen.

"Maybe it was nothin' more than this...this *curiosity* that
drove me out. Can't escape it sometimes, you know. Leavin' the
life I was in was the only threshold to findin' a real backbone—a
real strength inside myself. You learn yourself, and you become
your greatest company once you give into to the poundin' on
your spirits that tells you that you need change and you oughta
go live the life you're spendin' all your time thinkin' about."

A muted light came through the narrow hallway in the trees
and lit Echo's face. As much as I wanted to ask, to ask about
everything, all I could manage to do was listen, even if it was only
to the silence that sat between us.

"Bein' curious, bein' a seeker, bein' relentless for
answers...it's hell of a life. And the way I see it, Aydenn...what's
the other option? Is there one? Socrates said it right...an
unexamined life simply *ain't* one worth livin'. You gotta satisfy
your curiosities about life...no matter the
consequences...things'll work out if you've got a good and honest
heart. All's been written out for us. All we gotta do is live openly
and keep awake to witness the magic. Hell, read it in *Walden*—"If
one advances confidently in the direction of his dreams, and

endeavors to live the life which he has imagined, he will meet with a success unexpected in common hours." There's really no other choice, Aydenn. Happiness waits on the other side of our gumption to live, gumption to seek, to ask, to search, to go on when we're called to. This way you'll see things more clearly...this way you're not in the way of yourself anymore." I thought of Kristiansen again.

Maybe it was more than him *wanting* to go to Crete; maybe he *had* to.

"I got too crowded Aydenn," he went on.

"Needed more space to move around...was tired of not knowin' the world I lived in. I had this...this strong urge to just go...to be alone...out in Nature...for no valid reason. To travel to certain corners of places and find somethin' in myself, somethin' real and eternal. And I wanted to do it knowin' I was free. No connections, no obligations, no stuff."

My feet tingled in their numbness, still dangling down over the side of the bridge.

"And then I met a girl, and for a good, long minute there, all was well. All was light and a type of beautiful I hadn't thought existed."

The only thing identical about his eyes just then was the moisture that began to envelope them. Not only was I quiet; I sat completely still, blinking only if I had to.

"But even then, in the quiet hours in between butterflies, I felt the pangs, the pokes and the proddin'. I had work, undone. I had a callin', unanswered. A life, unlived.

"I...I left her, Aydenn. I left her for...for me. I wasn't happy. And...how can you make someone else happy if you ain't happy yourself...right? I wished more than anythin' that my big curiosity about things would just hush. But to extract one's curiosity is to halt one's pulse."

A spot of sun fought valiantly to peek through the iron gray clouds that galloped toward Mayhaw from somewhere else. The pine trees waved their arms in the breeze, not a care in the world. "I was tired of bein' indoors all the time...mentally...physically. It was time for things like...this." He didn't have to point. I knew what he was talking about. "And she didn't understand. She wanted to. But she didn't, and she couldn't. We were in some kinda love, married even, but both so young, and bein' young is a delicate time to handle freedom. I knew what I wanted...and I only had one choice."

Moisture in my eyes began to develop.

"It's been a hell of a journey, Aydenn. Everythin' I needed, nothin' I expected...may seem a little old to just be feelin' this way now...feelin' like it's taken me to where I need to be...spendin' so much of my life out here...."

For the third time, I thought about Kristiansen, on that plane to Crete. And for the first time, I spoke, using Echo's own words: "It's never about age. It's about experience. No two journeys are the same." He smiled right at me as everything disappeared except for his green and blue eyes.

()

Before I turned to walk the other way on the bridge that day, he said one last thing.

"Thank you, Aydenn....talkin' to you has made me realize a lot." His eyes were wet, but he didn't try to hide it. "You've given me the ear I needed...to realize that I'm finally ready. I've stood out in the rain long enough now. I've learned things I didn't think I could learn. I've felt things in my heart that I didn't know the heart was big enough to feel. Hell, I've even seen God out here."

He was thanking *me*?

"You've been a real friend...and I'll never forget you."

I could've asked why he'd chosen those last words—if he was leaving, or where he was going if he was. I could've wished him luck in finding *her* again, whoever she was. I could've even asked him if he'd finished writing whatever it was he was writing in that tent of his, in that delicate calligraphy.

But I didn't.

Instead, I gave him a nod accompanied by a smile, and that was it. The nod was one of friendship, maybe even of love. The smile was born simply from seeing him there, wearing the gift I'd just given him. It was Kristiansen's beret. I'd figured men with similar-sized thoughts must have similar-sized heads.

I jogged home under the fingertips of the storm as they reached for Mayhaw. I wondered if any airplanes were moving across the sky, way high above the iron grayness. It's strange how even above the most awful and hellish skies sits an unbothered blueness, calm and holy.

It's so damn brilliant how Nature has metaphors sewn right into it like that—like there's an undying serenity floating quietly above all tumult, and all will be well no matter what.

16

Christmas Eve could be sad.

It's a time when you really wake up to things like family and memories and which shoulders you can cry on and which ones you're always bumping into. Not having a father was one thing; not having a complete family on Christmas was another. It really pulled at my heart, shook me, tired me out. As I got older, it wasn't so bad. But it was different as a kid—not having someone to call *Dad* on Christmas stung like a thousand bees that you couldn't outrun.   But we did our best, my mother and I.

Late that morning, as the a.m. flirted with the p.m., she tidied up in between yawns and eventually wrote a list and was off to the big grocery store in town. Christmas Day dinner would seat and feed four this year.

While she was gone, I found myself dusting and vacuuming, hanging up the nicer towels, putting out the remaining holiday knick-knacks around the living room—along the mantle, the window sills. I wanted our house to look nice. I wanted it to look like a home. Maybe Aunt Jodie and Uncle Lou would like staying with us enough to do it more often. I'd have liked that, no matter how many times I'd have to dust.

I scooped up some firewood from the stack on the side of the house that sat quietly next to recycled newspapers and wine bottles. I situated it all in the fireplace for that night, and then pushed *A Christmas Story* into our VCR.

My mother would come home from the store, unload the groceries, get ready, put on earrings that matched her bracelet, and then she'd be off again. Like every holiday—Thanksgiving, Christmas, Easter—she'd spend a few hours feeding the homeless with her coworkers. And though I wished she was home the whole day on Christmas Eve, I guess I admired her for serving the homeless, in lieu of her eeriness about them in public. I even wondered if she'd ever seen Echo, maybe even served him dinner.

I busied myself well enough anyway, doing the *nothings* that kids dream of doing when the bell rings for Winter break every year. I flipped through some of the books Aunt Jodie and Uncle Lou had gotten for me over the years. I watched the words move with the pages, and I wondered who'd written them, and when, and why, and in what kind of chair they sat in to do it. Or perhaps they wrote them standing up.

I was excited to see them the next day, my aunt and uncle.

Perhaps I'd ask my aunt about the view from behind her camera, and how it was different and if it was better. Maybe I'd ask my uncle about the novel he'd written all but the last chapter of. He didn't talk much about his writing. Maybe that's how it has to be. Who has the energy to talk about what they're already talking about in their book? All he usually gave, when asked, was, "Ah, all meddled up with characters I may or may not have met before…we're getting there though."

They were good people, my aunt and uncle.

If you know good people, you should always remind them in your own ways that they're good. They deserve to know. I'd let them know by looking at their eyes when they talked. It's the only way to really see someone. You should always look at people in their eyes before you take in anything else about them. You see, we waste too much time *looking* at people instead of *seeing* them.

◌

Alone in a house that fought to keep warm, I waited for the sound of my mother's engine to pull up, hum, and disappear. It was past being dark outside, and I what-the-helled the situation and lit the fire anyway. I used a whole matchbook to do it. I pulled back the screen and swung open the damper. I ripped off a single match and lit it, then kissed it to the rest. The book went up in this little carnival-like blaze as the flame transferred down the line of matches. I flicked it in the fireplace to befriend the cold, dry wood. I shut the screen, hit the rewind button on the VCR, and as the tape sped off in reverse, I fell back onto the couch with my legs hanging over the arm. I got a tingle down my feet, and it was a similar feeling to the one I'd gotten on the bridge with Echo just the day before. It was the first time something *felt like yesterday* and it actually was.

All the lights were out except for the little white ones that dangled around the living room like snowflakes that wouldn't melt. I lied there with a blanket hanging down over my legs, tired and frustrated and alone. The fire flicked whatever light it could up onto my grandmother's painting that hung above me, along the wall. Big, crooked shadows moved across the ceiling ceremonially. The firewood had just started to crackle as I fell asleep.

I had a dream that I wouldn't remember. It was the kind of dream that lays you flat in a cold sweat and abandons you there to dry when you wake up. Soon, I would wake up—in the dark, in a sweat, with numb feet—to the sound of my mother jangling her house keys out in the cold.

◊

In a tired and distant voice, she actually apologized for being gone so long.

In the midst of removing her Winter layers, she put dinner out on the table. Two styrofoam containers, warm and moist on the bottom. "Good food at the shelter this year," she said. We ate the thick slices of honey ham and mashed potatoes and cornbread. From across the table, she looked discouraged, somehow let down. But I wouldn't ask about it. I'd just look up at her in between chews and sips and maybe bring up ordinary nothings to talk about.

Afterward, she changed into her Christmas pajamas. I changed too—the shirt I'd fallen asleep in had an uncomfortably cold dampness around the collar.

Before long, we found ourselves in the kitchen again, back to back at opposing countertops. She pulled out a stubborn cork and poured her wine as I got my tea together.

She filled her glass more than normal with a blood-like color. She pressed the cork back into its home and flicked off the kitchen light just as I started to dunk my tea bag.

I followed her out of the kitchen, into the living room, where we sat on the couch together—her, under a brown, fleece blanket; me, under my white and red one that had one of those wooden nutcracker men stitched into it. I turned the television on with one remote and pushed *Play* on another. I looked over at her just as the movie was starting. She was squinting into the fireplace. Her eyes were real thin and calm. It's a hell of a thing, a real personal thing, to be that close to someone who is somehow so far away.

17

The credits rolled up the screen, the VCR clicked, and the television went black.

I'd always wished that the movie was twice as long. My mother and I had both fallen into a slouch there, on the couch, under our respective blankets. The fire was nearly falling asleep. Just as I began feeling like we *did*, indeed, have this secret closeness between us, my mother climbed out of her slouch and waltzed stiffly into the kitchen to refill her glass.

She swept back into the living room that was blushing a deep red. Keeping her glass steady, she sat down on the floor, cross-legged, in front of what was left of the fire. Our humble hill of presents sat at her knee. It was Christmas Eve, so we could only open one. She picked hers out like a little girl. It was a long box with a big envelope strung to it, reading *THANK YOU*. She said it was from the Jeffreys. She'd just sold them a house. A glossy five by seven fell from the card's inside, landing in her lap.

She read the card's few words and picked up the photograph. She looked at it a long while, with a tilted head and a distant smile, and then handed it up to me. It was a middle-aged couple standing in front of a two-story house that was all decked out for Christmas. No picket fence. No loyal dog sitting at their knee. Instead, a small, bald and pale newborn, sitting in the crevice of the man's arm—safe from the entire world. I smiled at the image of a father holding his son.

My mother ripped open the accompanying gift just as I could've gotten sad that there were no pictures of my father and I like that. From a bored-white box, she pulled out a pair of something. It was a wooden spoon and spatula. For the kitchen. I didn't know what you'd use them for in particular, but they were real nice-looking. And I could tell she liked them. They must've known she cooked. Perhaps she was open with strangers like that. I wondered if other people knew other things about her that her own son didn't.

She put it all back into the box and looked up at me. It was my turn to pick a gift.

Leaning up off the couch a bit, I pointed at one, and my mother tossed it up to me. In its perfect squareness, I held what Dillon had given me on that last day of school. The red wrapping paper became vermilion in the firelight. I did my best to open it carefully. I mean, what's the point in wrapping something if the recipient isn't going to take more than three seconds in *un*wrapping it? I undid the hand-tied ribbon and peeled the gift open at the side. The paper slid off smoothly, maintaining a hollow, square shape. Into my lap, hugged by ninety-degree angles, the gift dropped.

It was the Rubik's cube!

I couldn't believe it. All the sides were the same color! He'd finished it!

I twisted it around in the dim light, my mother asking me how long I thought it would take to finish. A weightless laugh escaped me while examining it and touching each individual colored square. "It's...it's already finished." She let me have my time looking at it—in silence, in awe, in understanding. You see, Dillon and I hadn't been seeing much of each other. But in the wake of it, in the wake of school and preparing for college and having a girlfriend, he hadn't forgotten—about the Rubik's cube, about me, about our friendship.

Like many people forget to do, he remembered.

That's a best friend if I've ever known one.

◊

"How is Dillon anyway, Aydenn?" she started.

"He's...good." I could tell her eyes were up on me, but mine were still on the cube in my hands. "Got a girlfriend now. Together a lot. She drives him to school. Goes on vacations with them too." I felt her reaction, whatever it was. I went on, "But...still best friends, me and Dillon."

"Well good for him," she said, before taking a long drag from her glass.

"And what about you, Aydenn? Any little girls in your life? Any to bring to the ball next semester?" It was the first time she'd asked me about it: the first time she'd shown any curiosity about her son's love life, or whatever it's called when you're seventeen. It was oddly comforting, her knowing about Texana Hills' Senior Ball. But the topic of romance, I thought, had always deflated her. She hadn't had it since, well, my father. That's why she'd change the channels past certain movies, love stories; that's why she'd never asked me about it; that's why she hadn't tried dating or loving anyone else since my father had died.

I went along with it. I thought about the pretty girls I'd see around school or in town or behind registers at stores. Their eyes and naked collarbones and everything. They could have this smell about them too. They were delicate as hell. But the truth is, where I was in life just then, was everywhere *but* there. I wasn't ready for a girlfriend. I knew I wanted one. Just not yet. I had things to sort out in my own heart, my own head, before I could dive into anyone else's. I felt like maybe I had to learn *what* I loved before trying to seek out *whom* I loved. It made good enough sense. I felt a sort of responsibility to do it that way. Maybe it was because of Kristiansen and Echo, or even just my own human nature. Either way, I felt it: the curiosity about the self, about life—the blessing, not the doom.

"Eh, no, not really. Not really looking. Soon, but not too soon, I'll find one to bring home. A real pretty one. An honest kind of pretty." She smiled, looking into the fire. Perhaps that's all she could do.

I crossed my legs and sunk back into the couch even more, letting the Rubik's cube roll down my lap, then picking it up and dropping it and watching it roll down again. Right then, three words would come out of my mouth that would change everything. It wasn't how I said them. It was the words themselves. In that order.

"For right now, Mom, I'm just kind of taking it easy, moving with the wind. Focusing on school and making plans for after, and in the meantime, finding a good book or having a good jog, a good run when I can. Maybe I'll join cross-country when it starts up in the Spring. But for right now, I'm just sort of...*satisfying the me*, you know?" I said it with lightness, with confidence, waiting for an understanding nod of the head or smile from the woman who sat on the floor in front of me. Instead, her teeth clinked hard against her glass.

The crystal rang out unforgivably as she turned from the fire to look up at me. I let the Rubik's cube alone and looked back down at her. Disturbed and Perplexed got married right there on her face.

"What?" she said with a thin, loud whisper. "What do you mean, *satisfying the me*?" She stumbled on her tongue, getting louder. A simmering anger bubbled beneath her words. "What…what is *that* supposed to mean? Where did you hear that?"

It threw me.

"Wha—? Just somewhere. No big de—"

"Where, Aydenn?"

Her words were louder, more direct.

"Wh… Nowhere, Mom. What's the— "

"Aydenn!" she snapped, getting up onto both of her knees. A hard-cut shadow lined her jaw. She looked at me like I'd just spoken a different language. "Where…did you hear…those words?" She was talking to me like a child who'd just sworn for the first time. Frustration found and gripped me. "Mom, what the hell? Just a friend, relax. Nothing to chip your tooth over…hell."

"Aydenn, PLEASE," she begged, "PLEASE tell me where you heard that. The…the *satisfying the me.*" The image of Echo's face took over my thoughts—his new, clean-shaven face. Ever since I was young enough to really understand, my mother had always told me to stay away from the homeless, from the Northern Park especially. What was I supposed to tell her now? I wasn't going to sit there and be lectured on Christmas Eve. But she was looking right at me, into me, like she'd never done before. Her eyes were so vulnerable as she shrunk in the dying firelight. And it all suddenly felt so serious, like life or death depended on me answering her.

Still looking down at her, I gave her the stupid honesty she wanted. "A man I met, Mom. Just some man." I paused, looking into the fire that crouched behind her. "And I'll probably never see him again. So it's no big d—"

"But *who* Aydenn, *who*?!"

My heart bounced hard around my chest. She was scaring me. My eyes were back on her, harder this time. My voice got as loud as hers, maybe louder. "Just some guy! A nobody! Barely a somebody! You don't know him, so what's the difference?!" My whole throat swelled with a hotness. "And you want to know where I met him?! Do you want to know *that* too?!"

Her shoulders and her cheekbones sagged together. I could barely see her face. A cabernet glow flooded the lower half our living room. Big, dull shadows danced along the baseboards, trying to ignore my shouting. I didn't wait for her answer. "At Lake Wisley, Mom! The Northern Park!" I breathed deep, frustrated breaths, waiting for her to say something, anything. She didn't shout back. She sat back on her heels and came in just barely above a whisper. It wasn't a soft, kind whisper. Not a sweet or gentle whisper. It was a whisper born of a contracting heart choking her vocal chords.

"A h-homeless man, Aydenn? Was…was he homeless?"

With eyes still big from vexation, I looked down at this woman on the floor in front of me. For those moments, she felt like a stranger. I let out all my air, exhaling with closed eyes, worried for the woman who'd gotten worried over three damn words.

I found calm again, somehow. "Yes, Mom…he was homeless…*is* homeless"

Pain painted her stone face immediately. It stole the warmth right from the living room. "What's gotten into you?" I went on, concerned, "…all I say are three little words, *satisfying the me*, and you get like this."

Her glass dropped from her hand just as I said the three words again.

Red wine stained the carpet like murder. Her head followed suit, as she put her face down in her hands. She started scraping her fingers through her hair violently. I heard her nails against her scalp. You could almost feel the wetness clogging her sinuses as she demanded his name.

Without sanction, I was shouting again. "Mom! What the hell?! What is wrong with y—"

"Aydenn!" she screamed back up at me, violently topping my volume. "What was his name?!...what's...his goddamn *name*, Aydenn?!"

Looking at her face, anger pulsing in my own, I barked, "It was Echo! Echo! ECHO!" I wanted to lunge forward off the couch and grab her by the shoulders and look at her in the eyes and scream it a hundred more times.

She burst into tears like I'd never seen anybody do before— the same tears a boy cries when he sees his dog get hit by a car, right in front of him, just like that. They gushed out of her eyes, burning like little flames down her cheeks in the weak glow of the blinking fire. Between gasps, she fought to speak. Her words were soaked.

"His...his..."

I cut *her* off this time. "What, Mom?! What is it now?!" I lost control. I began to cry like her. "What is it?!" I shouted through newborn tears.

"His eyes," she coughed, "were...were they...." She was trying so hard, "...were they two...two diff-different...."

"Two different colors?!" I barked weakly. My eyes were wet and sticky. My chest was pumping up and down. I was angry. I hated her. I didn't want to be yelling like that. Not when she looked the way she did, small and weak, lifeless. I was scared. "Yes! One green and one blue! What the hell, Mom?! How—"

My voice stopped working when I saw her nodding painfully. Her eyes closed, and she bowed back down to the floor, forehead against the carpet right where her wine had stained like fresh blood. She cooed my name with a brokenness, *"Aydenn, Aydenn, Aydenn."*

I sat paralyzed under my blanket. Cold. My stomach shivered. Everything around me blurred except for the crippled woman in front of me—the woman who had always just been my mother. She flung up, looking back up at me with puffy eyes, strings of brown hair stuck on the sides of her face in layers of tears. Parts of her forehead were blotched wet with red from the carpet. She looked like hell. Through a sticky throat, she croaked, "Wh-where? Where is he?" I'd never seen such vulnerability in an adult before, and I never thought it would be from my own mother. I didn't understand. I didn't understand!

Why was she asking me these things? How the hell would my mother know Echo? And why was she such a goddamn wreck over it all? How could someone so strong—someone who'd gotten through the death of my father—now appear so damn weak?

I cried harder. She was so small and frail and helpless down there, my mother, like a child left in the rain. Like lightning on my heart, I felt a pang to just jump down from the couch and throw my arms around her shoulders recklessly and hug her for all seventeen years' worth.

But I didn't.

I could barely move. All but my voice was numb. "Mom!" I shouted, looking down at the back of her head as her face was in the carpet again. Her back swayed from side to side as if she'd just been stabbed in the stomach. "Mom!" I tried again.

But she didn't respond.

All her voice could do was repeatedly mumble *Echo* into the carpet that her lips were pressing against—the carpet that'd been soaked by red wine and unseen tears, the carpet that almost suffocated her.

I couldn't find any more words. My legs were far past numbness—still crossed, but dead. My stomach started shivering harder, jolting. I was scared. I could've thrown up right there into my own hands.

That's when she lifted her head. That's when she got up on all fours and turned away from me. That's when she began crawling out of the living room, her back at the last blink of fire, toward the hallway where our rooms were. I watched her go quietly, through wet and sticky eyes, and there wasn't another sound in the world other than her knees gliding across the carpet. Just before reaching her bedroom door, she got up, just barely, and limped the rest of the way. She was still in her Christmas pajamas.

She swept into her room and disappeared for what felt like forever.

I did the only thing I could do.

I waited, holding my breath, holding my tears, holding the world.

Back down the hallway, her legs just as weak, one of her arms rubbed against the wall to help her stand. Under her other arm, she was carrying something. It was a thin, beige shoebox. Her head was kept down until she made it over and sat on the carpet in front of me again, closer now. She looked up into my eyes in a way she'd never done before—a way, I guess, I'd always wanted her to.

With the shoebox on the carpet in between us, she looked down and lifted the lid from it. Heavy, round tears rolled down her face without sound. I got a hollow feeling in my chest. Not a lightness, nor a heaviness, but an emptiness.

From the shoebox, she pulled out a piece of paper that was folded into fourths. It rubbed against the cardboard as it slid out, making the sound of a shallow tide over sand. She handed it up to me. The corners were tattered. I reached for it with a heavy hand. It made its way snugly in between my finger and thumb. Holding it there, my heart lodged itself hard into my throat.

I looked at her imploringly. Her face was only half-lit by the sleepy fire to her right. She wasn't sad or beaten or anxious anymore. She wasn't even crying. She was lifeless. Still. Nothing. She was barely there. But somehow, she could mold the whispered, crooked words, "I'm...I'm sorry. I'm so, so sorry,

Aydenn. I...." She stopped as I looked back down at the folded paper in my hand, then started again, "I don't...I don't deserve to be a mother...your mother. And you don't deserve...I'm...I'm so...."

I wanted to stand up on the couch and scream *SPIT IT OUT!* right down at her goddamn face. My whole body pulsated hotter and hotter. I didn't know what was going on, with anything. I was crying harder and harder without even knowing it. I wanted to scream again, louder than before, louder than I'd ever screamed in my life. But I couldn't; my lips were sealed shut by sticky tears and spit.

As I unfolded the paper, my mother croaked once more, "I'm sorry, Aydenn...I...I'm sorry for who I've been and...for never...for lying to you...."

Anger split my lips open, "Just shut *up*, Mom! Shut *up*, PLEASE!"

She got as silent as a broken jaw. I wiped the wetness from my eyes roughly with the back of my wrist, heaving with my breath. The last flick of firelight breathed orange upon the unfolded paper. It was a letter. Words were written neatly but faintly, over the creases and across in straight lines.

18

The handwriting was too familiar.

Delicate.

Blue ink.

Calligraphy.

I'd seen it before.

I'd read it before, on my knees, in a dark tent.

I squinted through eyes that stung with dry tears to read the impossible words.

My sweet Emily, my wife,

This is no easier for me than it is for you. I've waded in ponderous tides with this, thought for miles about it. It's something that will not leave me alone. It's something I must do. And I must do it now. I must do it for the thing that starves, the thing that knows it's being swept under anything that will just barely hide it.

Perhaps I'll find something out there, discover things I didn't know I needed to discover.

I'm crowded, Emily. You know this. My mind. My whole body.

I need to see the space that's out there, the simpleness of it all. I need to give my feet the miles they ask for quietly from inside my tired shoes. I need to be happy. I want to be. More than that, I'm ready to be.

My mother sobbed heavily with hard breaths, in slow motion on the floor. Her words were barely alive, drowning in spit and tears. "He...he'd talked about...going...just *going* one day. Always wanted to...even before...before me, before us. Just...going! Going and living out there alone, living in the nowhere places and seeing everything. All those damn...books he read. Ob-obsessing right under my nose. One eye on me...the other on *that* life."

Her words stung my chest like a thousand hornets.

It was the first thing I'd been able to actually feel in several minutes.

I read on, with knots pulling themselves tighter in my stomach.

I'll be keeping my eyes wide for someone who's missing.

Not sure where he'll be, but I know he wants to be found. He doesn't want to be missing anymore. When I find him, I'd love for you two to meet. I think that would be beautiful, perfect even.

I won't be far Emily, not from your heart. I'll be somewhere—in and out of columns of trees, walking my feet across paths of dirt, stomach high in grasses, tree-lengths under the song of birds, ankle-deep in cool water, lying slim in a tent under a sky of no noise. I'll be out there, in the thick of it all, in the light of things, in the realness.

I'm sure I'll meet everyone I'm supposed to meet and see everything I'm supposed to see.

I'll travel to corners unknown as they soon become known.

I'll be far away, but still near, somehow.

A sunset won't pass that I don't think of you.

Each word I read made the letter heavier in my hands. My mother was lying still on the floor below me, wounded. I couldn't speak or feel or breathe. The only thing I could do was keep reading.

Maybe you'll understand some day. Maybe you won't. Perhaps we're not always meant to understand things.

I know this is salt on your heart, Emily. But this is my life. This is the person I'm supposed to be, and must be, at least for now. When one is called, through voices or dreams or winds or books, when one is called to his or her journey, what other option is there?

This is my chance to meet myself, a lifelong friend. My chance to meet wonders like simplicity and fear and appetite and shelter. And isolation. This is my ticket, Emily. My threshold. My time to actually write this book I've talked myself to death about—this book I told you about, with drunken breath, that very first night we met.

And to do it, I must go now. I must relinquish! Simplify! I must learn to understand the 'nothing' I have by nature, and how that 'nothing' is secretly everything. I must look in the direction of the wind, and stand out in the rain. And I must do it alone.

The pit of me hungers for satisfaction.

And I believe—the same way I believe in heaven—that the remedy is out there!

Only out there, can I satisfy the me.

There they were: the three words. She must've read them a thousand times.

Some mornings, Emily, I lie next to you and look at your eyes before you wake up. Beautiful, warm cocoons they are. And it hurts me, really breaks my soul, knowing that I can't love you as much as I should. And all because I don't love myself. I don't even know the self I should love. As I said, it's gotten lost. And I must go now, out into the clearings, and look for it, look for myself.

Ever since the death of my father, Emily, I've been astray without even knowing it. And though we're just married now, and though there couldn't be a worse time for me to realize all of this, I can't deny that it feels like the honest and right thing to do, really the only thing to do. My intuitive drum beats hard, drowning out everything around it, and it's all I can hear.

My back turned to ice.

I've taken very little. I won't be needing much.

I'll find my way along; I'll take the paths of others who find themselves—one way or another—homeless. Or perhaps they're only houseless. Perhaps home is where love is, and there can't be such a thing as homeless if there's even a tickle of love in your heart! I know I'll have the heaviest of souls at first, but I'll try to remember that it's best to travel light. I mean, the less I got, the less can get in my way.

Please don't be sad, Emily.

This is what I must do.

This is where answers stand tall, awaiting me, awaiting George Price.

This is where curiosity finds its backbone, where myself awaits me.

George Price.

It was the same two names that followed my own first name.

It was the name of my father.

I wish nothing more than to take this road and find you at the end of it.

It wouldn't be a miracle or a fingertip-touch of luck. It would simply be how it's supposed to be. All is written out, Emily, and I hope that you are written into my life; I hope that your face will illuminate the end of my journey. But I'm afraid that's all I can carry with me for now—hope.

I heard my mother's voice the same way you hear wind out of an open car window—loud but empty. "*I'll call myself Echo,* he said, *live like the homeless, greet life with nothing in the way…write a book about it…*I thought it was…a young and stupid thing…not a real thing," she trailed off, defeated.

I looked up at her and then back down at the letter.

These were words my father had written to my mother.

My *father*!

Please don't be sad, Emily.

When my father died in that fire, and my mother fell ill and went into the clinic, I was as lonely and cold as a teenager could ever be. No matter what anyone said—teachers, counselors, anyone, any age—nothing helped. A blackness slit open my soul. I felt it in every step I took, every breath I breathed in and let out. I swore I'd be empty like that forever. And having my father's firefighting helmet as a memory was just too sad, which is why you'll see I've left it behind.

Please do something with it, Emily. Something respectful. It helped me realize something invaluable, and I don't need it with me any longer. It helped me realize that I wasn't empty inside because I'd <u>lost</u> someone; I was empty inside because there was someone I <u>hadn't found</u> yet.

I never want to feel that loneliness again, Emily.

And so I'm off to find that person.

I looked at my mother again, over the glowing-orange, brittle letter. She was crippled, on weak knees, down there on the floor. Her eyes were on mine. An incredible, lukewarm anxiety flooded me, from my chest all the way down into my bowels. I could barely breathe words.

"*Echo…my…my father?*" My tongue swelled.

She inhaled quiveringly, as if to cry or say words or do anything to shatter the silence. We both knew I understood. We both knew I'd finally been pulled out of the shade of everything. We both knew that I had to finish reading the letter.

Everything slowed down. My mother and I were the only people on Earth just then.

For whatever it's worth to you Emily, my flower, I am sorry.

I cannot be sorry for my actions, only for how they might make you feel.

I just can't continue to dream, with my eyes open, of a life that I never lived, a chapter I never wrote. There's just something <u>out there</u> for me to see. It's so slight, and it has such a thin glimmer to it, but I know it's there—just *because something is difficult to see doesn't mean it's not there.*

You'll be with me each day, I'm sure, in some way—your name in the breeze, your eyes in the diamonds on the water. I'll be Echo, and you'll be Emily, and that's just how it'll be for now.

I must do this. This is my work.

What love I have is already yours.

What love I find will be yours, too, if that's how the story has been written.

> *From under the same sky,*
> *George*
> *(Echo)*

The letter fell through my fingers and floated down to the floor.

A remaining blotch of wine on the carpet soaked through the middle of it the same way a stab wound soaks through a white t-shirt. As if slipping out of a 17-year-long coma, my mother's voice was the first thing I heard. Her words were phlegmatic, deflated.

"A week later...I found out I was pregnant. We were barely married. And I was going to have a baby...you, Aydenn."

I couldn't look at her. I couldn't look at anything. My eyes wouldn't move. Nothing worked except for my heart, which was swelling up, putting pressure on my lungs. The whole living room was a hazy red, and my mother was barely there, ghost-like. With her head down, she dumped out the shoebox. A clumsy pile sat between us on the carpet. Things that I had never thought existed, did. A sepia-toned photograph sat right on top—my mother when she was younger, arm-in-arm with a man who looked just like—and it was—a younger Echo.

It paralyzed me down my neck and back. My legs were still

crossed, hot and numb.

Again, in her same deflated voice, "I just didn't want you to think…I didn't want you to know. I wanted to protect you from…from feeling abandoned." I felt her eyes on me—the same eyes that'd watched me grow up without a father; the same eyes that'd witnessed a boy become a teenager and then a man, alone. She went on, "I didn't want you to ever feel how I felt that night. It was…it was the only way to protect you, Aydenn."

I didn't say anything. Nothing would come out. Words wouldn't even gather themselves into sentences in my thoughts. It was as if I forgot every word I ever knew.

And it all really hit me right then, like a hundred fists to the stomach, all at once.

My father was alive.

He hadn't died in a fire. He hadn't even died. He was never a firefighter; it was *his* father that was. *His* father died in the fire. *His* father, my *grandfather*, was named Earl Price. It was *his* helmet that I used to try on in front of the mirror.

My mother had given me a false story all my life. To *protect* me. She'd been hiding behind it all along. Aunt Jodie and Uncle Lou—they knew too; they had to. What'd been kept in a dark closet, out of sight my whole life, was now spread out naked across our living room floor.

My father was alive, and I'd met him. I knew him, and I knew him well.

One last time, my mother spoke. The living room cupped its dark hands around us. We sat like shadows in a lifeless, orange glow, like Hell at night. I had barely enough strength to listen, barely enough strength to be alive.

"I tried Aydenn…I tried to find him. Years. So many. But nothing." She paused. "But I've never given up. Every holiday…Thanksgiving…Christmas…Easter…when I leave the house…when I leave you here alone…I've never gone to serve food to the homeless with coworkers, Aydenn…I go to every shelter I can make it to...to look for...for your father. That's where...that's where I was tonight even."

My eyes finally made it over to hers as she went on. Our eyes were only on each other's for a handful of seconds. Then, her head went down heavy, into her hands again, as she began to wail uncontrollably. She looked through her warm, wet fingers at photographs that were lying tired and cold in a pile on the carpet—photographs she'd always told me didn't exist.

Above her sobs, across the room, on the far wall by the kitchen, her car keys hung quietly on their hook. A hot jolt of something surged through my shoulders, down my arms and into my fingers. Pushed up from my insides, and then out of my mouth, tumbled the first word since I'd told my mother to shut up. It was also the first word I'd said as a baby.

"Mom."

It came out the same way a feather floats down to the ground. My mother was muttering my name apologetically, "*Aydenn...Aydenn.*" I said it again, finding the strength to move my legs and sit forward on the couch.

"Mom."

She looked up at me—the same way a prisoner, far away from home, looks from behind bars at a passerby for mercy.

Another hot jolt lashed through me, bigger this time.

I threw my blanket off and climbed up from the couch. I took five dizzy steps past my broken mother and lifted her keys from the hook. They made the loudest jingle of any Christmas. I turned back to her and put out my hands, down and right in front of her. Moving like she was older than she was, elderly-like, she slipped all ten, bony and cold fingers into my grip. I pulled her up to me. We were the same height. We stood there, the only two people on Earth. The fire was dead, smoldering, the room so black it had traces of blue. We looked at each other with only the strength to cry. I stuffed the keys into one of her hands and dragged her by the other, to the front door and out into the cold.

I can't remember if I even closed the door behind me.

We scuttled down the five steps and onto the sidewalk. There, just a few feet from our car, without coats on, we stopped. We were holding hands. We stopped because we both must've felt it. We looked up simultaneously.

Snow, finally, had begun to fall over Mayhaw.

With our hands like ice, I helped her get the key into the ignition.

The engine coughed to a start, muttering an ugly something from underneath the hood.

Thin, white snow was landing with light feet on our front windshield. I reached over my mother, over the wheel, to flick the handle for the wipers. They waved the snow goodbye for a little while. In reaching over her like that, our cheeks grazed each other's. The wetness from both smeared together, and I'll never be able to put that feeling into words.

I fell back into my seat, and without buckling up, I looked from her hands on the wheel up to her eyes. She squinted as she pulled away from the curb, whipping her car around hard on the black street. I didn't feel the anger I perhaps should have. I didn't feel the confusion or the sadness or even the anxiety, the dizziness. I didn't feel anything at all. I was just a hard-beating heart.

We lunged forward, snow collecting on the windshield only to be brushed back off again in a fury. Faster and faster, our wheels sprinted over the wet asphalt without caution. There wasn't time for caution. We cried softly in our own little way. It was the only thing we knew how to do; words were impossible at that point.

Up the road and deeper and deeper into the night we pulled ourselves. Startlingly soon, I felt a weight sink hard and heavy in my stomach as we jerked up the big hill in the road past my high school. The tall pines of Lake Wisley poked their pointed brows high up into the black and blue sky; I squinted out at them through the tufts of snow that relentlessly collided with our windshield.

From underneath our car came a loud and barbaric yawp as my mother dug her foot harder into the gas pedal. Faster and faster, we heaved ourselves into the thickness of night, the snow slapping itself against the glass in front of our eyes with a temper. And then, just like that, the old and familiar, knotty wooden sign jumped into view out of my passenger window.

LAKE WISLEY

I got the voice to yell, "*Here!*"

The car slammed to a stop. I jumped out while it was still recovering. I didn't even shut my door; I left it behind, bouncing on its hinges. I didn't wait for my mother either. She'd have to find her own way through the park, through the darkness.

The half-moon didn't give much light, but I knew the contours of the Southern Park well enough. I sprinted with clumsy strides and bad footing over the dampening dirt path. It wasn't until then that I realized I was wearing only socks, wet and thin. I ran on through the trickling snow with hollow and cold breaths, ripping holes into both heels.

As abruptly as our car back on the street, I jolted to a hard stop, standing opposite the bridge. From under the sign with the painted-red N, I squinted across its wooden planks. They'd turned an almost-white beneath the new snow. I looked back behind me for my mother.

Blackness.

A silence swallowed the air around me for a handful of seconds. Then, it spit it back out. I yelled with a thunder, beginning to move forward again. "Echo! Echoooo!" I sprinted across the bridge, into the Northern Park, right for his tent, his red tent, kicking up dirt and snow behind me with barely socks on my feet.

I shouted without limits.

"*Dad!*"

It was the heaviest my tongue had ever felt.

Closer and closer I got, tears freezing on my sticky face. A faint glow of light was flickering from inside his red tent. I passed our bench as the snow in my hair melted into freezing drops on my scalp, rolling down the back of my neck. Feet skidding to a muddy stop, I reached out for one of the tent flaps. Again, "*Dad!*"

My heart exploded as I threw it open.

19

Nobody was inside.

But everything was still there.

Everything was still there, except for his wound up stack of pages—his book.

His stout, red candle was lit, spreading a soft, familiar glow along the canvas walls of the tent. A deep and wet puddle of wax surrounded the burning flame. He couldn't have lit it too long ago; he couldn't have left too long ago either.

Before I could react—before I could shout his name again or look around into the blackness that surrounded me or rip at my hair and cry into the floor and roll over and disappear, I saw it. Right there, with one of its corners tucked under the candle, was an old envelope, smeared with dirt.

I crawled over and lifted it out carefully, the wax puddle tipped in ripples.

On the front were old stamps and addresses, all crossed out.

On the back, a pinecone had been faintly sketched in pencil. I reached into the already-torn-open side and pulled out the sheet of paper that'd been folded in half. Opening it, I found the same handwriting I'd just read in the letter back at home—my father's.

Blue and patient calligraphic words sat shoulder to shoulder across the paper in rows. I pinched my eyes shut as if to try and make the tears fall inward instead.

The first word I read was my own name.

Aydenn, my dear friend,

I don't know when you'll find this, but I hope it's soon that you do.

I've lit this here candle to keep these words warm while they wait for you. Hopefully it will burn long enough. It's Christmas Eve now, and I've taken my feet to the Earth once more. Movement is so important, you see! The beret you've given me has a familiar fit to it, and I even wore it on my way out of here this evening. Thank you, again.

I've left my books behind, as you might see. I won't be needing them any longer. They're yours to read and pass on, if you'd like.

You can probably guess where I've gone off to. This long journey of mine's finally whispered itself to a close. There's so much I've learned along the way—some things I'll write about, and others I'll never be able to put into words, which is perhaps how it's supposed to be.

Out here—throughout these years—I've satisfied the me, Aydenn.

I've seen the view from the top. It's beautiful, it really is, and I would say that I <u>hope</u> you see it one day, but I don't need to hope for something that I already <u>know</u> will happen. You're a real wonder, kid. A real seeker. Keep being that way. Never halt or restrain or wish off your <u>curiosity</u> about things—about the world and the people in it. Even when it throws you in a dark and damp ditch, it's only to test your spirit. The minute all the wondering and wandering starts to crowd you, and it begins to feel like a doom, remember that it's not. That doom is nothing more than a disguised blessing.

I'm touched that we made it into each other's lives.

Seems our paths just wanted to cross like that, or maybe they didn't have a choice.

I know it was brief, but there can be a whole lot of sunlight in even one moment. I think we needed each other in ways that neither of us knew about, and maybe we don't understand them now, but one day we will. We tend to realize the good things in life some time after they happen, when we hear them only as echoes.

You'll be an echo in my life, and I hope I'll continue to be the echo in yours.

My heart is what pulls me now, in the direction of someone whose face has haunted me, whose face I've thought of and missed in between moments for almost twenty years now. And I think I've found her again, right here in town! I found her name listed in a phonebook many weeks back, just as I stumbled upon this lake. Her name stuck out like a bright, yellow flower in Wintertime.

Emily Price.

Isn't that brilliant?! It's time to go to her. I know it'd be a hell of a love story. If it is to be, then it will; if it's not, then I'm back to trusting the universe. But the only way to find answers is to get moving.

So thank you again, Aydenn. Thank you for your presence with me and, of course, your ear. All I've told you—everything I've said about the ins and outs of things, and the magic hiding in everyone's life—it's been nothing more than my responsibility to pass it on. Wherever I end up, I won't be far from your thoughts, because echoes can never really disappear.

> "Failing to fetch me at first, keep encouraged,
> Missing me one place, search another,
> I stop somewhere, waiting for you."

Your friend, Echo

In spite of the cool snow beginning to clump down on the canvas heavy above my head, I felt the warmest rush of blood swallow every inch of me. I didn't know what it meant; I just knew it was warm.

It was then that I heard distant, heavy feet scamper across the bridge. They were my mother's. She crossed over, pattering into the clearing of the Northern Park.

"Aydenn! *Aydenn!*"

Her yells nearly got lost in the thick, snowy air.

She must've seen the crouched silhouette of her son in the glowing redness ahead. Her steps slowed, but were growing closer. And then, just like that, she was right outside of the tent.

Her long hands softly entered between the two flaps, dividing them open. She saw her son inside, kneeling down in the candlelight.

She whispered my name gently.

"Aydenn...."

I was still staring at the letter, at the words *Emily Price.*

My mother got down onto her knees and crawled into the tent, toward me. I looked up at her, and on all fours, she paused. The candlelight breathed the most delicate shadow across her face, and I looked deep into her eyes.

I looked deep into her eyes because, at that moment, that's all I could do.

THE END

ABOUT THE AUTHOR

Scott Duka is a graduate of
California Polytechnic State University San Luis Obispo,
where he studied English Literature and Creative Writing.

At present, he is teaching English in the Bay Area, California.

9 7 8 0 6 1 5 7 4 5 0 7 7